Francesca Scanacapra was [...] mother and Italian father, and [...] between England and Italy. He [...] nomadic with periods spent living in Italy, England, France, Senegal and Spain. She describes herself as 'unconventional' and has pursued an eclectic mixture of career paths – from working in translation, the fitness industry, education and even several years as a builder. In 2021 she returned to her native country and back to her earliest roots to pursue her writing career full time. Francesca now resides permanently in rural Lombardy in the house built by her great-grandfather which was the inspiration for her *Paradiso Novels*: *Paradiso*, *Return to Paradiso*, *The Daughter of Paradiso* and *Casa Paradiso*. Her novels *The Lost Boy of Bologna* and *The Sardinian Story* are also published by Silvertail Books.

Also by Francesca Scanacapra:

The Paradiso Novels:
Paradiso
Return to Paradiso
The Daughter of Paradiso

The Bologna Chronicles:
The Lost Boy of Bologna

Other fiction:
The Sardinian Story

CASA PARADISO

*300 Years in
the Life of a House*

Francesca Scanacapra

SILVERTAIL BOOKS • *London*

For my husband, Chris Lowe.
Thank you for everything, darling.

CRISTÓ LOVETTA

Lombardy, Duchy of Milan.

With the sunset to his back, Cristó Lovetta walked the step-worn stones of the ancient Via Postumia, following the eastward flow of the Delmona Canal. The waymark he had passed some two hundred paces previously announced only seven more miles to the village of Pieve Santa Clara.

It had taken Cristó just two days to travel from his starting point in Milan to the city of Piacenza. There, the road had been decent, with no shortage of carts whose drivers had let him cadge a lift in exchange for a few *centesimi*. To cover the far shorter route between Piacenza and Cremona had taken longer, but that section of road had been encumbered with checkpoints, manned by Spanish soldiers. They'd verified his work papers, specifically the proof of payment of taxes to the Duchy of Milan, and as everything was in order, they'd given him no grief. The authorities didn't usually bother guild-certified tradesmen like Cristó who had all their official seals and knew how to answer their questions; and he wasn't easily intimidated, even by armed soldiers. There were men taller in stature than Cristó Lovetta, but few broader in the chest or stronger in the shoulder. He had both the blessing of a robust constitution and twenty years of masonry to thank for that. Aged thirty-two, despite the strenuous nature of his work, he remained in solid form, with muscles as hard as the stones he cut and carved.

Stonemasonry was not for the faint of spirit. It demanded not only physical strength, but also artistry and an attentiveness to detail, not to mention saintly quantities of patience and unwavering dedication to the craft. Cristó had both an expert eye and a skilled hand and the vision and might to translate a flat image, or even just an idea, into a solid form of high-reliefs, bas-reliefs, carvings and intaglios. He was part beast-of-burden, part draughtsman, part sculptor. His work might be arduous, injurious to the body in a hundred different ways, and on hot days it could be testing, but it brought him immense satisfaction. He knew that with each chisel strike he was carving a little piece of history and took pleasure in the fact that his labours would endure for centuries to come. Yet it was not always the grandest designs which brought him the greatest fulfilment; it was the final few delicate touches, when he would etch his initials, 'C.L.', on his completed work. Often this carver's mark was placed somewhere destined to be hidden once the piece was set. But how it pleased Cristó Lovetta to think that one day, perhaps a whole millennium hence, a future stonemason's hand might uncover his mark during the course of a repair or a restoration and wonder: who was this man, 'C.L.', who had left this ghostly signature in the stone?

Conditions and circumstances permitting, Cristó had pledged to arrive at the new job on San Ruperto's day, which fell on the twenty-seventh day of the month of March, so he was a day ahead of schedule. Had he known the exact whereabouts of his destination, he would have continued walking until he reached it, but without precise directions, he questioned the wisdom of trying to find the place with nothing more than a waning moon to guide his path.

Now the sun was half-sunk behind the horizon, suffusing the sky with a coral-coloured light and turning the waters of the canal a mossy green. A sharp evening chill pierced the air.

Common sense was telling Cristó to find a place to stay for the night, but along this stretch of the Via Postumia, the few farmsteads he passed were deserted. Some had been burned down,

2

an indication of a visit by the black death. A fellow he'd walked with earlier that day said that the last outbreak had killed well over half of the region's population, and this was evidenced not just by the abandoned buildings, but also by the fallow fields surrounding them. The Lombardy Plain, an endless expanse of the richest, most fertile agricultural land, lay largely uncultivated. No beasts were pastured. There wasn't a soul to be seen.

Perhaps it was because his mind was already made up about stopping for the night that Cristó felt so suddenly overcome by weariness. The heavy pack of tools on his back seemed to increase in weight with every step he took. Still, with nowhere to stay he had no choice but to continue on his way.

As the daylight gave way to dusk, he came to a wooden walkway spanning the canal. Beyond it was a narrow track leading to the kind of farmstead known in this area as a *cascina*. From where he stood it was difficult to say whether the place was inhabited or not, but the track was clear, as though it was used regularly, and the long building in the near distance appeared to be in a decent state of repair. Cristó adjusted the pack on his back and made his way towards it. Even if the place was abandoned, he'd be able to camp out in a barn, perhaps light a fire and wash himself in hot water, and he still had a few provisions left. A hearty dinner would have gone down well, but failing that, the remainder of his bread and cheese would have to do.

Fortune smiled upon him when he found the *cascina* to be occupied. No doubt it had been a hive of activity in its time, and both a home and a place of employment for a dozen or more families, but now its decline was obvious. The main house had about it a run-down, decaying aspect. The workers' quarters were boarded up. Apart from a few piglets and a scattering of chickens, its only occupants were an elderly farming couple.

Once the farmer's wife had gone through the customary questions which might be asked of a stranger, she had been only too pleased to provide him with a room with a good bed and supper included for an extremely reasonable price. She also furnished him with a basin of hot water and tallow soap with which to wash himself, saying that they'd be having dinner as soon as her husband came in from the fields. Within the hour, Cristó was seated at the kitchen table with the farmer and his wife, enjoying a well-garnished *zuppa* of vegetables, beans and belly pork.

'So what brings a travelling stonemason to our parish?' The farmer asked, breaking chunks of bread and steeping them in his soup.

'I'm due to start work for the Marchesinis of Pieve Santa Clara. Do you know them?'

'Who doesn't know of the Marchesini family in these parts? I hear they're building a house the size of the Cathedral of Santa Maria Assunta. They're not short of money, that's for sure.'

Curious, Cristó asked, 'How did they earn their fortune?'

The farmer contemplated his *zuppa* before answering, 'Farming's a profitable business when you own the land. Old man Marchesini has connections to Spain. Unlike the rest of us folks, he's done all right for himself under the Spanish occupation. I'd heard he put money in ships. The vessels left our shores empty and came back from the New World filled with gold.'

There was no ignoring the bitter tone of the farmer's words. He continued, 'I've no problem with men making their fortunes. But when one man grows fat whilst a thousand others can't put a crust on the table, it sticks in my gullet. Men like Marchesini who've got into bed with the Spanish haven't been taxed like those of us who won't. He doesn't have to worry about a squad of soldiers coming to torch his crops if he hasn't paid his dues. And what business have those Spaniards got here anyway? If it was up to me, I'd –'

Before the farmer said anything else which could risk him

being reported to the authorities, his wife interrupted with, 'Do you have a family, Maestro Lovetta?'

Cristó stated that he did not. Had the same question been asked of him three years previously, he would have spoken of his wonderful wife and of his darling daughter, then aged not quite four. But even now, with a little time passed, any mention of his two beloved girls grieved him, for the black death had taken them. It would have taken him too, no doubt, if he had not been away working. The memory of returning home that dreadful day, euphoric at the prospect of his wife's welcoming kisses and of his little daughter leaping into his arms, only to be greeted by a black cross painted onto the door of his house and nobody inside it, wrenched at his gizzards.

To avoid the conversation turning to such maudlin matters, Cristó replied that travelling from job to job and staying in each place for as long as the contract lasted had never been conducive to settling down, and he began to speak of the different places he had worked. There were many, within the Duchies of Milan, Modena and Parma; in the Republic of Venice to the north and down as far south as the Grand Dukedom of Tuscany. He had worked further afield too. In his youth, he had served part of his apprenticeship in France, under the tutelage of one of Normandy's most celebrated stonemasons.

Following an excellent night's rest, Cristó was sent on his way the next morning, stuffed to the gills with breakfast. As directed by the farmer, on the approach to Pieve Santa Clara, he came to a brick bridge and crossed the canal, leaving the main artery of the Via Postumia and bearing north. He was now stepping onto the Marchesini estate. Here the fields which flanked the track were cultivated. A fine haze of sprouting barley, wheat and linseed crops carpeted the land, stretching far out of sight. Men were at work. Well-fattened cattle and sheep filled the pastures.

In the far distance, the snow-capped peaks of the mountains beyond Brescia were visible, giving an illusion of closeness, when in reality they were well over a week's travel away.

The main entrance to the Marchesini estate was marked by two tall, bevelled brick columns, capped with cornucopia finials, upon which hung an elaborate set of gates – a combined masterpiece of brickwork, stone-carving and black-smithery, and testament to the opulence of the landowners. Cristó passed through and followed a curving drive, and as he rounded the bend, he stopped, put down his pack and surveyed the site spread out before him. According to the information he had been given, work had been underway for two years. The foundations for the house were dug, with the main supporting walls half-built, up to first floor height. As the farmer had said, the place was enormous. At a guess, around four hundred men were at work, assisted by windlasses and crank-saws and horses and mules by the score. A lofty treadwheel hoist, driven by a yoke of oxen, was lifting a great cradle of bricks. The noise was thunderous – an unrelenting racket of hammering, chiselling and sawing; the tramping of boots and hooves; animal calls and orders being shouted. All around the boundary, various enclosures were partitioned, providing a separate workshop space for each trade; and beyond the picketed enclosures were rows of shelters and huts to house the workmen.

Cristó hailed a fellow to ask where he might find the architect, Montegatto, but Montegatto found him first. He hadn't yet picked up his pack when a voice called out, 'Lovetta!'

The two old friends embraced each other warmly. They had worked together many times. It was thanks to Montegatto that Cristó had been offered the job of heading the team of stonemasons when the position had become available unexpectedly.

'You've got me out of a fix, my friend,' said Montegatto. 'We had a sound fellow in charge of the stonemasons, until the poor chap took his thumb off with his chisel. It's a relief you could come.'

'The timing was lucky. Your message reached me just as I was finishing a restoration contract on the church of San Vittore. If truth be told, before I had word from you, I was thinking about taking the spring and summer off to prepare the houses for sale. Not much point in keeping them now. They're a responsibility I no longer want.'

Montegatto knew to which houses Cristó was referring – his former family home in the Duomo district of Milan and a second property close by, intended as a future wedding gift for his daughter.

'Anyway,' Cristó shrugged, 'It makes sense to sell up. The time's approaching when I might need a pension. A fellow can't be certain of how long he can toil before his back gives out, or when he might chop his thumb off with his chisel.'

Montegatto patted Cristó affectionately on the shoulder and as they made their way across the site he said, 'You won't have to lodge in one of the huts. I've bagged you some decent quarters in the stable block. You've got a stall to yourself, just next to mine.'

'What are the rations like here?'

Montegatto made a gesture to indicate that the food provided by the Marchesinis was adequate – an important element on any site. The old proverb said that it was the soup that made the soldier, and the same could be said for any tradesman. Workers needed to be well fed, as meagre rations were the quickest path to mutiny.

'The basics are all right,' Montegatto assured him. 'The bread's decent, and there's usually plenty of it. For most meals there's polenta, and sometimes you'll be lucky enough to find a piece of meat in the *zuppa*. But locals come here to sell food every day. You'll be able to get eggs, cheese and fresh milk, even pies, or cake, on a good day. In this region, the summers fry you and the winters freeze you, but there's never any shortage of food.'

Montegatto took Cristó to the workshop to introduce him to the team of stonemasons who were busy cutting plinths and sills. Lying on the ground by the boundary of the enclosure were several large blocks of limestone, still in raw form. They had travelled all the way from the Cave del Baggero quarries, near Lake Como, Montegatto explained. Just as well the canal ran through the Marchesini property, or they would never have managed to transport them.

'These are the stones destined to become the dining hall fireplace I mentioned in my letter,' said Montegatto, taking a scroll of parchment from his jacket and spreading it out flat on one of the blocks. Sketched upon it was the schema for a fireplace of monumental proportions, measuring ten feet in height and twelve in breadth. Its opening was in Gothic arch form and its mantel was embellished with an intricate tracery of lozenges, quatrefoils and fleur-de-lys. In the centre of the over-mantel was the Marchesini coat of arms, depicting two herons with their necks bent to form the shape of an 'M'.

'What's Marchesini like to work for?' Cristó asked.

'Fickle as a feather in the breeze. He has a new idea every time the wind changes direction. Apart from that, he's all right. At least he's got more money than sense and he pays on time. But we don't see much of him, to be honest. He comes down whenever he can for a look then takes himself back to Milan. Sometimes he's called to Spain. He's a senator.'

Montegatto pronounced the word 'senator' through clenched teeth. The title could easily have been exchanged with the word 'traitor'.

Cristó took up his tools on the Monday following San Ruperto's day, as pledged. He began by roughing out the shapes of the blocks which would eventually come together to form the fireplace. This was quality, fine-grained limestone, perfect for sculpting, but there was a lot of preparation to do before he'd be unpacking his roundels and detailing chisels. At a conservative estimate, Marchesini's monumental fireplace would take a year to complete.

He was barely an hour into his work when a woman's voice was heard outside the enclosure calling out, '*Panin'!*'. The din of chiselling and hammering stopped immediately, and from one moment to the next, the workshop emptied. As he was on his way out, one mason turned to Cristó and grinned, 'Florenza's here with her stuffed bread rolls. The best you'll ever taste. She bakes them herself and crams them full of cheese and pickles. Quick, come and get one whilst it's warm!' Cristó put down his mallet and followed him. His mouth was already watering at the prospect of a warm, stuffed *panin'*.

Outside the enclosure, Florenza was standing in the midst of a crowd, selling her *panin'* as fast as she could take them from her basket. She was a young woman, but sombrely dressed in a long black tunic. Her head was entirely covered by a widows' cowl, falling past her shoulders and fastened under her chin.

It was only when Cristó reached the front of the crowd that he saw the little rosy-cheeked girl, half-hidden behind Florenza's skirt. Her fair ringlet curls were tied up in a pom-pom on the crown of her head. She looked three, or perhaps four years old, at a guess; approximately the same age as Cristó's own daughter had been the last time he had seen her alive. The sight of this child holding onto her mother's skirt made the breath catch in Cristó's throat – such an ordinary, everyday thing, yet so extraordinarily precious, and so easily vanished. The agony of his own recent losses, which he kept strictly hidden from public view, swelled inside him, threatening to burst out right there and then. He closed his eyes to steady his nerves, and when he opened them again, the little girl was looking directly at him. But rather than shying at the sight of a stranger, particularly one as big and burly as himself, she gave him a great beaming smile, ducked behind her mother for a moment, then popped back out again, inviting him to play peek-a-boo. The feeling of love for his daughter ambushed Cristó, and without the slightest concern for the circumstances, he joined in the game. The little girl's giggle trilled like a lark's call.

He paid for his *panin'* and went to sit on one of the limestone blocks to eat it. As the mason had promised, it was delicious; made from a golden-crusted bread with a soft, light crumb and crammed full of pickles and cheese. Every flavour-filled bite was worth savouring. Cristó was about halfway through when something made him look up. Florenza's little girl was standing a few steps away, with her eyes fixed on him.

'Hello,' he said gently, because he didn't want to scare her, but she seemed not in the least bit wary. When he asked her name, she told him that it was Nella. In the same sentence she also told him that she liked strawberries, but she didn't like onions; that she had a cat called Alfredo, but he was lazy, and that her Papá was an angel. With that, the introduction was complete.

Nella ran back to Florenza as soon as her name was called. Cristó watched as mother and child hurried away. Nella, who was skipping along behind Florenza's black skirt, stopped mid-skip, turned, gave her beaming smile and waved good-bye. Cristó waved back, but struggled to form a smile. His lip was trembling. It was not just the stone dust which he wiped from his eyes as he finished his *panin'*.

From that day on, conversations with Nella became part of Cristó's morning routine. He would go to rest on one of the limestone blocks to eat his *panin'*, Nella would clamber up beside him and sit swinging her legs and talking. She was a lively little girl, curious about everything and bright as a star. Their dialogues covered a whole range of topics – from all they saw around them; to nature and animals; to their personal tastes in matters of food – as her confidence in him grew, more than just occasionally, she would pinch the cheese from his *panin'*. Quite why Nella had singled him out, he couldn't say, but those few moments of daily connection between childless father and fatherless child were like a curative balm to Cristó's grief-injured heart.

Some of the tradesmen found these interactions odd, even suggesting that they were a ruse on Cristó's part to win Florenza's affections, but nothing could have been further from the truth. The stonemason was not yet sufficiently mended to be thinking of that sort of thing; and in any case, even if he had been, making any kind of advance towards a widow who was still dressed in her mourning attire was not only inappropriate, but also highly disrespectful. Even the most uncouth knew that. He had exchanged a few words with Florenza when she had come to ensure that he posed no threat and that Nella wasn't bothering him. Following that, their conversations had been friendly, but fleeting. Florenza was inevitably in a rush. When she was not selling *panin'*, she was fetching or delivering workmen's washing. Often, on his way to or from the village, Cristó would spot her at the communal lavoir by the brick bridge, standing knee-deep and bent over in the water scrubbing laundry. The young widow worked every hour God sent to provide for herself and her daughter.

Spring that year was fine. Sunny, and peppered with occasional showers. Perfect weather, with temperate days and cool nights. The fruit orchards burst forth pink and white blossom as the landscape exploded into green, with crops shooting up so fast that you could blink and they'd grown another inch. By mid-May the first hay harvest was gathered.

Marchesini's colossal Gothic fireplace took shape at a steady pace. Being away from Milan was good for Cristó, as was Montegatto's company. Once the day's labours were over, the two old friends would sit together in their quarters, putting the world to rights. Speaking aloud the troubles in his mind proved itself a cathartic experience. Cristó's grief, which had so often expressed itself through anger; the blaming of himself for not having protected his family; even the feeling that without his wife and daughter his own life counted for nothing, gradually settled into an acceptance of the facts. His had not been the only door scored with a black cross. Along his street of forty houses, twenty-eight had been marked, and of the remaining twelve, seven had been unoccupied before the plague had struck. Whether it had been God or luck to spare him, he'd never know, and as Montegatto reminded him many times, there was little point in trying to settle on an answer. It was better to look ahead, Montegatto said, to welcome tomorrow's opportunities, than to dwell in the sorrow of yesterday. As spring warmed to summer, the stonemason began to feel more at peace.

The high season brought with it a sticky, humid heat. Occasional thunderstorms, which came and went abruptly, only served to thicken the atmosphere. Distant rumbling would whisper the warning of an impending deluge. As the clouds darkened to a purple grey, cries of *'Tempesta! Tempesta!'* would echo across the site, followed by a mad scramble to put under cover anything which might spoil. These storms were biblical in their ferocity. The heavens unleashed a mighty roar. Jagged veins of lightning tore the sky apart. The rain fell not in drops, but in sheets.

By August, the heat became so intense that it was visible, shimmering above the sun-scorched crops. The flat expanse of the Lombardy Plain, held within the embrace of the Alps to the north and the Apennine Mountains to the south, was commonly known as *La Padella*, the frying pan, and for good reason. A relentless sun blazed with a roasting, skin-sizzling heat. Deaths from sunburn and sunstroke were not unheard of.

During this time, building work either slowed to a crawl or ground to a halt altogether. In the searing heat, heavy lifting sapped even the mightiest of muscles. The bricklayers were forced to set aside their trowels, defeated by cement which dried faster than they could spread it. Wood warped. Roofers' tar turned to soup. For many of the tradesmen, most of whom were away from home, August was a long-anticipated opportunity to reunite with their families. Only a skeleton crew remained holding the fort on site. Montegatto left for most of the month. With no family to return to, Cristó stayed put, intending to continue working on the fireplace, but even beneath the shelter of an awning, his hands were too slick with sweat to grip his tools. Much of his time was spent seeking shade and elusive whispers of breeze. And yet, despite the unforgiving climate, with each passing day, Cristó felt increasingly settled in his surroundings. He liked this place, with its level landscape, its vast sky and the distinct rhythm of its seasons.

September marked six months since the stonemason's arrival in Pieve Santa Clara, and as the summer heat waned, the germ of an idea began to take root in his mind. He was certain now that he would not return to live in Milan. The place was too hectic, too crowded, and too filled with memories of his wife and daughter. Part of him had always been drawn to a life in the country. Why not here? he thought. Property was cheap compared with the city. If he sold his old family home in Milan, he could buy a new house for himself – a place with a bit of land, with broad, open views and no ghosts. And he would still have money left over, and a second house which he could either sell or rent out to bring him long-term income. Perhaps it was too soon to think of full retirement, but easing off a little would spare his body from the injuries which might otherwise force him into it. Marchesini's fireplace was reminding Cristó of that every day. It was half-complete, and his elbow was giving him jip.

No sooner had he put out the word that he was looking for a house, locals began coming to him, eager to sell their properties. There was no shortage. The black death had led to a surplus of vacant homes inherited by those lucky enough to have escaped it – not that Cristó was keen on the idea of a plague house, because he couldn't be assured that the pestilence didn't linger inside, even after the property had been emptied and the period of quarantine had elapsed. Neither did he want anything too hemmed-in by neighbours, nor in the middle of nowhere; and certainly not by the bank of the canal, which risked flooding and would draw in the damp and the fog in the winter and attract plagues of mosquitoes in the summer. He went to look at a number of houses in various locations and states of repair. You could certainly get a lot for your money here. One hopeful vendor, who was quite obviously in a dire economic situation, proposed to him a whole *cascina* on the southern boundary of the village at a giveaway price, comprising a stately eight-bedroom house and four enormous barns – an impressive spread, but just too ridiculously big for one man on his own.

Having viewed a whole host of properties, none of which had been right for one reason or another, Cristó amended his plan. He rather fancied the idea of building his own house to his exact specifications, from foundation to chimney pot. He had the skills and the money, and once his contract with Marchesini was finished, he would have the time, so there was no reason not to.

A fellow came to see him proposing a plot for sale. Good building land, he said – roughly six acres with two wells, but not susceptible to flooding. It was currently rented to a woman who grew vegetables there, but if Cristó wanted to buy the plot, he'd tell her to leave.

'Head in the direction of the village and cross the canal,' the fellow said, 'About a quarter mile after the brick bridge, you'll see a fenced allotment on the left. You can't miss it,' so the following afternoon, Cristó made his way there.

From the way the owner had described it, Cristó had expected to find nothing beyond a large field and a few rows of cabbages and beans. Instead, within the enclosed plot was a spectacular, burgeoning garden. In between neat lines of carrots, onions, beets and greens, all manner of currant shrubs grew, surrounded by yellow calendula, frondy pink cosmea and tangles of nasturtiums with orange trumpet flowers. The lavender stood at shoulder height. Beyond were beds of strawberries and melons and tall stalks of maize. An intoxicating herb scent permeated the air so densely that it was almost palpable. This was a true Garden of Eden.

Cristó called out to announce his arrival, but the only reply was birdsong. Nevertheless, he opened the gate and went in.

There were just two constructions in the centre of the plot – a brick oven and a small, rundown wooden outbuilding with a straw roof and patched daube walls, which looked a gust of wind away from collapse.

Cristó stood for a time, imagining how fine a house would look in this spot. He already had an idea in his mind of its design – relatively simple in plan, with a central arched front door, two windows on either side and five above; built in brick with limestone lintels and sills. South-facing, perhaps nudging more towards south-east, to get the best light. What views his house would have, over a vast panorama of fields and pastures and copses of woodland. In the far distance the foothills of the Apennine mountains drew a smoky blue silhouette against the sky. From here, he could enjoy both the sunrise and the sunset. There was ample room for a barn too. This spot felt just right.

Having spent a while building his future home in his mind,

Cristó made his way deeper into the garden and found himself in an orchard of peach saplings with lines strung between them and rows of men's linens hanging out to dry. It was through the gaps in the laundry that he saw a young woman digging the ground. When she noticed him, she seemed surprised, but not displeased to see him, and gave a cordial greeting, as if they had already met; although he couldn't say that he recognised her, because he would have remembered. She was striking, with a head of long, wild curls as dark and shiny as freshly-hulled chestnuts. It was only when Nella bounced out from behind her, squealed his name and came running towards him that Cristó realised the woman was Florenza. Unshrouded, without her black tunic and widow's cowl, her appearance was entirely different. But when he stated the reason for his visit, her welcoming smile disappeared.

'And if you build a house here, where am I to go?' She asked.

She staked her spade into the ground, wiped the sweat from her face with her apron and eyed him with a fierce expression. 'When my husband died, I was left with nothing but a child inside me. I've put almost five years of my life into making this garden and every *centesimo* I've earned from scrubbing workmen's stinking laundry into having that oven built so I can bake bread to sell.' Then, pointing to the outbuilding, she said, 'And that shack may seem like nothing to you. A man of your size could boot it over with a single kick. But it's my home. The roof over mine and my daughter's head, and before I built it, I slept under hedgerows and canvas with my baby. And you would take my home and my garden and my means to make a living to build yourself a fancy house? Get out!'

Cristó apologised for the intrusion and left. As he made his way back to the site, he kicked himself for his insensitivity. He'd got completely carried away. Whatever had driven him to start jabbering on about the magnificent house he planned to build without consideration for rendering a hard-working widowed mother dispossessed and destitute? What part of him had, in those few moments of madness, thought it reasonable to forsake little Nella's needs and cast her into a life of insecurity? A home built on the ruins of Florenza's livelihood would be no home at all. When he reached the grand gateway which marked the main entrance to the Marchesini estate he stopped, turned and re-traced his steps. He went back to speak to Florenza, and that conversation marked the point at which everything changed in Cristó's life.

The master stonemason from Milan did indeed purchase those six acres of land. On the spot where once a brick oven and a wooden shack had stood, he built a splendid house – symmet-rical in design with two windows on either side of its arched front door and five above. There wasn't another like it in the village, with such pretty, intricate brickwork. Only Villa Marchesini could boast the same finely scroll-carved limestone lintels and bull-nosed sills. People would stop to admire the house, and to appreciate the glorious, blossoming garden in which it sat, filled with every kind of vegetable and fruit, and vibrant sprays of flowers.

There was just one word which could truly capture the essence of such a heavenly home, rising out of this Garden of Eden. On the twenty-seventh day of March 1640, three years to the day since his first arrival in Pieve Santa Clara, Cristó Lovetta registered the house as 'Casa Paradiso'. The name on the title deed was not his, but that of his new wife, Florenza.

1658

OTTORINO BOCCHI

The comforts of the marital embrace remained elusive to Ottorino Bocchi, which was most frustrating, because a man such as himself – hard-working and blessed with an amiable temperament – should have no trouble finding a wife. He still had his hair and most of his teeth, which were things women appreciated; and he wasn't offensively ugly. On the contrary, whenever he studied his reflection in still water, the face which looked back at him was not bad at all. Yet for all his many positive attributes, which also included sensibility and generosity and wit, Ottorino's success with the fairer sex was hampered by one big problem. That one big problem was his smallness.

From a distance, those who did not know Ottorino mistook him for a boy of around twelve, when in reality, he was a man closer to thirty. His precise height was impossible to measure as everybody used different scales, but suffice to say, if he stood up straight, he could just about see over a cow's hindquarters, unless she was one of those massive Chianinas, of the type most commonly used to pull ploughs.

Being the issue of many generations of herdsmen, there wasn't an awful lot Ottorino Bocchi couldn't tell you about cattle. Some even said he was possessed of a special affinity. His innate understanding meant he knew how to keep a cow content and productive; when to pasture her and when to confine her. He could spot signs of discomfort or disease early on and administer the appropriate remedies – such as turpentine for horn and hoof troubles; juniper poultices for wounds, and plaisters of hot ale to cure skin infestations caused by fly-strike. Not much could be done about consumption, but parsley and fennel kept the worst of the coughing at bay.

Amidst this extensive trove of herdsman's wisdom, Ottorino was also an authority on breeding. He knew that within their marrow, cattle carried essences of their forebears. When a cow and a bull blended their blood, it was like joining two streams into one river. Some characteristics passed down from one, some from the other, with certain elements being more dominant. Long since Ottorino had come to understand that what was relevant to cattle was also relevant to people. His own parents were a case in point. Both were significantly lacking in stature, and every one of the seventeen children they had produced was afflicted with the same deficiency, and in some cases, it had been compounded. Ottorino himself was one example. The top of his head barely brushed his father's moustache. Yet some of his sisters, who were approximately his height and had married quite tall men, were the proud mothers of children whom nobody would consider too short.

Ideally, Ottorino would prefer a wife who was beautiful and who appreciated his qualities, but above all, he sought one that was big. The bigger the better as far as he was concerned. He wanted her not only tall, but also meaty – the kind of wife that fattened-up well. Whilst he was under no illusions that the offspring they would bring forth would be giants, he could quite reasonably expect them to be sturdy, and of a respectable height.

Having exhausted all the possibilities in his native village and tried his luck in countless places beyond, Ottorino had still not come close to corralling a wife. Although he had offered himself to numerous women of imposing dimensions, none had been receptive to his advances. Some had even been hostile, or ridiculed him, which had hurt; and really, there had been no justification for that. The worst types were the ones who led him on, who accepted his gifts and fooled him into a sense of hope, only to reject him. He'd spent a small fortune on trinkets and love-tokens, and he must have picked half of the flowers in Lombardy, not to mention the wages wasted on sweet treats for all of those ungrateful witches. Thrice over he'd run out of fingers on which to count the number of times his heart and his pride had been crushed.

Still, Ottorino Bocchi was not a man easily beaten, for what he lacked in stature he made up for in determination. Now, finding himself working for the Marchesinis of Pieve Santa Clara, his search for an appropriately sized spouse could start afresh.

One early September day not long after his arrival, during his noon rest hour, Ottorino was on his way to purchase snuff. Along the road which led from the Marchesini estate to the village, a little way beyond the canal, there was a house with an arched front door. A barn was under construction adjacent to it. Ottorino stopped to look, not so much at the handsome house, nor its pretty garden; more at the barn, and most specifically, at the men who were building it. Impressive specimens, all of them. The very essence of vigour and masculinity. There was one older fellow and three others in various stages of growth, from adolescence to early manhood. These were the fellow's sons, Ottorino deduced, for there was no ignoring the family resemblance – broad, muscled shoulders; chests like barrels; arms thicker than his own legs. The eldest lad was already taller than his father and almost as strapping, with the middle one not far behind. Even the youngest, still fresh-faced and without a whisker, had the makings of a mighty man. They scaled the ladders with stacks of bricks and buckets of mortar as though the heavy burdens weighed nothing at all. What Ottorino wouldn't give to sire such sons!

But when the girl came out of the house, all else disappeared. Never had Ottorino laid eyes upon such a creature of towering beauty. Her tawny curls caught the September sunlight like the burnished coat of a prize French Aubrac. Her bearing was graceful. Her stride, even and steadfast. She must be blessed with straight legs and sound feet. And she carried her head well, with a proud stretch to her neck – a sure marker of health and good breeding. This maiden would be the bell-cow of any herd.

Evidently she was not yet at the peak of her maturation, for she might have been only around fifteen years old, but for such a girl, Ottorino could wait. She was already tall, standing a clear head and shoulders above him, and despite being a little on the lean side for his liking, she nevertheless disposed of generous breadth at the girdle and an ample buttery for her age. Another couple of good grass seasons in the pasture and that fine heiferette should be ready for mounting.

Ottorino's gaze followed the girl as she made her way through the garden. With her back to him, she stopped in the vegetable plot and bent over to tend to some plants. He might have devoted his entire noon break to the admiration of her well-balanced haunches and firm rump, had a man with a barrowload of pumpkins not pulled up at his side. Assuming that Ottorino was looking at the barn, the man commented, 'It's coming along well.'

'Yes,' agreed Ottorino distractedly, turning his head in its general direction, although his eyes were still fixed on the girl.

'That Cristó Lovetta could build you a palace from a pile of rocks,' said the man.

'Who?'

'Cristó Lovetta. The fellow up there on the scaffolding with his sons. Fine lads, they are. All three of them.'

Realising that the man was party to information which might be useful, Ottorino pointed to the girl in the garden and asked, 'Is that his daughter?'

'Yes. That's Carolina. She's the apple of his eye, that one.'

So now Ottorino knew her name. Oh, sweet Carolina! Her name rolled off the tongue like a song!

'Thank you,' he said, tipping his cap, 'Good day.' And he left the man standing looking at the barn.

Under different circumstances, Ottorino might have angled for an introduction, but his past encounters had instilled in him the importance of a favourable first impression. In his tattered work clothes, with his hands and face grubby and his boots caked in manure, he knew that his spark of appeal flickered faint. Also, not having picked his teeth clean for several days, he was conscious of what might be caught between them.

Ottorino was resigned to the fact that on initial meeting the first thing any woman would observe was his small size, and there was nothing he could do about that. Therefore, it was important to balance this disadvantageous characteristic with something more positive. It was preferable to be perceived as 'a short, but well-dressed fellow', or 'a modestly-sized man with a lovely smile', rather than 'a stinking, scruffy little arse-worm', or suchlike. He'd been called worse. Experience had taught Ottorino that women, for all their many gracious features, could be extremely cutting – and not always polite. With Carolina Lovetta, the very jewel of maidenhood, he resolved to cast himself in the most flattering light.

Before he knew it, the noon rest was over and Ottorino was back at the Marchesini farm, realising as he passed through the entrance that he had completely forgotten to go to the village for snuff. As the afternoon progressed, his thoughts strayed and he struggled to concentrate on his cows. His heart was taken; his mind bewitched by that most beautiful of creatures in the garden. He knew that he would not sleep a wink that night unless he laid eyes on her once more, so after the dusk milking, with his workday at its end, Ottorino set off for Carolina's house.

Twinkles of firelight quivered from the downstairs windows. Ottorino stood on the verge by the gate, stretched up on his tiptoes and craning his neck. Yet even if he had been as lofty as

Goliath himself, he would not have been able to steal a glimpse of Carolina. He was just too far away to see into the house. When darkness descended, he scaled the gate; then, as stealthily and silently as a cat, he slipped into the garden and crept towards the illuminated windows.

The family was seated around the kitchen table – Carolina, her three brothers, her mother and father. How glorious his sweetheart was, with her pretty face brightened by the firelight glow!

Disappointingly, the mother was of moderate build, although clearly the father, Cristó Lovetta, disposed of the dominant characteristics, for the children she had brought into the world were all robust. Carolina did not have the beefiness of her brothers, but that was to be expected as no cow ever matched the stature of a bull. Nevertheless, Ottorino could predict with a high level of certainty that the essences which Carolina carried within her blood would contain enough mass to make up for the deficiencies in his, and this would pass on to their offspring.

On the table sat dishes piled with polenta and sausage; one platter of cheeses and another of *salumi*; pots of pickles and mustard and fruit *mostarda* in jars. Right in the centre were two crusty loaves cut into slices thick as millstones and a golden pat of butter the size of a brick. Such quantities of food! Worthy of a feast more than an evening's supper – but just as well, as the three Lovetta sons had appetites like buffalos. They took second helpings almost as generous as their first. Yet to Ottorino's dismay, despite there being plenty to spare, Carolina did not. This was the time in her development when food in good quantity was important for growth. At the yearling stage, Ottorino always fed his heifers well, adding supplements of forage and grain, even blood soup to their fodder. This strengthening was vital, so that when the time came, they'd take the bull well; and once in calf, the quickening would bear fruitful issue.

'Dine heartily, my sweetheart,' willed Ottorino as he watched Carolina eat; and there he remained, with his eyes just cresting the edge of the windowsill; until finally, dinner was finished and the table was cleared.

The family transferred to a second room on the ground floor. Outside, mindful that his feet should not disturb the gravel, Ottorino followed and observed as Cristó Lovetta set about building up the fire in the hearth. And what a hearth! A fully-grown steer could stand side-on in its opening. As the father laid the fire, the mother lit lamps, and now, bathed in light, a luxurious parlour revealed itself. Ottorino brought his face closer to the pane to take in the dresser and cabinets – even pictures on the walls and upholstered chairs. He'd seen such fancy rooms through the windows of the wealthy, although never had he set foot inside.

Ottorino pricked up his ears, trying to discern words of the family's conversations, but only the vaguest of fragments carried through the glass. These murmurs were lost when the father and eldest son took up mandolins, and the youngest, a fiddle; and their voices lifted into song. As the mother and middle boy laid out a game of cards, Carolina, seated close to the fire, busied herself with embroidery. Ottorino was glad to see that she liked to sew, although he hoped that aside from this charming pursuit she was adept at practical tasks, such as making clothes, darning and mending. Needle skills were a valued virtue in any herdsman's wife.

At last, after what felt like a whole night of waiting, Carolina kissed her mother and father good-night and left the room. A minute later, a glimmer of candlelight appeared upstairs and Ottorino was rewarded by the vision of Carolina standing framed in the top right-hand window and twisting her curls into a braid. Seeing her undress as she prepared herself for bed would give Ottorino a better understanding of her stage of development. A good thickness of fat covering the ribs, back and shoulders would be a heartening sign; although unless up close and in a better light, he would have no way to determine the ripeness of her teats, nor whether her ingress had swelled.

Yet despite his eagerness to cover her, as a seasoned herdsman, Ottorino knew the importance of patience. *Fill the pail steady, for haste spills the milk*, the old saying went – and there was much wisdom in this. Being too quick to couple, even if a heifer showed signs of the heat, could cause problems with both first and future calvings, and the last thing Ottorino wanted was that.

As he watched, hardly daring to blink lest he should lose a precious second, Ottorino's anticipation grew to the point where he thought he might burst. But a moment later, having finished braiding her hair, Carolina closed her bedroom shutters, and Ottorino was left deflated in more ways than one.

The smitten herdsman returned night after night but was always denied the pleasure of seeing his beloved undressed. For the present, he could bear the frustration, because another matter vexed him more. To acquaint himself with Carolina through a pane of glass was a vain pursuit if she remained oblivious to his very existence.

The problem of his shoddy clothes could only be resolved after pay day, which was not for another two weeks. Ottorino had formerly owned a good set of garments. However, having left his previous employment in a hurry, he'd had no time to gather his things. That calamity owed its cause to a woman, but that was another story, and not worth getting upset over again now.

Explaining that he needed a change of clothes to wear on days of Holy Observance, Ottorino asked for an advance on his wages; and judging this as perfectly reasonable, the farm steward subbed him a whole month upfront. The clothing Ottorino bought from the market comprised a linen shirt, breeches and a waistcoat – all formerly owned, but in neatly-patched and largely un-stained condition; canvas boots and a wide-brimmed straw hat. It was these last two items with which he was particularly delighted. The boots were constructed with thick wooden soles and a heel, and the hat with a deep crown. Between them they gave Ottorino an advantage of a whole hand-span in height.

Every day, the instant the noon bell rang, having previously scraped his teeth and chewed sage leaves to freshen his breath, Ottorino stripped off his work clothes and leapt into the cow trough, where he scrubbed himself thoroughly with a stiff grooming brush. Once washed, he quickly pulled on his new outfit. Without a minute to waste, he dashed from the farm at a sprint, only slowing to catch his breath at the brick bridge. On his approach to Carolina's house, he slackened his steps, adopting a nonchalant stroll, and as he reached the gate, further lessened his pace.

It was there that he would find a reason to stop. He might crouch down to re-tie his laces, or take off his boot altogether and shake out an imagined stone. There was always some flower or butterfly to admire on the verge, or a bird to observe in the sky; and of course, there was building progress on the barn to be reviewed. Evidently, Ottorino's interest lay not in these details, as his aim was to catch a glimpse of Carolina. At times fortune favoured him, other times not. Yet aspiring to see her was one thing; more crucially, he sought her recognition. Regrettably, in this matter luck was elusive. When in the garden, Carolina was always occupied with one or other thing and usually her mother was with her. Furthermore, Ottorino had caught her father's eye, which had not been his intention. Whenever Cristó Lovetta spotted him, he would put down his tools and regard him with suspicion.

Having employed this tactic for a week without success, and even tried whistling to attract Carolina's attention, Ottorino remained invisible, except to her father. A more direct strategy was now necessary, and the perfect circumstances arose the next time he saw her.

It was a blustery day and Carolina was hanging out washing. Her mother was nowhere to be seen. Her father and brothers were working out of eyeline on the other side of the barn. Siezing the opportunity, Ottorino took off his straw hat and with a flick of his wrist, sent it spinning over the gate. The hat landed, not where he had intended, somewhere on the ground near Carolina, but instead lodged itself in the branches of a pear tree.

'Excuse me!' He called out, standing on his tiptoes and drawn to his full height, as without his hat, he had lost a few valued inches. Finally, after so many unrewarded efforts, Carolina saw him, left her laundry and came towards the gate.

With each approaching step, her resplendence unfolded. Up close, the loveliness of her face arrested Ottorino's soul, for Carolina had a rose-coloured, lightly freckled complexion, like the velvety muzzle of a Cream Charolais. Her eyes were as long-lashed and brown as those of a pure-bred English Jersey. Ottorino found himself too overcome to do anything but gaze at her beauty.

'Are you looking for someone?' She asked in a tone which was not in the least unfriendly.

'I'm looking for you,' Ottorino sighed with his most heartfelt smile, and upon hearing this remark, Carolina seemed puzzled, so he gathered himself, mindful of not spoiling his chances by speaking too impulsively. It was then that love-struck Ottorino remembered his hat.

'Please pardon the intrusion, sweet Signorina,' he said, feeling a flush creeping up his neck, 'but a gust of wind robbed me of my hat and it has landed in your pear tree. Would you allow me to retrieve it, please?'

'Of course,' she said and undid the latch on the gate. For an instant Ottorino stood frozen, for to him this felt not like a simple opened gate, but the dissolution of all barriers to their love. It took all of his restraint not to kiss Carolina there and then. But just like young calflets, women took better to a guarded approach. Sudden movements could startle them, as could loud noises. Best to keep his gestures gentle, his voice, soft. Then, and only then, might he hope for a tender caress.

As Ottorino couldn't reach his hat, Carolina unhooked it from the branch and returned it to him. At this point his intention was to begin a conversation, and he had a list of appropriate subjects previously compiled in his mind, but as he was about to comment light-heartedly on the weather, Carolina's father's voice boomed down from the scaffolding, 'Who's that, Carolina?'

'Just a man come to rescue his hat, Papá,' she called back, and before Ottorino knew it, she had ushered him from the garden and closed the gate.

He would have remained longer and continued talking from the verge, but from up on the scaffolding, Cristó Lovetta was eyeing him in a threatening manner, which rather spoiled the intimacy of the moment. Anyway, Ottorino couldn't be late for his afternoon shift, so he wished Carolina the most blessed of days and sauntered away, humming cheerfully and with his hands clasped behind his back. He counted ten steps twice before looking over his shoulder, hoping that she would be watching as he made his way up the road. If she was, he might be so bold as to blow her a kiss; but when he turned, with his lips already puckered, Carolina was nowhere to be seen.

Nonetheless, as Ottorino lay on his haybale bed that night, his mind whirled with thoughts of love. Considering the encounter with a little perspective, he reasoned that he should probably have told Carolina his name. No matter. The first threads of an introduction had been spun, and maybe the mystery of the hatless stranger in the garden would intrigue her.

Although they were only just embarking on their romantic journey, there were future practicalities to consider; and with all important matters in life, just as in herdsmanship, planning and foresight were crucial. There might not be the opportunity to take Carolina to meet his family until the following spring, but in the meantime, she would introduce him to hers. He hoped that her father would be swayed with ease. Whether they would marry in his home village or in Pieve Santa Clara, they could decide together. Ottorino and Carolina Bocchi – how perfectly their names combined! As a married man, he would be entitled to spousal lodgings on the Marchesini farm so he wouldn't have to sleep in the cowshed anymore. And once they'd welcomed a minimum of three children into the world, he could apply for larger quarters – two rooms instead of one, even a cottage with an upstairs and a downstairs if one came available. He should start saving for some furniture, and all the other household things like pots and pans and bowls and spoons; as well as bedding and blankets. He would start scouring the markets for items of good value and keep his ear to the ground for news of deaths in the village. There should be bargains to be had at the post-mortem auctions.

With his wealth of experience in matters of wooing, Ottorino knew that the next stage of his courtship must involve gifts, but finding something suitable in Pieve Santa Clara proved impossible. The selection of ribbons, beads and lace handkerchiefs was very limited, not to mention rather pricey; and having spent almost the entirety of his wage advance on new clothes and a pouch of snuff, his funds were insufficient to buy even the most modest of favours. In any case, any man off the street could gift such commonplace items. Ottorino required a meaningful token, infused with feeling and originality, and crucially, one that could be obtained free of charge.

The first milk of the day, known as the ambrosia, was the

creamiest; so with dawn barely broken the following morning, a full hour before the arrival of the dairymaids, Ottorino went to tap Marchesini's prize cow. He drew only a modest amount, just enough to fill a pint pot, so the petty theft would go unnoticed. In the silky sumptuousness of that ambrosia, the richness of his feelings would be impossible for Carolina not to understand.

As soon as the noon bell sounded, Ottorino washed and changed and left the farm with the pot tucked into his waistcoat. Tempting as it was to run, he was mindful of not shaking it too much. The last thing he wanted was to churn the precious ambrosia to buttermilk. All the way to Carolina's he prayed that she would be in the garden without her mother and that her father and brothers would be occupied elsewhere, and both his prayers were answered. Carolina was blissfully alone, picking pears from the very tree which had ensnared his hat. This in itself felt like a sign of forthcoming blessings. Was she thinking of him as she plucked the pears from that tree?

'Pardon me, Signorina,' he called out, this time giving a little friendly wave, and just like the previous time, Carolina stopped what she was doing and came to the gate. Today she seemed to Ottorino even more radiant.

'A small token for you, Signorina,' he smiled, holding up the pint pot, 'to thank you for returning my hat.'

'Oh,' replied Carolina, clearly surprised. 'Really, there's no need,' and she seemed reluctant to accept it.

'On the contrary, Signorina. You were very kind,' insisted Ottorino, pressing the pot into her hands; and now that he had Carolina's full attention, undisturbed by anybody who might meddle in their confidences, he seized the chance to impress her with a speech he had prepared and rehearsed in advance.

Ottorino elaborated at length on the craft of herdsmanship, making insightful connections between animal husbandry and Holy matrimony. Many parallels could be drawn, he said. The tending of livestock and the institution of marriage required the same kind of commitment. Both demanded patience, dedication and understanding to ensure an enduring bond.

Reading Carolina's lack of interruption as a mark of her agreement and gladdened that she would not be the kind of wife to butt in, Ottorino continued, 'Young maidens, just like yearling heifers, each have their own dispositions. Some are docile, others more headstrong; and whilst some show fondness easily, others are slower to yield.' Ottorino paused and Carolina lowered her gaze – a clear sign of submission. Greatly encouraged, Ottorino drew in a deep breath and went on, eager to reach the climax of his speech. With his voice rising, he declared, 'Yet these differences in temperament respond to one thing –' Now gasping, and with his eyes ablaze with passion, he cried ardently, '– and that thing is *love!*'

Carolina threw the pint pot back at him, saying that she could not take it because her father would not approve, and bolted into the house. Disappointment dropped in Ottorino's stomach like a stone.

For several days, he was too upset to see her. He went about his duties distractedly, driving the cows late into the parlour; ignoring orders from the farm steward; forgetting to shut gates. Then all at once it dawned upon him that he was being very selfish. His wounded pride was one thing, but what of Carolina's feelings? She might think that his sentiments were wavering, or worse, that he had lost interest altogether. After all, she had not said that she did not want him. The only reason she had turned down his gift was the fear of her father's objection. This final realisation sent a sour surge of bile to Ottorino's gullet. What sort of a father would deprive his daughter of love?

Ottorino Bocchi – he, of all the men in God's green pastures, stood as tall as the mightiest oak. Cristó Lovetta would not fell him. He would return to Carolina's that very night and throw a pebble at her bedroom window. She would look outside and then he would declare his love. 'Run away with me, my sweetheart!' he would say; and of course, at first she might show reticence, for the fear of her father must be strong. But from the depths of his heart, Ottorino knew that their love was woven within the fabric of destiny. They would escape together, and that very night, their shared life would begin.

As Ottorino's thoughts spun with dreams of elopement, being a man of sound sense, he was nonetheless mindful that practicalities must be considered. Initially, at least, they would return to his home village and live with his family in their hut; just until he found new employment, which shouldn't take long for a man with his herdsman's experience. He might even ask for one of his old jobs back. All the misunderstandings which had led to his prior dismissals should be forgiven and forgotten by now.

Fired with burning determination, Ottorino changed into his good clothes, and with a veil of dusk falling, headed for Carolina's house.

As always, he stole into the garden, darting between the shadows to evade the full moon's light. Furtively, he crept to the kitchen window and peered over the sill. A platter of roast lamb and vegetables sat in the middle of the table. Ottorino could smell enticing wafts from outside. The family was laughing at some shared joke, even Carolina. How well she hid her heart's wounds behind that pretty smile! Yet in that moment, Ottorino's lovelorn gaze turned from his intended to her father, that heartless brute of a man. With his nose just an inch from the windowpane, Ottorino Bocchi fixed his glare on Cristó Lovetta, sending him curses of piles and gut-worms and dysentery, and a long and torturous death. Suddenly, their eyes locked and Cristó Lovetta yelled, 'Oi!'

Ottorino shot out of the garden, leaping over the gate with a single bound, and diving into the ditch on the other side of the road – and just in time, because Carolina's father and brothers came out of the house. Lying face-down in the ditch, Ottorino held his breath, fearing that the panicked drumming of his heart would blow his cover.

'Where did he go?' He heard their voices say, and they didn't have to search for long. The hands of Carolina's elder brothers grabbed Ottorino by his scruff and the seat of his britches and lifted him from the ditch as if he was made of air.

'Yes, that's the little rat,' Cristó Lovetta said. 'Get rid of him.'

Ottorino's end was nigh. He was outmatched both in numbers and strength. How would they kill him, he wondered. Would they beat him, or tear him limb from limb? Whichever means they chose would be painful, so all he could hope for was that it would be quick. Yet to his great surprise, that moonlit autumn night Ottorino Bocchi did not meet his maker. The Lovetta brothers carried him by his arms and legs as far as the brick bridge where, with a stern word of warning never to come back, they lobbed him over the side and into the Delmona Canal. Ottorino landed in the shallows by the lavoir, still alive. He even managed to hang on to his hat.

Once more, the sweet wine of love had turned to vinegar, and once again through no fault of his own. Cristó Lovetta would see to it that he was dismissed from his employment, so there was little point in returning to the Marchesini farm; not even to collect his work clothes and his snuff. Still dripping, Ottorino took to the road with no idea in which direction he was heading and walked all through the night. This time his shattered heart could never mend and love again.

Many miles and hours passed. As the first glint of dawn pierced the horizon and day dispelled the remnants of the night, Ottorino stopped. There, driving a small herd of cows to pasture was a girl – a true giantess in both stature and substance; a bounteous, undulating landscape of rolling hills and valleys. The abundance of her bosom and the breadth of her hips carried the promise of their children yet unborn. Never before had Ottorino laid eyes upon such overflowing perfection.

Siezing the opportunity, he took off his straw hat and with a flick of his wrist, sent it spinning into the field. It landed just a little distance behind the girl.

'Excuse me!' Ottorino called out, standing on his tiptoes and drawn to his full height. 'Please pardon the intrusion, sweet Signorina, but a gust of wind robbed me of my hat and it has landed in your pasture. Would you allow me to retrieve it, please?'

1680

CAROLINA LOVETTA

Casa Paradiso was a respectable establishment of excellent reputation, catering for select paying guests. It was both owned and run by Carolina Lovetta, now in the thirty-sixth year of her life. She was a woman of many talents – resourceful, industrious and highly-esteemed within the community.

Carolina had written signboards placed along the Via Postumia advertising rooms to let, which worked well to attract the right calibre of clientele, because only those who were able to read could follow them. Her lodgers included merchants, members of the clergy, men of law and men of letters, as well as a regular traffic of artisans, particularly those associated with the luthiery crafts. With Pieve Santa Clara being situated not quite twenty miles from Cremona – a city world-renowned for the manufacture of the finest stringed instruments – Casa Paradiso was perfectly positioned as a rest-stop. Even Maestro Antonio Stradivari himself, the most famed of Cremona's violin-makers, had stayed with Carolina on numerous occasions. His employees and fellow luthiers were frequent guests, and Maestro Stradivari even recommended Casa Paradiso to his clients.

That crisp late autumn morning Carolina was seeing off Signor Zucca, a *cordaro* by profession, procurer and spinner of strings for musical instruments. He always overnighted at Casa Paradiso to rest both himself and his horses on his way to and from the sheep pastures of Colazzo. Sheep gut made for the most prized strings, not just for the bowed instruments, such as violins, violas and cellos; but also for lutes, guitars and mandolins, all of which were produced in Cremona.

Carolina came out of the house just as Signor Zucca was bringing his four packhorses from their stabling in the barn. He was a charming man and Carolina was very fond of him. Now advancing in years, dear Signor Zucca was still remarkably fit and sprightly, although over the long time Carolina had known him, his eyesight had diminished considerably. These days his vision had dwindled to almost nothing in one eye, and the other wasn't far behind. He could still make out bright colours and vague forms, but little else. Carolina did worry about him travelling long distances without being able to see, but Signor Zucca would brush off her concerns, saying that it didn't matter that he was as blind as a mole because his horses knew the way and he just let them lead him. He still undertook the eighty-mile return trip between Pieve Santa Clara and Colazzo on foot so as not to overburden his pack-animals.

In exchange for the delicious sheep's cheese he brought back from each of his trips, Carolina would send him on his way with provisions for his onward journey. No financial transaction would be involved. Carolina was more than happy to enter into these kinds of barterings with her most loyal clients. Signor Zucca's favourite victuals were her stuffed *panin'*, baked and filled to her mother's exact recipe. Carolina had prepared a half dozen of them for him that morning. They were still warm from the oven.

'Your rations, Signor Zucca,' she said as she handed over the package of *panin'*.

'You do spoil me, Signorina Lovetta,' he smiled affectionately, breathing in the aroma of the bread and cheese and pickle. As he placed the package in one of his saddlebags, he added, 'The weather's holding fair, so I should encounter no delays. I will be back on San Bruno's day.'

'A room will be waiting for you,' Carolina replied. 'Godspeed. I wish you safe travels,' and she kissed him on the cheek, which was a gesture reserved for only her favourite guests.

This time Carolina was particularly looking forward to Signor Zucca's return, as he had pledged to bring back twelve *bracci* – the equivalent of around ten yards – of woven woollen cloth. Carolina had given him the money in advance to purchase it. With this cloth, she planned to make herself a hooded cloak. Signor Zucca had one such cloak in an olive shade of green, which Carolina had always admired for the softness of the wool and quality of the weave; although olive was not a flattering colour for her, tending to sallow her rosy complexion. The fabric she had asked Signor Zucca to procure was indigo blue, and obviously, her own cloak would be fashioned in a more feminine style. Carolina already had the fastenings and the silk lining for it, acquired from another of her regular lodgers – a haberdashery merchant who passed through twice a year on his way to and from the port city of Venice.

There was no denying that Carolina enjoyed her luxuries, although her generosity extended well beyond herself. Whilst profit-minded with her customers, because business was business, she was generous to a fault with those she loved; not that the Lovettas wanted for anything. Her father had seen to it that her three brothers were solidly set up in their trades – two in masonry, and her middle brother as a cabinet-maker – and they were all doing very well. Her older sister, Nella, despite not being a Lovetta by birth, upon her marriage, had received a house with the deed in her name. Cristó Lovetta had been firm in his belief that women should dispose of independent means. It was for this reason that Carolina had inherited Casa Paradiso in its entirety.

Carolina remained unwed entirely of her own volition. First and foremost, because she had never encountered a suitor worth the trouble of marrying; but also, having been raised in a household with four men, she was well-acquainted with the ceaseless ministering required to sustain them. How bachelors survived without feminine guidance, she could not fathom, and many lacked the capacity, which was why such a number of them remained living *in perpetuum* under their mothers' roofs. Whilst she respected the fact that men worked hard, and often their jobs were physically arduous; women's work was no easier. Within any marriage, wives bore the weight of household management, kitchen duties, laundering and the myriad of tasks essential for husbands' functionality – not to mention the bearing of children, which was potentially lethal; followed by the raising of them – a constant occupation in itself. And in many matters, even beyond the domestic sphere, women were obliged to do men's thinking for them, as well as all manner of other things which they could quite easily be doing for themselves. That being said, Carolina harboured a fondness for masculine company and welcomed gentlemen warmly into her home. But she reasoned that if she was to provide all the forementioned services – with the exclusion of child-bearing, obviously – why not levy a fee for her efforts?

Carolina watched as Signor Zucca made his way up the road, heading North, and led at a sedate pace by his horses. His olive-green cloak was being lifted gently by the breeze. Once the cavalcade had disappeared from view, Carolina went back into the house to oversee the girls who came each day to undertake the cleaning and the laundry. Casa Paradiso brought in more than enough income to allow for hired help. Nevertheless, nobody could accuse Carolina of sitting idly as others toiled. She was continuously busy. Everybody said that she took after her mother in that respect. Aside from all the accounting and organisation required to keep the guesthouse running smoothly, she did all the cooking, providing wholesome, generously-portioned meals for her guests, many of whom elected to stay with her for the food just as much as for the clean, comfortable rooms, the feather beds and cordial hospitality.

As she was preparing a marinade for that evening's joint of beef, there was an urgent knocking at the door. The man Carolina found standing on her threshold, whom she had not encountered before, gave a rather confusing impression. Preceded by an elaborate bow, in painstakingly respectful tones, he introduced himself as Signor Dellarocca-Barbarosa, Devotional Antiquarian and Curator of Sacred Objects.

The fellow wore a coachman's coat, several sizes too big and burgundy in colour, and embellished with two symmetrical columns of large brass buttons – an expensive garment, no doubt, but looking somewhat weathered and with three buttons missing. The coat certainly didn't match his footwear. His boots were of a rustic type and far from new. What was more, beneath his coat, Signor Dellarocca-Barbarosa did not appear to be wearing any britches. Over his shoulder, he was carrying a sack.

However, when he explained to Carolina what had happened to him, his ill-assorted apparel made sense, as did the fact that he had fresh-looking cuts on his face and knuckles. The carriage in which he had been travelling the previous night had been held up by a bandit. A robber brandishing a blunderbuss had stolen his clothes; although mercifully, the brigand had spared him the humiliation of stripping him of his undergarments. The coach-driver had been kind enough to lend him a coat and his manservant had given him his spare boots. Of his personal possessions, aside from a small sum of money, which had been concealed beneath the bench of the carriage, all that remained was contained in the sack.

Carolina could not suppress her shock. Armed crimes of such aggression were unheard of in the region. 'Have the Constables of Justice been informed?' She asked.

'Yes,' assured Signor Dellarocca-Barbarosa. 'I have sent my manservant back home to Novara to fetch replacement clothing and belongings, with instructions to stop in Cremona and call in at the High Constable's Offices to report the malefaction. I felt indisposed to travel with him as the assault has left me most grievously shaken. It is for this reason that I find myself in need of safe shelter. I require a few days of calm repose to settle my shattered spirits.'

Still aghast, Carolina inquired, 'Did you get a good look at your assailant?'

Signor Dellarocca-Barbarosa shook his head. 'Alas, rendering a precise description of the villain is impossible as he was clad in black from crown to heel, with his visage concealed behind a mask. The sole mark which could unveil his identity is that he was ill-spoken and employed the coarsest and most blasphemous of tongues.'

On hearing of this dreadful incident, Carolina felt very sorry for the poor fellow and invited him in, saying that a room had been vacated that very morning. With a second bow he stated, 'I am most heartily obliged, and express my sincerest gratitude for extending to me such a generous and noble favour, Signora.'

'It's "Signorina",' corrected Carolina. 'I'm not married.'

The moment Signor Dellarocca-Barbarosa stepped into the kitchen, he made a sound of surprise and admiration, which was a reaction Carolina was well accustomed to from those entering the room for the first time. The larger part of the gable end wall was taken up by a Gothic fireplace of monumental proportions, measuring twelve feet in breadth by ten in height and carved with an intricate tracery of lozenges, quatrefoils and fleur-de-lys.

'Good heavens!' Marvelled Signor Dellarocca-Barbarosa, 'Never before have I beheld such a resplendent hearth!'

'This fireplace was sculpted by my father,' Carolina explained. 'It was originally intended for the dining hall of Villa Marchesini, but Signor Marchesini changed his mind about the decorative style of the room, so my father purchased the fireplace from him

40

and installed it here when he built this house. Formerly the Marchesini coat of arms was engraved on the over-mantel, but now you can read the initials of my parents, Cristó and Florenza Lovetta, carved within the central shield. Each of the surrounding acanthus leaves represents one of my three brothers, and the two roses represent my sister, Nella, and myself. The Tau cross was carved in memory of my father's first daughter, who succumbed to the plague.'

As was her habit with new lodgers, and in order to avoid any misunderstandings, Carolina stated her prices; firstly, for the room with breakfast included. Lunches and evening meals incurred an additional cost and were to be requested with prior notice. Hot baths could be reserved at pre-determined times, but not on washdays. Laundry services were provided with a fee applied to each individual item. All payments to be made in advance. Within her establishment, the rules were simple – respect and good manners must be practised; rudeness, rowdiness and drunkenness were not tolerated. Engaging in immoral behaviour would result in immediate eviction without reimbursement of any monies already rendered. Therefore, aside from wives or provably close relatives, no female guests could be received in the rooms.

Having agreed to all the costs and conditions, Signor Dellarocca-Barbarosa reached into his coat and took out a purse, the contents of which he tipped out onto the kitchen table to reveal an assortment of coins originating from various regions. These were all familiar to Carolina as she was accustomed to lodging guests from foreign places who paid in their local currencies. It was all acceptable to her. Money was money, wherever it came from. Aside from a handful of copper *centesimi*, which were of negligeable value, there were a couple of silver Florentine *scudi* and a silver *bolognino*. There was only one small gold coin, a Venetian *quartarolo*, worth one fourth of a *ducato*. Carolina did a quick calculation in her mind and assessed that this money would be just about enough to pay for three nights with breakfast, but no lunches, dinners, baths or laundry; or alternatively, two nights inclusive of all the supplementary services. When she stated this, Signor Dellarocca-Barbarosa looked somewhat crestfallen.

'Regretfully, I was robbed of all my other coinage,' he lamented, 'and it will take my manservant a minimum of ten days to make his way to Novara and return here with further supplies. At which point I can guarantee, Signorina Lovetta, that you will be recompensed in full for any debts I incur during my sojourn. Have my assurance that I am a gentleman of honour, and my word stands as my solemn bond.'

Carolina had no problem with her regulars, whom she knew and trusted, paying late if unavoidable circumstances arose, but pledging credit to a stranger made her uncomfortable. She ran her home as a commercial enterprise, not a charitable institution, and she had costs to cover. Hesitantly she asked, 'What was it you said you did for a living, Signor Dellarocca-Barbarosa?'

With a grand gesture, he replied, 'I am a Devotional Antiquarian and Curator of Sacred Objects.'

'Meaning what, exactly?'

'I deal in the purchase, sale and valuation of religious effects, mainly icons and relics. In fact, when my carriage was ambushed, I was en route to the Holy See in Rome to offer my expertise concerning the provenance and appraisal of several items purported to have belonged to Jesus Christ himself.'

Before Carolina could ask how he, or anyone else for that matter, could determine whether an item had belonged to Jesus one thousand six hundred and forty-seven years after His death, Signor Dellarocca-Barbarosa placed his sack on the table and began to take items from it. Each piece, he proclaimed, carried with it its own history of sanctity and wonder; and laying out a variety of brooches and medallions, he declared, 'Every one of these treasures is not only a masterpiece of artistry, but more importantly, a portal to the Divine – an intermediary between the realms of heaven and earth!'

With one of the pieces held reverently in the palm of his hand, he stated, 'Here we have a representation of Santa Lucia, defender of poets and scribes. And here –' he continued taking another, '– here we have the Mystic, Santa Teresa.' Then, having rummaged through the contents of the sack as though seeking something specific, he held up a tin pendant, saying, 'This piece may be of interest to you, Signorina Lovetta, for upon it is engraved a likeness of Sant'Anna, whose intercession is recognised in assisting nubile ladies in the search for a husband.'

Carolina crossed her arms and stated firmly that such a piece was of no interest to her whatsoever. Signor Dellarocca-Barbarosa gave a regretful nod, placed the icon back in the sack and went on to introduce San Cirillo, San Gervasio and San Giustino – all of whom guarded against a variety of disasters and misadventures.

Despite being a woman of faith, Carolina was not convinced by icons. You could find pedlars at every fête and market selling such trinkets, and most of it was tat. Sensing that Carolina was not greatly impressed, Signor Dellarocca-Barbarosa said, 'I detect, Signorina Lovetta, that you are a lady of discerning tastes and not spiritually stirred by these relatively conventional Holy representations,' so he reached into his sack again and took out a leather case containing several small glass vials. In a reverential tone he stated, 'Held within these vessels are the tears shed by the Madonna di Luvigneto – a miracle of which I am certain you would have heard spoken. The statue cried tears for three whole days, following which many extraordinary instances of healing were reported, such as infections of the pox being cured and the lame once again being able to walk.'

Carolina had indeed heard of the purported miracle of the crying Madonna. She had read about it not only in the *Gazzetta Lombarda*, but also in newssheets from far-off regions which her clients carried with them. Quite a collective frenzy had been stirred up by those who believed it to be true. For others, including many within the church, it was no more than a fraud, cooked up as a money-making scheme to attract gullible pilgrims. Carolina tended more towards the latter. She was also sceptical when presented with a number of vials supposedly containing the blood of the martyred San Sebastiano, despite being told that a single drop of this divine substance had resurrected a man from the dead.

Signor Dellarocca-Barbarosa leant forwards and lowered his voice, as though what he was about to reveal was of the utmost confidentiality. 'By the grace of God, and His magnanimous celestial benevolence, my assailant was not a man schooled in sacred matters, for despite having stolen my money, my clothes and numerous valuable personal items, he fled without taking the most precious of my treasures.'

In a ceremonious fashion, he laid upon the table what seemed to Carolina to be little more than a collection of household junk, comprising bits of wood and metal and scraps of cloth. Inhaling deeply, as if drawing into himself some mystical energy, Signor Dellarocca-Barbarosa presented a sliver of rib bone belonging to Sant'Agnese – very popular with sailors as protection from shipwrecks, allegedly; a strand of hair from the head of Santa Corona, protector against plagues and epidemics; a piece of fabric originating from the Sudarium, imprinted with the sweat of Jesus, and otherwise known as the Veil of Veronica; and most priceless of all, the very nail which had pierced the right hand of Christ on the cross.

Signor Dellarocca-Barbarosa granted Carolina a moment to appreciate the extraordinary value of all that was laid out before her, then proposed, 'As a mark of my recognition for your kind offer of accommodation and nourishment, I am prepared to part with any one of these prized items as payment for my board and lodging.'

Carolina surveyed the array of supposedly sacred wares spread across her kitchen table and replied, 'I'd rather take the money, thank you. Would you like to see the room?'

As Carolina led Signor Dellarocca-Barbarosa towards his quarters, he stopped at the foot of the staircase and gasped in wonder, 'Never have my eyes been witness to such a sublime ascent!'

Indeed, the staircase at Casa Paradiso was very beautiful, and just like the kitchen fireplace, everybody remarked on it. It was cantilevered, with each stone tread fixed only on the wall side, thus giving the impression that it was floating as it curved its way upwards; or more evocatively, in the words of Signor Dellarocca-Barbarosa, that its steps appeared to be carried upon the seraphic wings of angels.

'Am I to presume that this masterpiece of masonry is the work of your father?' He asked, and Carolina confirmed that it was.

'And this fine smithery? Was this also wrought by your father's dextrous hand?'

'No,' replied Carolina. 'The ironwork for the balustrades was designed and commissioned by the renowned architect, Montegatto, a lifelong friend of my father's, and presented to my parents as a wedding gift.'

Once he had pronounced himself satisfied with the amenities, Signor Dellarocca-Barbarosa informed Carolina that he would be taking the full-board option for the two nights which his available money would cover. After which, he would leave his fate in the hands of The Almighty. As a gesture of goodwill, and in view of the fact he had just been through a harrowing experience, Carolina offered him a late breakfast, free of charge, which he accepted using so many long words wrapped up in such complicated sentences that it took Carolina a few moments to work out whether he wanted breakfast or not.

So that Signor Dellarocca-Barbarosa wouldn't have to walk around in his undergarments, or keep his coat on, Carolina gathered together a few items of clothing to lend him which had been left behind by previous guests. She then inquired whether he would like to take a bath. Casa Paradiso had an indoor laundry room adjacent to the kitchen, installed by Carolina's father to save her mother the backbreaking chore of washing clothes in the communal lavoir by the canal. A water pump fed directly into a copper cauldron, which in turn fed into a stone trough. The trough doubled up perfectly as a bathtub, from which the dirty water could be emptied into a drain-hole in the middle of the floor. As Carolina had intended to soak Signor Zucca's sheets that morning, she had already lit the brazier under the cauldron and the water was piping hot. Laundry usually took precedence over bathing, but taking into account the exceptional circumstances, she was happy to let Signor Dellarocca-Barbarosa use the water for his bath. Signor Zucca's sheets could wait. For this kind gesture, her new guest declared his appreciation using yet another elaborate tangle of flowery words.

Carolina left him to his ablutions and made her way to the village to purchase a few things for that evening's dinner, and it was there that she received a very troubling report. Everybody was talking about it. A second robbery had taken place along the Via Postumia the previous night. Signor Marchesini's coach had been held up by an assailant armed with what was initially thought to be a blunderbuss, but was subsequently suspected to be a stick, carved into the shape of a shotgun. Following a brief tussle, Signor Marchesini's driver had seen the robber off with a few cracks of his whip. Nevertheless, the man had made off with several precious rings and an undisclosed – but clearly not insignificant – sum of money, as well as Signor Marchesini's clothes. Thankfully, nobody had been seriously hurt. Still, this was very unwelcome news. The presence of a bandit in the area was going to be bad for business. Carolina worried for Signor Zucca, who was due back in just a few days' time. She informed Signor Dellarocca-Barbarosa of what had occurred the moment she returned home, adding that Signor Marchesini had arranged for a division of Constables of Justice to patrol the Via Postumia after dark.

'Such tidings are of most grievous concern,' declared Signor Dellarocca-Barbarosa with a troubled expression. 'Let us pray that the good men of the law apprehend this wicked rogue and bring him swiftly to justice, so that rightfulness and tranquillity may be restored to the denizens of this fair land.'

'Yes, let's hope they catch him. This unfortunate business is making the locals jumpy,' agreed Carolina.

That evening, aside from her new lodger, Carolina's dinner guests comprised two wine merchants, a glove-maker and a botanist associated with the apothecary trade. Signor Dellarocca-Barbarosa commandeered the conversation entirely, giving a dramatic, move-by-move re-enactment of the attack to which he had been subjected. Although, he emphasised, he would not reprise the foul language used by the brigand, particularly in the presence of a lady and four distinguished gentlemen, as it had been of the most obscene kind. Contrary to the report given of Signor Marchesini's heist, Signor Dellarocca-Barbarosa had no doubt that the blunderbuss used during his assault was real, as he had seen the weapon's brass muzzle glint in the moonlight and had heard the clacking sound of its hammer being cocked. He then speculated at length on modern-day theories concerning the inherent flaws, moral failings and spiritual corruption of the criminal disposition. Miscreants and malefactors, he maintained, could in certain circumstances be cured by means of religious intervention; and he pontificated at length on matters of mystical enlightenment, repentance, exorcism and flogging. Having exhausted the subject, and his table companions along with it, he began to speak of the many celebrated figures whose fortunes his icons and Holy relics had transformed. The dinner guests listened politely, but ate their food rather more quickly than usual. In the end, one of the wine merchants parted with a whole *denaro* in exchange for a small flask of water, in which Santa Sigismunda was purported to have washed her hands. Carolina suspected the vintner had made his extortionately-priced purchase not out of belief in its sanctity, but more to shut Signor Dellarocca-Barbarosa up. Using the excuse of having an early start the following day, the two wine merchants, the glove-maker and the botanist retired to their rooms immediately after dinner. Having lost his audience, so did Signor Dellarocca-Barbarosa.

'Such restorative slumbers I have enjoyed!' Signor Dellarocca-Barbarosa announced as he strode into the kitchen at breakfast time. 'The very arms of Morpheus did cradle my being, gifting unto me the essence of most sweet repose. The tumults which yesterday besieged by spirit have dissolved into the night's air, and serenity has been restored to my soul.'

'I'm happy to hear you slept well and that you're feeling better,' replied Carolina, assuming that was what he meant, as she laid out bread and butter and fruit preserve. Signor Dellarocca-Barbarosa tucked heartily into his breakfast, and having complemented the craftsmanship of the fireplace once again, he turned his attention to the Marchesinis, asking, 'I surmise from what I have heard told that the family's fortunes are abundant?'

'Well, yes, there's no denying the fact that they're wealthy, but a large part of their money went on building that enormous house of theirs. The family is allied with the Spanish Habsburgs, but if the rumours are correct and the Austrian Habsburgs take over control of the Duchy of Milan, who knows whether people like the Marchesinis will be able to hold onto their estates?'

'Your words provoke much contemplation,' mused Signor Dellarocca-Barbarosa. 'I possess certain holy artifacts which may, by their divine virtue, assist in safeguarding their fortune, even to augment their treasury beyond their riches of prior days. Perhaps I will bestow a visit upon them this very morning.' He paused for a moment before suggesting, 'Given the preceding interests between the illustrious landowners and your father, might I venture to declare that I have been dispatched upon your recommendation, Signorina Lovetta?'

Carolina replied that he absolutely could *not* tell the Marchesinis that she'd sent him. Signor Dellarocca-Barbarosa accepted her refusal without argument, saying that in that case, he would go for a walk instead, to admire the verdant theatre of God's creation. Carolina was rather relieved to have him out of the house, but he'd barely been gone five minutes when her eldest brother, who was one of the village *consiglieri*, called by to give news that there had been yet more highway robberies the previous night.

'I thought the Constables of Justice were supposed to be patrolling the Via Postumia,' said Carolina.

'They were. The road was crawling with them. But the heists took place on the south side of the village, just off the Via Aeterna. It's got to be the same thief who held up Marchesini and your lodger. Same description – masked and dressed in black, armed with something that looked like a shotgun, in the dark, at least, and using some very unpleasant and threatening language. He demanded money and items of jewellery, then he stripped them of their clothes. Seems like this thief's putting together a new wardrobe for himself as well as filling his coffers.' Carolina's brother paused for a moment and his expression darkened. 'But the fellow he accosted after that was a skinner by trade, and he took his fleshing knife. So now the robber's not just armed with a stick. He's got a blade. A big, sharp one.'

'Oh, sweet Mary, Mother of God!' Gasped Carolina.

'Keep your wits about you, sister. Tell your guests not to venture out after dark, or to carry anything of value with them. They'd be wise not to wear their best clothes either.'

Carolina did just that, but not everybody heard or heeded the warning, because that night yet another robbery took place, this time along a relatively minor track to the West of Pieve Santa Clara, and as was feared, this time at knife-point. A spice-trader, whom Carolina knew as she regularly gave him her custom at the market, was relieved not just of his week's takings and a fine leather waistcoat and hat, but also of a valuable five-pound bag of cinnamon. WANTED posters appeared all around the village. Signor Marchesini put up a reward of five gold *scudi* for any information leading to the apprehension of the thief. A farm labourer could not hope to earn half that sum in a year. On account of his dark clothing, the marauder was now being called 'The Black Bandit'.

On the third morning of Signor Dellarocca-Barbarosa's stay, once he had polished off a considerable amount of breakfast, Carolina inquired what he intended to do next as his money had run out. Signor Dellarocca-Barbarosa replied in a voice which expressed absolute confidence, 'Having rendered prolonged supplications to San Giuda, known for his assistance in dealing with desperate financial tribulations, the answer to my pecuniary inconveniences was revealed to me. San Giuda enjoined me to venture into the village, pledging that therein I would encounter a soul in want of divine succour. Therefore, this day I will endeavour to locate this individual and vend unto him one or more of my sacred effigies. Rest assured, Signorina Lovetta, that you will have your money.'

Although Carolina doubted that he'd find any willing buyers in the village, she wished him luck, at the same time wondering which saint she should invoke to make Signor Dellarocca-Barbarosa employ less headache-inducing language. She also warned him not to come back late, and certainly not after dark, as The Black Bandit was now armed with a deadly knife.

'Good heavens! This turn of events gives rise to great concerns. Are the constables not yet upon the ruffian's heels?'

'No. According to my brother, they're no closer to catching him.'

'This brigand does indeed lead the constables on a merry chase,' replied Signor Dellarocca-Barbarosa, sighing deeply. 'The Black Bandit is as elusive as a shadow at dusk.'

Signor Dellarocca-Barbarosa made his way out after breakfast with his sack slung over his shoulder and returned not long before supper time, sporting a dandy new ensemble comprising a knee-length jerkin with matching mustard hose – a rather garish yellow shade, in Carolina's opinion. You wouldn't be able to miss him, even at a distance of five hundred paces on a foggy morning. His new outfit was completed by laced leather thigh-boots and a black felt hat embellished with pheasant feathers.

'I have enjoyed the most blessed and lucrative day!' He announced, bounding into the kitchen. 'San Giuda bestowed upon me a generosity beyond my expectations. I encountered not one, but three pilgrims bound for the Holy Shrine of San Girolamo. How heartened they were at my coming! They were in sore need, for they were so terribly afflicted by debilitating physical maladies that they were fearful of perishing before their journey's conclusion.'

'What did you manage to sell them?' Carolina asked, somewhat surprised that he had succeeded in finding such a number of exploitable pilgrims in Pieve Santa Clara.

'To the first, a vial of the Madonna di Luvigneto's tears, which quickly disabused him of a plague contracted at sea and granted him the relief of walking without burden. To the second, a woman afflicted by hysterical suffocation, I furnished an icon of Santa Bernadina, and within moments she found herself able to draw breath. The third pilgrim was a gentleman suffering from such acute rheumatic palsy that his hands were swollen to twice their normal size. I therefore parted with a fragment of hallowed board, originating from the very table at which the Last Supper was served, and so transported was he with joy and thankfulness that not only did he render the agreed sum thrice over, but also bestowed upon me this fine suit of clothes.'

Then, taking a leather pouch from the inside pocket of his new mustard jerkin, Signor Dellarocca-Barbarosa tipped out its contents, sending a shower of gold coins jingling across the table. In a rapturous voice, he declared, 'Pray avail yourself of all the monies you require to meet my expenses for the ensuing month, Signorina Lovetta!'

'For the next month? Is your manservant not due back from Novara within the next few days? Will you not be continuing your journey to Rome?'

'I have sent word to my manservant to abide until such occasion that the brigand is seized. I harbour no desire to imperil him unduly. Yet that notwithstanding, so splendid is the comfort that I enjoy in your home, and so delectable is the artistry of your culinary creations, that I am resolved to tarry a while longer before resuming my travels to Rome. As His Holiness the Pope and I are in amiable fellowship, I am certain that He shall find no offence if I arrive a trifle tardy.'

'You're friends with the Pope?' Queried Carolina, taken aback.

'His Holiness and I have partaken in a most cordial amity extending over a considerable measure of time, since long prior to His ascension to the Papal throne. I have stood both as a confidante and a counsellor to His Holiness, as well as His esteemed servant in affairs of sacred relics.'

Despite having more than a little trouble believing Signor Dellarocca-Barbarosa's claims of friendship with the Pope, Carolina refrained from asking searching questions. She did not wish to discourage him from parting with the considerable quantity of gold scattered across her kitchen table, which in its entirety would be enough to cover well over a year's board and lodging. She might well need it. Since the news of the robberies had made its way onto the pages of the *Gazzetta Lombarda*, several guests had postponed their stays until further notice, and passing trade had been reduced to nothing. Travellers were keeping off the Via Postumia, and in many cases circumventing Pieve Santa Clara entirely. As Carolina counted out the appropriate sum to cover the month, she advised Signor Dellarocca-Barbarosa to avoid going out with any amount of gold coinage on his person, even during the daytime, because who was to know where The Black Bandit was holing-up?

'Your tender solicitude for my health and preservation enkindles a warmth in my bosom, Signorina Lovetta,' he replied with his hand clutched to his heart, and quite clearly moved.

The villagers of Pieve Santa Clara were granted a night of reprieve, when no heists took place. Although, as Carolina's brother commented, this was no certainty that The Black Bandit had moved on. There simply weren't any people out and about to rob. The mayor had imposed a dusk curfew, and nobody was foolhardy enough to disrespect it. But the subsequent night, things took a very nasty turn.

During the hours of darkness a man was awoken by a stirring in his bedroom, to find The Black Bandit standing over him, pointing a long knife at his throat. Unless the man gave up his valuables, The Black Bandit threatened using very sinister language, his entrails would end up scattered in the Delmona Canal. Evidently, the terrified man had let the robber take anything he wanted. This was the first of three incidents that night, all following exactly the same pattern of people being awoken to find The Black Bandit standing over their beds, and all accompanied by the promise of evisceration and disembowelment.

The community of Pieve Santa Clara was in uproar, berating the authorities for their inefficacy. Now they weren't even safe in their own homes! The priest opened the church as a sanctuary for women with small children. Mothers and their young slept in the pews at night whilst their menfolk remained guarding their houses, armed with whatever came to hand. Carolina, who had turned down the offer of spending the night at one of her three brothers' houses, nevertheless barricaded the doors and slept with her rolling pin beside her in bed. The village blacksmith received so many requests for window bars, chains, padlocks, bolts and latches that he simply couldn't keep up with the orders. Signor Marchesini doubled the reward for catching The Black Bandit to ten gold *scudi*.

By now, Carolina was most concerned for Signor Zucca's safety. It was San Bruno's day, so she was expecting his arrival at any moment. She prayed fervently that he would reach her before darkness fell. As she waited, she set about preparing Signor Zucca's favourite dish of *tortelli* stuffed with artichoke, followed by pork loin with rosemary. To accompany the sheep's cheese which he would bring, she had stewed some pears. As an additional treat, in recognition for going to the trouble of procuring her indigo cloth, she was kneading the pastry for a quince tart.

At around six o'clock in the afternoon, as the light was beginning to fade, Signor Zucca's four packhorses appeared in the yard. Carolina set aside her rolling pin and went outside to welcome him and to lend a hand stabling the animals, relieved that he had made it without incident. But he was nowhere to be found.

The horses, which were normally placid animals, seemed extremely out of sorts. Their nostrils were flared and their ears pinned back. They were jerky on their hooves.

'There, there, my lovelies,' Carolina said reassuringly, attempting to soothe them as she led them into the barn, but they tugged on their halters, tossing their heads and wrenching the reins from her hands. Nevertheless, she managed to tether them in their stalls and unsaddled them of their loads. When she gave them hay and fresh water, they would touch neither. On opening the saddlebags, Carolina found them to be filled with bundles of dried sheep-gut, but when she looked inside the pannier in which the old *cordaro* transported his provisions and personal possessions, it was empty. There was no sign of her cheese or indigo blue cloth either, and most worryingly, still no Signor Zucca. This was a very poor portent indeed.

Carolina called one of her domestic girls from the house, instructing her to run as fast as she could to the brick bridge where a watch-team of constables was stationed, and to tell them to send out a search party. The gentleman they were to look for was elderly and nigh-on blind, slight in stature, and wearing a long olive-green cloak. He would have been approaching Casa Paradiso from a northerly direction. The girl left immediately and was back not long after, assuring Carolina that the search for Signor Zucca was underway. It was starting to get dark. And now Carolina was also concerned for Signor Dellarocca-Barbarosa, who had not yet come home.

When at last Signor Zucca appeared, he arrived not via the road, but emerged from the shrubbery behind the house. The poor old man was trembling and in tears and wearing only his undergarments, which were torn and caked in mud. As well as all manner of cuts and bruises and abrasions, he had a bloody injury to the side of his head.

'Oh, my Good Lord!' Shrieked Carolina, bundling him into her shawl. Signor Zucca was in such a frenzied state of shock that she almost had to carry him into the house. All he could do was to apologise repeatedly for his unseemly state of dress. He had been too ashamed to walk along the road in his braies, so he had shooed off his horses, confident that they would make their way to Casa Paradiso, and he had come across the fields. But he had been utterly disorientated and unable to see where he was going. He had banged his head when he had fallen into a ditch.

Once Carolina had calmed him sufficiently, cleaned his wounds and furnished him with a robe, he told his story: a fellow, who had been very friendly to begin with, had walked with him for a while, and they had enjoyed an entertaining exchange; until suddenly, he had felt the cold, sharp prodding of a blade to the side of his neck. At this point, the fellow's cordial conversation had turned to the most spine-chilling of menaces. Even his voice and his manner of speaking had changed. Unless he surrendered all he had of value, the brute had vowed to cut off his fingers, then to pluck out his eyes and feed them to the crows. What was more, he had threatened to slit the throats of his horses.

'I was so very frightened, for both myself and my animals,' Signor Zucca stammered, 'for I believed the man's pledges to be deadly serious. So I told him to take anything he pleased. But the villain was furious to find that my panniers contained little else apart from sheep-gut. It was then that he demanded that I should take off my clothes.'

'Were you able to distinguish anything at all which might be of help in identifying this brute?' Carolina asked. 'Was he by any chance dressed in black?'

'No,' replied Signor Zucca, shaking his head with absolute certainty. 'The only thing which my fogged eyes discerned was that he was dressed from head to foot in a very vibrant shade of mustard yellow.'

Instantly, Carolina's blood congealed in her veins. 'I shall inform the constables,' she assured the old man, but said no more. She then settled Signor Zucca into his room and told him to bolt the door and not come out under any circumstances.

No sooner had Carolina returned to the kitchen than Signor Dellarocca-Barbarosa swept in. Over his mustard ensemble he was wearing Signor Zucca's olive-green cloak.

'Behold, Signorina Lovetta!' He proclaimed, twirling on his heels and causing the cloak to billow like a sail. 'Is this not the finest mantle that you have ever seen? Pray, bestow a moment's regard upon its resplendent hue, akin to olives plucked fresh from the sacred Gardens of Gethsemane! I chanced upon a peddler, his sight so dim that he was nigh to blindness. Upon his clouded eyes I did lay a shred of Veronica's Veil, and lo! His vision did become as lucid as the waters of Siloam!'

Assessing that she found herself in a very perilous situation, Carolina steeled her composure and smiled, 'That is indeed a beautiful cloak, Signor Dellarocca-Barbarosa. Clearly the peddler was very grateful for your help.'

'Indeed! And as I hold to the belief that a kind deed ought not go unrequited, I come to you bearing gifts.'

With a majestic flourish he pulled from his sack a wheel of sheep's cheese and a roll of indigo blue cloth. 'I wish to bestow upon you, Signorina Lovetta, in recognition for your generous hospitality, not to mention your virtues, numbering more than the stars in the heavens, these tokens of my esteem.'

'Really,' said Carolina, swallowing hard to steady her voice. 'You're too kind, Signor Dellarocca-Barbarosa.'

He replied with a gesture of false modesty, and holding up the roll of indigo blue cloth, he proclaimed, 'I am of the inclination that this hue will bring the bloom of summer roses to your fair complexion, Signorina Lovetta. You shall surely be the object of every gentlewoman's envy in the village,' and turning his attention to the cheese, he added, 'and tonight, we shall partake in a feast befitting a sovereign – a repast of such splendour as to rival the banquets of kings!'

At that very moment, Carolina's brother arrived at the house to say that so far the constables had been unable to locate Signor Zucca, but the search was ongoing. He took one look at the expression on her face and asked, 'What is it, Carolina?'

'This man is The Black Bandit!' She cried, ducking for safety behind the table.

'What?' Spluttered Signor Dellarocca-Barbarosa. 'Are you bereft of colour discernment, woman? I am clearly not clad in black, but in the most conspicuous shade of saffron!'

Carolina's brother, knowing that his sister would not make such an accusation without irrefutable grounds, sprang forwards to grab the villain, and in a swift countermove, Signor Dellarocca-Barbarosa pulled the fleshing knife from his boot. It was some twelve inches long with a blade a quarter inch thick. He lunged at Carolina's brother, but was arrested mid-thrust by Carolina cracking him on the head with her rolling pin, and he fell to the floor, stunned. By the time he came around from his daze, his hands and feet had been securely bound.

'Release me, you bastards!' He yelled, flailing on the kitchen floor like a fish on a hook. 'I'll wrench out your innards! I'll mash your brains! I'll stick my foot so far up your fundaments that you'll be choking on my bootlaces for a week!' The constables came to take him away shortly after.

With The Black Bandit apprehended, peace returned to the community of Pieve Santa Clara. Signor Dellarocca-Barbarosa – not his true name, evidently – was sent back to his native Novara to enjoy the amenities of the Broletto gaol, an establishment in which he had quartered on previous occasions following convictions for sundry acts of larceny and confidence trickery. Within its dank and impenetrable walls, he enjoyed the comforts of sleeping without pillow or mattress on the floor, but cosy in consort with the three dozen new companions who shared his two hundred square foot cell. They were a spirited, and frequently capricious, lot – comprising vagrants and knaves, bruisers and scufflers and dispatchers, and violators of every kind. Hardly a moment passed which was not brimming with lively diversions. The prison menu, if a little lacking in variety, comprised mainly gruel, garnished with a sprinkling of millet, and the occasional added delicacy of gristly matter which was trickier to identify. Bathing and laundry services were not provided.

Along with an outfit of black clothes and a stick carved into the shape of a shotgun, a stash of loot was located in the hayloft of Carolina's barn. All items were returned to their rightful owners. It was not long until regular guests and passing travellers came back to Casa Paradiso.

Quite a legend grew around Carolina, who herself was simply glad for life to get back to normal. Although, it had to be said, her business experienced a significant upsurge, with the curious clamouring to stay in the very place where the infamous Black Bandit had lodged, and eager to hear first-hand accounts of how Carolina had foiled him. A correspondent from the *Gazzetta Lombarda* came to write down her story and published an article headlined: *Heroine of the Hearth! Daring Landlady Nabs Elusive Outlaw!* Following its publication, Carolina received numerous offers to purchase her rolling pin.

All in all, what with the increased traffic of guests and the reward of ten gold *scudi* conferred by Signor Marchesini, Carolina Lovetta did rather well out of the whole thing.

UGO LOVETTA

The Lovetta boys, Ugo and Moreno, were fraternal twins, and although not dissimilar in appearance, they were like day and night in temperament. From the moment he had torn his way bawling into the world, it was clear that Ugo was the more forceful character. He did all he could to assert his dominance and to torment his brother with pokes and pinches, shoves and slaps. This caused not only Moreno, but also their parents, significant anguish.

'What am I to do with that boy?' Ma Lovetta would despair. She couldn't leave the twins alone for a minute or set them down to sleep in the same bed. The moment her back was turned, Ugo would start on Moreno, who despite his placid nature would not take his brother's attacks without defending himself.

Dealing with Ugo's aggressive tendencies became evermore difficult as the boys grew. Scuffles and tussles escalated to fights involving sticks and stones and all manner of improvised weapons. When he wasn't physically attacking his brother, Ugo delighted in trying to get Moreno into trouble for things he himself had done. He was never believed, and this led to more problems. Ugo would protest his innocence, say it wasn't fair and rile that his parents showed blatant favouritism towards his twin brother.

Many said that Pa Lovetta was too soft and what Ugo needed was a good walloping to bring him into line. Pa Lovetta was a big, gentle man who did not believe in raising his mighty hand to anybody, let alone to his own children. He was driven to do so only twice when the circumstances had been life-threatening.

The first time, when the boys had been eight years old and he had caught Ugo chasing Moreno with a pitchfork and clearly intending to cause him permanent damage with it. The second time, for throwing a brick through the kitchen window. Pa Lovetta struck his son not for smashing the glass, but more precisely because at the time Ugo lobbed the brick, he had been aiming it at Moreno's head. Ugo took the spankings whilst laughing at his father and showed no remorse. He resolutely refused to apologise to his brother.

The incidents with the pitchfork and the brick were not the last of the brothers' altercations. However, when Moreno began to grow bigger than Ugo, and by the age of eleven had overtaken him by over three inches in height and several pounds in weight, Ugo's enthusiasm for picking fights with his brother decreased. He turned his attentions to other forms of baiting instead, such as mocking his twin with smart-mouth jibes and jeers and name-calling. Moreno could give as good as he got, and often he did, although most of the time it was easier to ignore the insults and get on with his own things. Unlike Ugo, Moreno was always willing to assist his mother around the house and garden and loved nothing more than going out for the day to help his father in the fields.

Bored with goading his goody-goody twin brother, Ugo sought other amusements, and there was entertainment a-plenty to be had with his best friend, Aldo. As far as Ugo was concerned, Aldo was the brother he should have had – a partner in crime who shared his tearaway spirit. What a tight little gang they became! They were both boisterous in nature and keen to throw their weight around. Many of the boys in the village were scared of them. Picking on those who were smaller and weaker provided Ugo and Aldo endless thrills. They also developed a taste for practical jokes, such as letting livestock out of their enclosures, scrumping and setting things alight. Whenever the priest, or the mayor, or some angry villager turned up at Casa Paradiso with a face like thunder, Pa Lovetta would greet them with the same weary words – 'What's Ugo done now?'

By the time the twins turned thirteen, it was clear to the Lovetta parents that if something was not done to regulate Ugo's behaviour, he would end up either in prison, or dead – and sooner rather than later. He was old enough, and certainly big enough, to go to work, but with his unruly reputation, finding someone willing to employ him was easier said than done. None of the farms would have him, and as he had expressed a visceral contempt for working the land, even if one of the local farmers had been desperate enough, or foolish enough, to give him a chance, Ugo wouldn't have gone anyway. Trying to force him was more trouble than it was worth. The blacksmith and the wheelwright refused to consider Ugo, both stating that they did not trust him around their fires. Similarly, various carpenters, masons and roofers expressed concern about giving Ugo access to sharp or heavy tools. Ugo was a liability, they all said, and most of them added that if Moreno wanted a job, they'd be happy to employ him instead. Eventually, after much asking, begging and prayer, Pa Lovetta managed to secure an apprenticeship for Ugo at the local sawmill as a general labourer. The sawmill boss had the reputation of being a tough, no-nonsense fellow. Pa Lovetta hoped that he would be a positive influence on his errant son, and that he would teach him the things which he had failed to, such as respect, compliance and a good work ethic.

The sawmill, which was powered by a colossal waterwheel, was located on the bank of the Delmona Canal. Ugo was not allowed inside, and certainly nowhere near the sawing mechanisms. His job was to help move the wood around the stock yard and to load and unload the timber which arrived by barge. To say that he began his career as an apprentice labourer with enthusiasm would have been an exaggeration, but he didn't go entirely unwillingly. Being endowed with the sturdy Lovetta constitution, he was keen to show off his physical prowess. Despite being two-and-three-quarter inches shorter than Moreno, he was every bit as strong, stronger probably, and keen to prove it. He was also attracted by the prospect of earning what seemed to him at the time, a serious amount of money.

The other sawmill workers didn't go out of their way to be friendly towards Ugo and he didn't like the boss one bit. Being told what to do and when to do it got on his nerves, especially if he was charged with some menial task. He almost jacked in the job on his very first day when he was ordered to do some sweeping. The only thing which stopped him was the thought that people might call him a failure if he walked out. So, despite harbouring a deep resentment towards the boss and his workmates for treating him like an inferior, and towards his father for having forced him into the job in the first place, Ugo gritted his teeth and went to work. He learned the hard way that if he didn't turn up when he was supposed to, or was lazy, or rude, his wages would be docked, and once he had come to terms with the fact that no work meant no pay, that was incentive enough to ensure that he stayed within the rules, more or less.

The prospect of money was the only thing which got Ugo out of bed every morning. He scrupulously spent every *centesimo* of his wages in the village tavern on Saturday nights. The Lovetta parents worried about their son's taste for drink, particularly in view of his relatively young age, but no amount of concern or admonishment dissuaded Ugo.

Every Saturday night without fail, Ugo went to get a skinful of beer with Aldo. Aldo had money in his pocket too since he'd got himself a job driving a delivery cart for his uncle, and he was equally eager to spend it on drink. What boozy fun they had, and not just in the tavern, but after closing time too! They dared one another to do all sorts of rascalish things, from urinating on doorsteps and in the fountain, to graffitiing obscene pictures on walls. One night they even broke into the church and cut the rope of the Sanctus Bell. There was nothing more hilarious than waking up the sleeping villagers by rapping on their doors; or by standing in the piazza singing off-key songs at the tops of their voices. Often Pa Lovetta would discover the evidence of Ugo's Saturday night exploits the following morning, such as the time he awoke to find three stolen sheep in his vegetable garden munching on his runner beans. Ugo swore that he hadn't stolen the sheep. He had simply borrowed them, although he couldn't remember who from. Random objects often appeared – shop signs; enough fiddles, drums and concertinas to set up a band; a selection of potted plants; all manner of laundry – in particular ladies' undergarments of every shape and size, plucked from washing lines. The list was long and varied. Pa Lovetta was acutely embarrassed and did his best to return the pilfered items to their owners. For his part, Ugo just laughed at all the moaning and moralising, and Aldo laughed with him.

Moreno said that rather than wasting it all on drink, Ugo should give some of his wages to their mother for housekeeping, but Ugo didn't go much on that idea, and as neither of his parents had asked, he saw no reason to offer. It was easy for Moreno to say, because he earned hardly any money at all. On this matter, Ugo mocked his brother for not having enough brains to leave the fields, to which Moreno replied with a question, 'How much intelligence does it take to sweep sawdust and shift planks of wood around for a living?'

This comment, amongst others, further spoiled the sour relationship between the Lovetta twins. Ugo reckoned that Moreno was envious of him. He told anyone who would listen that his brother was not only jealous, but stupid and weak too. He didn't like it when people disagreed, and even less when they leapt to Moreno's defence, but Aldo agreed with him whole-heartedly, and his was the only opinion which really mattered.

By some miracle, Ugo managed to complete his three-year apprenticeship as a labourer without being fired. However, once qualified, the sawmill owner declined to offer him a permanent position. Ugo didn't care one jot, because he realised that there were better things to do than sweep sawdust and shift planks of wood about for a living, and it had come to his notice that the pay wasn't that good anyway. He knew that a young man of his strength and ambition was worth far more. During his time at the sawmill, he had become friendly with the men who worked on the canal barges. They were more his type of workmates – rowdy, hard-drinking and always up for a laugh.

The Delmona Canal had been an important artery for commerce since before Roman times. A continuous traffic of horsedrawn barges, known as *chiatte*, transported goods between the towns and villages along its eighty-mile route. Seduced by the prospect of adventure and long-distance travel, Ugo got a job as a *mozzo*, which was the most junior position aboard, but he was to be paid twice as much as his measly sawmill wages.

Ugo set off on his maiden voyage one fine spring day, brimming with trepidation and excitement in equal measure. As a *mozzo*, he was called upon to assist wherever and however he was needed aboard the *chiatta*. Aside from deck-scrubbing and emptying the bilges, sometimes he helped the horse-driver. Other times he added his strength to the navigators who steered the vessel by means of pushing long wooden poles into the canal-bed. He also kept an eye on the merchandise along with the cargo-men, ensuring that the load was balanced and secure. By sunset that first day, when the crew moored-up to make camp, the *chiatta* had travelled over thirty miles, which was the furthest from Pieve Santa Clara that Ugo had ever been. The day had been both thrilling and exhausting and never had Ugo been so keen to lay his head down. He then discovered that his *mozzo* duties included remaining awake most of the night to keep watch for thieves. Nevertheless, despite the hard work and sleep deprivation, Ugo loved his job.

It wasn't all work and no play. There was no shortage of watering holes along the canal, many of which catered solely to the barge crews. Unlike the tavern in Pieve Santa Clara, these were raucous places, filled with noisy banter, laughter, bawdy songs and colourful curses. The drink was cheap and plentiful and brawls were common. And oh, the women! Never in his life had Ugo encountered such friendly ladies! During his second week as a *mozzo*, Ugo met a girl who invited him to put his hand up her skirt and subsequently relieved him of his virginity for a very reasonable price.

Barge life suited Ugo well, and it was not long before he was promoted from *mozzo* to *barcaiolo*. The job was not dissimilar, except now he didn't have to scrub the decks, or empty the bilges, or stay up all night watching for thieves. Best of all, his pay was doubled.

With Ugo gone for weeks at a time, an unfamiliar peace descended upon Casa Paradiso. Ma and Pa Lovetta would worry about Ugo getting into trouble, or falling drunk into the canal, but for Moreno, his brother's absence was a long-overdue relief. He continued working with his father and at the age of nineteen he married his sweetheart. The newlyweds remained living at Casa Paradiso.

Ugo was rather insulted to discover that the wedding and feast had taken place in his absence and suspected that it had been done on purpose. He didn't think a lot of Moreno's wife. She was a pale, flat-chested little thing and about as exciting as drizzle. He had a good laugh about her mosquito-bite tits with Aldo and speculated about all the things which would, or wouldn't, be going on in the marital bed. By now Ugo had enjoyed more than his fair share of ladies and considered himself quite an authority on the pleasures to be had in female company. During his three years working on the barges, he'd had six different women – two of them unpaid and one of them twice.

With the newlyweds living at Casa Paradiso, and within no time at all a baby on the way, Ugo decided that the time had come for him to find a place of his own. He worked hard, so his rest was important. The last thing he needed was to have his leave disrupted by some bawling brat. His family made no effort to dissuade him, so he rented a small cottage on the bank of the canal. It was cheap, and some might say for good reason, as aside from its very modest size, it was in a pretty tattered state. Not only that, but its position so close to the water drew in the damp and the fog. In the bitter depths of winter, when the canal froze, it was insufferably cold. During the summer, it was infested by biblical plagues of mosquitoes. With the canal being both a trade artery and a sewer, in hot weather the smell could take some getting used to. None of this bothered Ugo, particularly as he spent more time away than at home. But when he was back in Pieve Santa Clara on leave, he enjoyed having his own space, isolated from his parents' nagging and his brother's sanctimonious lecturing. That in itself was enough to mitigate the house's less agreeable aspects.

Unlike Moreno, Ugo had no designs on getting married. There was far too much fun to be had as a bachelor for a wife to spoil. He certainly didn't want kids, and he became all the more certain of it when Moreno's son, Rosolino, came into the world. Ugo went to take a look at his newborn nephew more out of duty than anything. The kid was a bit funny-looking, in his opinion. It didn't have the Lovetta constitution, taking more after the mother's side. He was quite glad when nobody made him hold it. He had a private laugh to himself, not just because the baby was scrawny, but mainly because of what they'd named it.

'Rosolino' meant 'Little Rose'. What a thing to call a boy! That kid was going to get teased like there was no tomorrow. Aldo thought it was funny too and they spent a good part of that evening in the tavern getting a head start on all the possible nicknames for a boy called 'Little Rose'.

Now all the more certain that he would remain a carefree bachelor for life, Ugo returned to his job on the *chiatta*, until one evening in a tavern on the outskirts of Mantova, he met a girl called Nunzia. From the moment he set eyes on her, love struck him like a lightning bolt and all other women ceased to exist for Ugo. Their romance took off with the force of a whirlwind and sent them tumbling drunkenly into the long grass by the towpath. In his besotted, post-coital rapture, Ugo asked Nunzia to marry him, which she did the following day. It was a hastily organised ceremony, with the church sacristan and the priest's housekeeper brought in as their witnesses. After exchanging their vows, rather than the customary wedding feast, they had a lock-in in the tavern. What a party that was! And with everyone enthusiastically buying drinks for the newlyweds, the whole thing didn't cost Ugo a bean. Ugo had no regrets about not informing or inviting his family. After all, they'd held Moreno's wedding in his absence and without his knowledge. The snub evened things out.

The bride and groom returned aboard the *chiatta* to Pieve Santa Clara, but the marriage encountered its first teething troubles within moments of the newlyweds disembarking from the barge. Nunzia was mightily unimpressed by the marital home. Maybe Ugo had painted a rather rosy image of his waterfront dwelling. Although he had not wildly exaggerated its attributes, he had certainly glossed over its negative aspects. He couldn't remember having made some of the claims that Nunzia said he'd made, although he couldn't deny that he might have. It wouldn't have been the first time he had spouted reckless promises to a woman whilst intoxicated.

Admittedly, if Ugo had had the slightest inkling that he'd be returning home with a wife, he'd have tidied up before his departure, but that wasn't Nunzia's greatest objection. She griped that the house was so small there was barely room to turn around in it. And where was the furniture? True, the cottage was rather sparsely equipped with only the items which had been left by the previous tenant. There was a bed, and the frame was in a reasonable state, but Nunzia said that the mattress smelled as though someone had died on it, and Ugo couldn't be certain that this wasn't the case. The table only had three of its legs, but Ugo had made it usable by propping it up with a stick. For the rest, he improvised with crates and buckets and anything which came to hand. It hadn't ever crossed his mind to buy proper furniture. Still, he understood how a wife would expect some home comforts, so he pledged to replace the mattress and buy some sheets. With his next pay-packet, he promised to get a new leg for the table and some items for the kitchen. He also agreed that as soon as the finances allowed, he would rent a bigger house in a more pleasant location.

Ugo had taken a week off work to enjoy his honeymoon; and enjoy it he did. From the moment the mattress was replaced, the newlyweds' love-nest rang to the music of creaking bedsprings and blasphemous cries of ecstasy. When the time came for Ugo to rejoin the barge crew, he was loathed to go, but with all the things he'd promised to buy Nunzia, he needed the money. Nunzia waved him off from the dock, weeping into her handkerchief.

During his absence, Ugo missed his wife terribly and counted the days to his return. However, he came back to Pieve Santa Clara to find, to his great dismay, that Nunzia had been spending her evenings not at home, as a wife should, but in the village tavern. And it wasn't just the fact that she'd run up a considerable debt there. A tavern was no place for an unaccompanied

69

married woman to be, surrounded by packs of ogling drunks; and Nunzia was an eye-catching girl who dressed to expose her attributes to the greatest advantage.

'So it's all right for you to go out and enjoy yourself, but not me?' Nunzia said, and Ugo's answer was, 'Yes'. It was obvious to anybody that different rules applied to men and women. He had no objections to Nunzia having a good time, but only if he was with her. Nunzia was having none of it. In order to avoid the situation getting out of hand, Ugo asked Aldo to chaperone her when he was away, which Aldo did because he was a true and trustworthy friend.

However, this arrangement wasn't to Nunzia's liking. She argued that if she'd wanted to spend her evenings with Aldo, she'd have married him instead. She complained at length about Ugo's absences. What was the point of having a husband if she hardly ever saw him?

With a heavy heart, Ugo gave up his job on the barge and managed to beg his way back to a position at the sawmill, this time as a wood-stacker, which was only a small step up from being employed as a general labourer. His workmates weren't any more friendly towards him and the boss was still a prick. The work was dull compared with the travel and excitement of working on the *chiatta* and the pay cut was going to hurt, so now they wouldn't be able to move to the bigger house he'd promised Nunzia; but at least he could be home every evening.

In ideal circumstances, Ugo would have returned from his hard day's work to a hot dinner on the table, but Nunzia didn't know how to cook, which rather disappointed Ugo as he had presumed that all women could. To begin with, he'd let it slide, thinking that she'd make an effort to learn the basics, at least. Perhaps, he had suggested, she could get a few lessons from Ma Lovetta, but Nunzia had no such ambitions.

'I didn't get married to be a cook and a cleaner and a maid,' she said, and this fact was clearly demonstrated. Nunzia wasn't keen on housework, and therefore didn't do any, so it didn't take long for the house to fester. The neighbours complained about the smell and the flies, and the infestation of cockroaches. The landlord said that if it wasn't sorted out immediately, they'd have to look for another place to live. By the time they'd been married for a year, Nunzia still hadn't changed the sheets on the bed. But if ever Ugo mentioned the state of the house, Nunzia would make eyes at him and do that wiggly thing she did and then his mind would be taken elsewhere entirely.

All of this might have been easier to manage if money hadn't been so tight. Ugo's sawmill pay simply wasn't enough to make ends meet. It would have been, had he not had Nunzia to support and had they both not been so keen on a tipple. In order to save money, he had a go at brewing his own hooch. It was so repugnant that Nunzia said even being in the same room made her eyes water, and she refused to try it. Ugo attempted to drink it with Aldo, but just one glass gave them the runs and left them half-blind for a week.

Whenever Ugo mentioned tightening their belts, Nunzia would fly into a rage. She was surprisingly handy with her fists for a woman of her size. He didn't know what he would have done if Aldo hadn't bailed him out. Aldo was doing all right for himself since he'd established his own delivery rounds and bought his own donkey and cart. But even Aldo's generosity dried up. When Ugo asked him for a loan to cover his rent for the third month running, Aldo said, 'I'm sorry, mate. It's not that I don't want to lend you the money. I simply don't have it.' Ugo knew this to be true because a friend as good as Aldo would have helped if he'd been able to, and he hadn't yet paid him back for the last two months of rent.

It was Nunzia who suggested that Ugo should ask his family for money. He said that there was no point because they didn't have any, which Nunzia refused to believe because they had that big house, Casa Paradiso, and apart from farming the land around it, they also owned a fair amount of livestock.

'How did your parents pay for your brother's wedding and feast?' She asked.

'They sold a calf and slaughtered a couple of pigs, I think.'

'And how did they pay for *our* wedding and feast?'

Ugo frowned, somewhat confused, and replied, 'Our wedding cost nothing and we didn't have a feast.'

'Exactly. So don't you think they owe you something?'

To this, Ugo wasn't certain quite what to say. Although he could see Nunzia's point, if truth be told, he felt deeply uncomfortable about going to his parents for anything. He hadn't had an awful lot to do with his family since word of some of the comments he'd made about Moreno's wife's flat chest and the ridiculous name they'd called their son had got back to his brother. Some ear-wigging busybody at the tavern must have listened in on his private conversation with Aldo and spilled the beans. But Nunzia wouldn't let the matter go. She poured herself a generous tankard of wine, knocked it back and asked, 'How did your father afford to buy that big house in the first place?'

'Casa Paradiso's been in the family for years. He inherited it.'

'So he was *given* a house? He didn't even have to sweat and toil to buy it?'

Nunzia poured a second tankard of wine and said that by rights, part of the house should be Ugo's and that it was greedy for Pa Lovetta to be keeping it all for himself.

'How much rent does Moreno pay?' She demanded.

'None. He works with my father to grow their food and raise the animals if there's surplus they sell it and just share out any money they make. And if there's anything to be spent on the house, they go halves, I think.'

Nunzia made a noise of disgust. Moreno and his family were

living there in that big, comfortable house free of charge whilst Ugo had to pay a landlord for the privilege of living in a dingy little hovel by the canal? That wasn't right by anybody's reckoning! She began talking about property ownership laws, which Ugo suspected she was making up as she went along, and by the time she had drained her third tankard, she was in a furious, indignant rage about how the Lovetta family, and Moreno in particular, had stolen from Ugo what was rightfully his. She had a good mind to go to Casa Paradiso right now, she said, to tell the Lovettas exactly what she thought of their thievery. Ugo managed to stop her, and only just, by promising to go and have a word with his father the following day.

It took a couple of stiff drinks for Ugo to swallow his pride and to summon the pluck to make his way to Casa Paradiso. He lingered down the road for a while, trying to concoct some feasible reason for needing some money which didn't involve admitting to his family that he didn't earn enough of it, and that what he did earn was spent on the things they'd always said he shouldn't waste it on. Perhaps he could pretend to have been injured, maybe even put on a limp, and claim he couldn't work. Or he might say that Nunzia was pregnant, even though she definitely wasn't because she took herbs to stop it. A hundred different excuses whirled around his brain. He had to have a swig of grappa from his hip flask to settle his nerves. Once the hit of grappa possessed him, he reminded himself of what Nunzia had said about his parents paying for Moreno's wedding, and that, along with another swig from his hip flask, was enough to awaken his courage. He didn't need to make up an excuse. He was well within his rights to demand a sum at least equal to that which had been spent on his brother's wedding. Now filled with the certainty of being in the right, Ugo drained the dregs of his flask and marched purposefully into the yard.

There was no sign of anybody outside, so he headed for the

kitchen door with a big, friendly smile fixed on his face. He knew he'd have to do a bit of buttering up before he could demand his money. He might even, at a push, offer to hold the baby, although he made a mental note not to call it by one of the nicknames he'd thought up with Aldo. He was slightly regretting those last couple of swigs he'd taken from his hip flask because grappa tended to loosen his mouth and he knew all too well that thin-skinned Moreno had no sense of humour. Before he opened the door, he took several deep breaths to clear his head.

But the moment he walked into the kitchen and took in the scene laid out before him, his reason for coming to Casa Paradiso left him entirely. Moreno was by himself, standing in a cloud of steam and ironing bedsheets. Ugo had to rub his eyes to make sure the drink wasn't giving him visions, but it was true. Moreno was actually *ironing*! Ugo burst out laughing so hard that it caused him a pain in his side. Honestly, the only thing which would have made the spectacle funnier was if Moreno had been wearing a dress! Moreno gave his twin brother a withering look and growled, 'What do you want?' But Ugo was laughing too much to speak.

The visit lasted less than two minutes. Ugo remained only long enough to be told that Ma and Pa had gone to visit Ma's friend in the village and that Moreno's wife was upstairs seeing to the baby. But Ugo couldn't leave without asking the obvious question: how come Moreno was doing women's work?

'Because my wife's expecting again and she's tired. And Ma struggles with her arthritis,' came the reply, 'Now what do you want?'

Realising that there was no point in asking Moreno for money, Ugo shrugged and said, 'I just thought I'd pop in to say hello.' He then added, 'And to see the baby.'

Clearly Moreno took this for the nonsense that it was. Ugo

never 'popped in', unless he needed something and he certainly didn't believe that his brother had any interest in the baby.

'Ma and Pa will be back for supper. And Rosolino's teething, so it's not a good time. And you stink of booze. Don't come to this house unless you're sober.' With that, Moreno gestured towards the door, indicating that the visit was over, and resumed his ironing.

Well, thought Ugo as he made his way out, that hadn't gone to plan; although it wasn't his fault that he'd failed in his mission. If Ma and Pa had been home and Moreno hadn't been ironing, the outcome would have been different.

As he was heading home, a creeping feeling of dread overcame Ugo. Nunzia wasn't going to be happy, and she had quite a temper on her when she didn't get what she wanted. He'd probably end up with another black eye, and he was running out of reasons to explain them away to his workmates. But then, as if by some divine intervention, Aldo drove by on his donkey and cart. What a relief it was for Ugo to see his friend! They could talk things through about the best way to deal with Nunzia, but before he got onto that, he just had to tell Aldo about the scene he'd just walked in on at Casa Paradiso.

Aldo laughed so hard that it made him cry. Moreno, *ironing*, really? He'd have given anything to see that! He then said, 'Fancy a couple of ales at the tavern?' and obviously, Ugo replied that he did. They had quite an evening, and more than just a couple of ales. As the drink soaked in, all they could talk about was Moreno-the-Housewife. Ugo recounted to all the other patrons what he'd just witnessed, adding all manner of dreamt-up details, and even acting out the scene with theatrical flourishes. Some of them thought it was mildly amusing, others less so. One man admitted that he often helped his wife with the domestic chores. Ugo had always had a funny feeling about that fellow anyway.

Word of this got back to Moreno, and two days later he turned up at the sawmill in the middle of the lunch break. Ugo was sitting with his workmates, and the moment he saw his brother, he said something about Moreno only being allowed out because he'd done the washing up, which he thought was hilarious, especially because all his workmates knew about the ironing. Moreno came over to him and without a word of warning threw a punch with the force of a twenty-pound ball hammer, knocking Ugo clean out, right in front of his workmates. Everyone who'd witnessed it said that Ugo hadn't crumpled. He'd been out cold before he'd hit the floor and gone down straight and rigid as an iron bar, landing flat on his back. His skull had hit the ground with a cracking noise which had made even the tough sawmill men wince. They'd left him lying unconscious on the floor whilst they finished their lunches. The first Ugo had known of it was when he'd been woken up by a kick in the ribs by the boss, who was telling him to get up and get back to work. Ugo was acutely embarrassed, but went to load up the timber as though nothing had happened, even though he couldn't see straight and he had a terrible headache. After that, Ugo chose to have nothing to do with his brother and both Aldo and Nunzia, who agreed that Moreno had overreacted, said it was probably for the best.

Still, this did not resolve the money problem, and now things were getting desperate. Ugo tried in vain to find another job locally which paid more than the sawmill, but he was either unqualified or unwanted. Regretfully, he said to Nunzia that he had no choice but to go back on the barges, promising that he'd only do it until something else came up in Pieve Santa Clara. He expected Nunzia to throw a tantrum, but thankfully, she spared him. In fact, she was very encouraging, saying that it was a sensible idea. This time, she didn't stand on the dock weeping into her handkerchief. Instead, she saw Ugo off with a smile and a wave. Nunzia was a girl with a good heart, Ugo thought. Clearly she didn't want him going away on an argument, or saddening his departure with her tears.

Ugo supposed he'd be away for a fortnight, but good weather and favourable winds brought him back a day early. He docked in Pieve Santa Clara with a healthy wage-packet in his hand – enough to repay Aldo his loan, to cover the rent arrears and the debt at the tavern, and with some to spare. He couldn't wait to show Nunzia. He'd even bought her a gift of almond biscuits in a fancy presentation box. They'd be celebrating tonight!

But the moment he opened the door to his house, just as he was about to call out, 'I'm home, my little *polpettina!*' Ugo froze, for there, on the kitchen table were Nunzia and Aldo, going at it hammer and tongs. They were making so much noise that they didn't even realise he'd walked in.

Had anyone been asked how they thought Ugo Lovetta might react on discovering such a scene, most people, including Ugo himself, would probably have said that he'd knock ten bales out of Aldo. Conjugal murders happened for less. Instead, Ugo stood paralysed, sobbing uncontrollably, with his box of almond biscuits clutched to his chest.

It was Nunzia who spotted him first, and the look on her face alerted Aldo, who looked over his shoulder to see Ugo standing in the doorway, gasped, 'Oh, Christ!' and fled from the house so fast that he didn't even pause to pull up his britches.

'Well, what did you expect?' Huffed Nunzia, climbing off the table and straightening out her dress. 'With all that time you've spent away, you've practically thrown me into Aldo's arms.'

Once Ugo had gathered himself sufficiently to ask how long it had been going on, Nunzia told him that it was since he'd taken his first trip on the *chiatta* after they'd got married. As far as she was concerned, their marriage was over because in this pit of a place, if the mosquitoes and the damp didn't kill her first, she risked dying of boredom. She was going back to Mantova and Aldo was coming with her. Within the hour, she had packed up her things and gone. The lovebirds were spotted heading out of the village that very afternoon on Aldo's donkey and cart, and as a final farewell, Nunzia had taken Ugo's wage packet with her.

Betrayed by his wife and best friend, Ugo knew that he was going to be a laughing stock, if he wasn't already. People must have known that Nunzia and Aldo had been carrying on behind his back. He could imagine what cuckold names they'd been calling him at the sawmill and in the tavern. With his humiliation spread all over the village like a pestilence, he'd never be able to show his face in Pieve Santa Clara again.

There was nothing to drink in the house, apart from the barrel of home-brewed gut-rotting hooch, but at least it was strong. Ugo rolled the barrel into the bedroom and took to his bed, fully intending to drink himself to death – an objective which he hoped he would achieve quickly. Failing that, he would have to be patient and perish slowly, from either misery, or starvation, or both.

Ugo wept for what felt like a week. For exactly how long he lay in his hooch-poisoned stupor, he could not say. After a period of time which he was later to learn amounted to eleven days, he came round vaguely, with his ears ringing and his sight still blurred by the drink. There were voices in the room and arms lifting his trembling body from the bed. Those voices in the room were calling his name. Were these angels, perhaps? Ugo thought it unlikely, and as there was only one other option, he put up no resistance, resigned himself to his fate and willed himself back into unconsciousness.

Ugo re-awoke in different but familiar surroundings, in his childhood bedroom at Casa Paradiso, to realise that the voices he had heard and the arms he had felt lift him belonged to his father and his brother. News of Nunzia's departure had reached them, and as nobody had seen Ugo for some time, they had grown concerned. Moreno and Pa had found him languishing half-starved on his intended deathbed, in a room so rank and filthy that it was a wonder he hadn't been consumed by the rats.

Now Ma was by his bedside with a bowl of warm chicken broth, speaking in a gentle voice and saying, 'Come now, Ugo. You need to get your strength back, my boy.'

The Lovetta family nursed its black sheep as though all their past differences counted for naught. They neither judged, nor condemned, and nor did they ridicule. All they did was to care for Ugo; and it was amidst this flood of compassion that the events of Ugo's life collided with his conscience. Hitherto they had largely managed to avoid each other. An inner voice told him that he had brought every element of his misfortune upon himself, and when at last he found the courage to express it aloud, all that he could say was that he was sorry. He spent the remainder of his recovery in inward contemplation, looking back at Ugo Lovetta the boy, the adolescent and the man, and came to the realisation that there hadn't been very much to like about him, and he wouldn't blame anybody else for feeling the same.

It was his previous treatment of Moreno which darkened his conscience the most. Seeing his twin as the family man, and now a father of two, taking on the responsibilities of head of the household, Ugo felt nothing but admiration. Casa Paradiso was a cheerful place to be. There was no shouting in this house, no jibing, no sulking, and certainly no chaotic, drink-fuelled quarrels. Everybody did helpful things for each other without having to be asked, for no reason other than making life easier. Moreno and his wife were loving parents, just like Ma and Pa.

One evening, after Ma and Pa and Moreno's wife had gone to bed, Ugo found himself alone with his brother – although not quite alone, because little Rosolino had been grizzling, and in order not to wake his parents and to allow his wife and new baby a few hours of undisturbed sleep, Moreno had brought Rosolino down to the kitchen. Ugo watched as his brother paced the floor with Rosolino in his arms, bouncing him gently and humming a lullaby.

Quite how they had got onto the subject, Ugo could not recall, but as he sat by the fire with his brother opposite, and the now sleeping Rosolino nestled on his chest, Moreno commented that in life, one way or the other, everyone got the lot that they deserved.

'You didn't deserve the way I treated you,' Ugo replied, and Moreno half-smiled.

'You could sometimes be a bit indigestible,' he said, 'and a hefty pain in the arse for poor old Ma and Pa, if we're being frank. But I learned a lot from you, Ugo.'

'What could I possibly have taught you?'

'You taught me the importance of kindness and consideration, and how much poorer life is without them. You made me thankful for having the parents we have and the home we have and taught me to appreciate all the things you were so ungrateful for. I suppose I could say that you showed me how *not* to be. I wouldn't be the man I am today if it wasn't for you.'

Ugo remained at Casa Paradiso for three months and made himself useful almost to the point of getting under everyone's feet. He went out to work with his father and brother in the fields and did all he could for Ma and Moreno's wife around the house and garden. He even helped out with Rosolino and the new baby.

Eventually Ugo returned to his work on the barges, travelling far, well beyond the reach of the Delmona Canal, and only returning to Pieve Santa Clara every now and then.

Upon Pa Lovetta's death, he renounced his inheritance and gifted his half of Casa Paradiso to Moreno.

DON ROSOLINO LOVETTA

Rosolino, seated at the head of the top table and dressed in his stiff new cassock, reminded himself that he was now officially Don Rosolino Lovetta. It would take time, he thought, to adjust to such an esteemed title, and a miracle to feel deserving of it. Most of the village had been invited to the celebratory banquet, held in honour of his recent ordination as a priest. The number of attendees was such that trestle tables had been set up in the yard in front of his father's house.

Rosolino's father, Moreno Lovetta, was seated to his left, along with Rosolino's four sisters. Other relatives also had places at the main table, although Rosolino wasn't certain exactly how most were related to him, or to each other. To his right was the parish priest of Pieve Santa Clara, Don Bergoglio, now rather long in the tooth, but bullish as ever.

Don Bergoglio rose to his feet, tapped his tankard with a spoon and began by recounting the events of the auspicious day, some eighteen years previously, when he had happened upon seven-year-old Rosolino Lovetta alone in the church with his nose in a prayer book. As Don Bergoglio regaled the audience with his version of events, Rosolino cast his mind back to that pivotal moment.

'What are you doing?' Don Bergoglio had bellowed. Startled by the interruption and knowing that he would be in trouble for helping himself to the prayer book without permission, Rosolino had nevertheless replied truthfully, 'I'm reading, Don Bergoglio.'

The priest had scoffed at what must surely be a lie. This Lovetta boy, the issue of illiterate peasant parents, *reading*?

Snatching away the prayer book and cuffing Rosolino with the back of his hand, Don Bergoglio had cried out, 'Nonsense!' But it was true. Rosolino really was reading, and how he had learned to do it had come about as the result of a fortunate encounter the previous Easter, when the Lovettas had received a visit from a distant cousin by the name of Omfrio Cacciatore. The fellow had been born a long way away, in the city of Piacenza, which remained his place of residence. He had come to Pieve Santa Clara to call upon, and in some cases meet for the first time, members of his extended family.

This distant cousin was unlike anybody Rosolino, or the rest of the Lovettas for that matter, had ever encountered. He used a lot of perplexing words as he spoke of a book he had written, entitled *A Treatise on the Noble Art of Gentlemanly Comportment in Matters of Seduction*, and he recounted how his work had been greatly celebrated within elite societal circles. Although this might as well have been explained in a foreign language to Rosolino, he understood that this man was very important. As far as Rosolino knew, the only other person to have written a book was God, who had written the bible, and he knew this to be a fact because every Sunday at Mass, after the readings, Don Bergoglio would say, 'This is the word of the Lord.'

Rosolino was mesmerised as much by Omfrio Cacciatore's discourse as by his manner of dress, for the cousin was attired in a bright blue silk waistcoat, coupled with a matching pair of tight britches which were fastened with pearl buttons at the knee. Over this striking ensemble, he wore a long velvet frock coat with flared lace cuffs. Rosolino was particularly impressed by the man's wig – an elaborate, powdered arrangement, coiffed into a tall bouffant style with little sausage-like ringlets which fell over his temples and his ears.

On setting eyes upon this exotic individual, Rosolino's little sisters had run to hide. For his part, Rosolino had felt somewhat mesmerised, but he was not afraid because despite his unusualness, cousin Omfrio seemed to be a very nice man. Aside from describing his book, he cracked jokes and even told funny stories. Therefore, when the fellow struck up a conversation with young Rosolino, asking him all manner of questions about his likes and dislikes, and how he enjoyed filling his time, the small boy was not too nervous about responding. He only found himself at a loss when Omfrio Cacciatore inquired whether he knew his letters.

Hoping that he would not disappoint anybody by failing to answer in the right way, Rosolino had admitted that he did not. He had then glanced at his father, fearing that he might somehow have brought shame upon the Lovetta family. But rather than laughing at him, or scolding him, Omfrio Cacciatore had led the little boy to stand in front of the door of the house, beside which, set into the wall, was an engraved stone the size of a brick. Rosolino had never paid any attention to it before. It had certainly never crossed his mind that the marks upon it were writing.

Cousin Omfrio had explained to him how each spoken sound corresponded to a letter of the alphabet, and how each letter could be written as a symbol. He then broke the word into things he called syllables – PA-RA-DI-SO – and taking a stick, he scratched them out into the dust by the doorstep, pronouncing each syllable out loud as he wrote it.

Somehow Rosolino had made a mental leap and he had asked whether the first syllable of the Lord's Prayer, the *Pater Noster*, would therefore be written in the same way as the first syllable of Paradiso. Omfrio Cacciatore's delight at the boy's agility of mind was evident. 'Yes! Yes!' He'd cried, clapping his hands, 'That's exactly right! What a clever boy you are!' He had then reached into the pocket of his frock coat and taken out a gelatine sweet wrapped in gold paper and presented it to Rosolino as a reward.

Rosolino had never seen such a fancy sweet, let alone found himself in possession of one, and he was uncertain what he was expected to do with it. He was probably going to be told to share it with his sisters, which he would have done without complaint, but Omfrio Cacciatore said, 'Eat it up, little lad!' so Rosolino had done just that, placing it in his mouth, wrapper and all.

There followed an intense exchange between cousin Omfrio and Rosolino's father on the subject of school. Rosolino had not heard of a place called school before, but from what he could deduce from the conversation happening above his head, little boys went there to learn their letters and Omfrio Cacciatore was saying that Rosolino should go too.

Moreno Lovetta had shifted uncomfortably and said, 'School? Well, perhaps if there was one in the village I'd send him for a little while. But the thing is, I need Rosolino here. If I had another son, well, maybe things might be different, but I'm not getting any younger and with my bad knee and everything ...'

Exactly how the conversation had ended, Rosolino did not know, because his mother had sent him to do something useful and fetch some kindling. But as he was taking his leave, Omfrio Cacciatore had bent down so that their faces were at the same level, shaken Rosolino's hand as though he was a big boy and said, 'I wish you all the best for your future studies, young man.'

The moment the fellow had gone, Rosolino had assailed his father with questions about the place called school and whether he could go there to learn his letters. Moreno Lovetta had told him not to get his hopes up, or better, to forget about it entirely; but being and inquisitive boy, Rosolino had been unable to erase the matter of reading from his mind. Over the days which followed, he stood for long periods of time in front of the door of the house, staring at the engraved stone beside it, studying the shape of the writing and taking a stick and scratching the letters into the dust, just as Omfrio Cacciatore had done. He felt rather pleased with his efforts, until it dawned upon him that although he could read and copy out one word, there were hundreds, possibly even thousands of other words, and he had no idea how to read or write those. Learning them all was going to take an extraordinarily long time; and where would he find them? 'PARADISO' was the only written word at Casa Paradiso.

Although there was a copy of the bible in the village church, Rosolino knew for certain that he wouldn't be allowed to look at it. Don Bergoglio would probably box his ears just for having the audacity to ask. But eventually, the boy's curiosity became too overwhelming, and finding the church empty one afternoon, Rosolino crept up to the altar with the intention of sneaking a quick peep.

He found not just the bible, but four different books, stacked in a neat pile to one side of the lectern from where Don Bergoglio gave his sermons, yet he was too nervous to take one. He knew that he was doing something naughty, and doing it there, in the House of God, made it significantly worse. Having spent a considerable amount of time wrestling with his conscience, Rosolino looked up at the cross above the altar, and pledging to the crucified Christ that he meant no mischief, and that he would put it back exactly as he had found it, he took the smallest of the books.

This little leatherbound volume revealed itself to be a collection of common prayers, and this was most fortuitous as Rosolino already knew some of them by heart. He located what he suspected might be the *Pater Noster* on the second page and began to work his way through it, picking out the letters he could recognise and guessing or deducing the rest. With this as his basis, he then moved onto a prayer which turned out to be the *Ave Maria*, and so on and so on. It took only a few surreptitious reading sessions for Rosolino to be able to read even the prayers which he didn't know from memory, or had never heard recited at all – quite an achievement, as the meaning of most of the words he deciphered was far beyond his understanding.

That day, when Don Bergoglio discovered him, Rosolino had just mastered the *Symbolum Apostolicum*, but the priest resolutely refused to believe it. Flexing his fingers in preparation to give the boy a proper hiding for his insolence, he had opened the book at random and pointed to an obscure prayer – a devotion to Santa Caterina – and ordered, 'Read that!'

Rosolino focused his attention and began, '*O sancta Caterina, quae barbaros a patria pellisti ...*' Such was his concentration that he barely drew breath as each carefully pronounced word left his mouth. He certainly did not notice the look of incredulity on the priest's face. As he reached the end of the prayer, Rosolino braced himself, ready to feel the strike of Don Bergoglio's hand again, but rather than administering a beating, the stunned priest asked him to read another prayer. He couldn't believe how the Lovetta boy was able to read words and phrases which he could not possibly have encountered before, and what was more, in Latin!

When, in answer to the priest's question on the matter of writing, Rosolino had volunteered that he could do that too, Don Bergoglio had marched him to the sacristy, invited him to sit at his desk and furnished him with a quill and parchment. Rosolino, who had never come across such equipment, admitted that he could only write on the ground with a stick, so Don Bergoglio had taken a piece of charred wood from the fireplace and encouraged Rosolino to use that instead of the quill, saying that if he found it easier, he could form his letters on the flagstone floor. He then added that Rosolino could write absolutely anything he wanted. Rosolino duly obliged, scratching out, *PATƎR NOSTЯEO QUIES IN CELAIS*. Don Bergoglio was dumbfounded. Despite the misspellings and crude formation of the letters, Rosolino's endeavour was recognisable as the first line of the *Pater Noster* to anybody who had basic notions of reading.

Don Bergoglio's decision had been made there and then. The sign was as clear as that given by God to the prophet Elijah. A boy of such intelligence would be wasted toiling in the fields. Rosolino Lovetta must, without argument or doubt, become a priest; and there was no better establishment to prepare a boy for such an important vocation than the *Collegio Francescano* in Bergamo. This was the institution where Don Bergoglio himself had received his education. He wrote a letter to his former school that very day, asking to be informed of costs and of any bursaries which might be made available to the family of a gifted boy of very modest means. By the time Don Bergoglio broached the matter with Rosolino's parents, their son had already been accepted to the *Collegio Francescano* and the starting date for his education had been set.

On hearing that her young son was to be sent all the way to Bergamo, Rosolino's mother had wept wretchedly, lamenting that sending her little boy away would be worse than having her heart torn out. His father too had been shaken, and he voiced the same concerns as he had to Omfrio Cacciatore on the matter of needing his only son's help in the fields. Don Bergoglio had admonished them both, saying that there was no room for self-ishness in this situation, and quoted several verses from the Book of Proverbs to prove it. The Lovettas had put up only moderate resistance, assuming that the priest, being a man of virtue and learning, knew better than they did.

But when Don Bergoglio mentioned the school fees, Rosolino's father said that it would be impossible to provide such a sum – and not just once, but every year. Not to worry, Don Bergoglio reassured him, for he had made arrangements. The bursary he had secured covered a good part of the costs, and he had spoken to Signor Marchesini, who had pledged his sponsorship to cover the outstanding amount. The priest remained vague with the details, failing to mention that Rosolino's benefactor expected repayment with interest. Don Bergoglio also omitted to say that the loan was to be secured upon the only thing of value the Lovettas owned; the house built by one of their antecedents, which had been in the family for almost a century and a quarter, Casa Paradiso. As Moreno Lovetta could neither read nor write, it was Don Bergoglio who signed the mortgage contract on his behalf.

With a heavy heart and saddled with a debt amounting to half a year's wages, the Lovettas had waved good-bye to seven-year-old Rosolino, ignorant of the fact that they would not see their only son again until his twelfth birthday, and after that, once he was able to walk the seventy or so miles from Bergamo alone, for just two weeks every other summer.

Thus over the years which followed, Rosolino became immersed in a world of penury, prayer and piety and received rigorous instruction in the subjects of theology, scripture and spiritual philosophy. All lessons were taught in Latin, including Greek. Aside from this weighty curriculum, adherence to strict discipline, both moral and physical, was expected. Good behaviour went largely unrewarded. All other types of behaviour were punishable. Just as well that Rosolino found his schoolwork manageable. Being a diligent student and driven by the incentive of making his parents proud, he passed every one of his exams, often with merit or distinction; even during the last term of his third year when the whooping cough nearly killed him. Despite a state so weakened that he had to be carried to the examination hall, a delirium-inducing fever and a propensity for fainting each time a coughing attack overcame him, Rosolino had nevertheless sat each test. Unfortunately, his essay analysing the question of Eschatological Hermeneutics and the Paradoxes of Divine Providence and Human Agency was disallowed because he had coughed such an amount of blood over the page that it had rendered his closing argument difficult for the assessor to read. Considering this, it was nothing short of a miracle that he achieved an overall pass grade. Had he not, he would have been forced to repeat the school year. The prospect of that had been so excruciating that being skinned alive, like San Bartolomeo, or roasted to death on a gridiron like San Lorenzo would have been preferable. His family couldn't afford the fees as it was. Burdening them with a supplementary year of expenses was unconscionable.

Every month without fail, Rosolino would write a letter to his mother and father, and as neither could read, Don Bergoglio took charge of communicating its contents. The priest would tell them that Rosolino was happy, that he had many friends, that he enjoyed his schoolwork, and that his devotion to God was growing by the day. There were occasionally a few grains of truth in this, but the priest was careful to redact anything which might worry or upset the Lovettas. It was perfectly normal for a small boy to miss his family.

Don Bergoglio would compose a reply on behalf of Rosolino's parents in which he would take great pains not to dwell on the subject of home, aside from repeating how proud his mother and father and sisters were of his achievements. It was more beneficial to motivate the boy than to pander to his brooding. Don Bergoglio was certain that given time, Rosolino would come to see the value of his vocation; and he was proven right, because as one year led into the next, and the next after that, the tone and content of Rosolino's letters changed; or rather, matured. He no longer spoke of missing his family and longing to return to Pieve Santa Clara, but instead kept to theological subjects. Don Bergoglio brimmed with pride at the quality of the boy's rhetoric and the precise structure of his arguments.

Rosolino came back to the present just as Don Bergoglio was

concluding his speech. '... and we thank God for choosing Rosolino for this Holy Vocation; for giving him the grace and fortitude to respond to God's calling, and devotion to His service.' Then, with a ceremonious gesture, the priest presented Rosolino with a brass pocket watch – a congratulatory gift from the parishioners of Pieve Santa Clara – adding that it had taken six months to collect the money for it. Rosolino's name was engraved on the back of the case. Don Bergoglio nudged Rosolino sharply with his elbow and hissed, 'Speak!'

For all the hundreds of hours he had spent practising sermons, Rosolino's nerves at the prospect of public speaking had not diminished. The few lines of humble gratitude he had prepared left him entirely. With his body trembling, he stood up and blurted out a single sentence, 'I will be undertaking my duties in the service of God and thank you for the watch,' and sat straight back down again.

The gathered diners, who had expected something rather more impassioned, and certainly a good deal longer, stared at him silently, in anticipation of more. Rosolino was saved by the arrival of great platters of lard-fried bread and dishes piled with coppa, capicola, prosciutto and salami.

On seeing the magnificent spread, a loud cheer arose from all those seated around Rosolino, with the obvious exception of his sisters. He overheard his second youngest sister mutter, 'Half a pig's worth of meat for the golden boy's *antipasto*,' as she cast the sourest of glances in his direction. The other sisters exchanged whispered words behind their hands. Rosolino could guess what they were saying, for it was clear that they felt nothing but disdain for him. They blamed his fancy education for the hardship the family had endured, and this ruinously expensive feast was the final insult to add to a long catalogue of grievances. Whilst Rosolino had been busy with his highfaluting books, they'd gone to bed with rumbling bellies and they'd had to share shoes in the winter. Not only that – the family's dire economic situation was clearly evidenced by the dilapidated state of the house, every brick of which was now mortgaged. Over the years, their father's health had suffered, and the constant financial worries had sent their mother to an early grave. And to what end? The world wasn't short of priests!

Relieved that the attention had turned to the feast, Rosolino began to pick at the food on his plate, but he could swallow none of it. At the *Collegio Francescano* he had been nourished almost exclusively on bread and bean soup, with a little fish or meat every other week. He knew, even without trying it, that the food laid out before him would be too much for his delicate digestion. The same applied when the beef-filled *marubini* were brought to the table, served in a broth so rich that it gleamed with puddles of chicken fat. Still, with everybody so occupied digging into the food, nobody was talking to him, and for this Rosolino was very grateful. But the moment the ribs and chops and cutlets appeared, the very question which Rosolino had been dreading came from Don Bergoglio – 'Any news on your first posting?'

'Not as yet,' Rosolino replied, forcing a smile, and this was an outright lie, for he had learned on the very day of his ordination that he was to be sent to the province of Lecce, right down in the heel of the peninsula, some six hundred miles away – a journey that would take a minimum of a month from Pieve Santa Clara. As his annual leave was to amount to only one week, not including the Sunday, it did not take an educated man to work out that he would probably never return to Casa Paradiso again. He had kept this information from his father, knowing how upset he would be, for since he had first left to follow the calling imposed upon him, Moreno Lovetta had taken it as a given that once qualified, his son would return home to take up the post of parish priest of Pieve Santa Clara. With Don

Bergoglio clearly past the age of retirement, the position was his for the taking. Rosolino didn't have the heart to tell his father that wasn't the way things worked. He was being sent to Lecce and there was nothing he could do about it.

Still, perhaps it was better like that, for far away from home his family would never know of his dismal priestly talents. All the books he had read had not prepared him for life in Holy Orders. He was no leader, no shepherd of souls. If a parishioner were to come to him for guidance, what could he tell them? No doubt he'd be able to regurgitate a few scraps of scripture, but what practical use was that? The humble country folk seated around him had forgotten more about everyday life than he could ever know. In the village of his birth, his kith and kin were little more than strangers, and he could feel how critically they judged him for having plunged his family into poverty. His sisters had been right to say that nobody was here to celebrate his ordination. They had just come to gorge themselves on the free food.

Rosolino felt suspended between two worlds, neither of which he belonged in. He was not a true man of God, and neither was he a yeoman of the earth. Beside his father – a sturdy man, endowed with the mighty Lovetta constitution – Rosolino looked as though he was made of twigs and paper. His body was scrawny, rickety and stunted from years of undernourishment. He stood barely five feet tall and wouldn't tip the scales at more than ninety pounds, even if his cassock was dripping wet. Whereas his father's hands were the size of shovels, calloused and stained from working the soil, Rosolino's were small, soft and pink. There were no calluses on his crooked little fingers, just an indelible inky mark from holding a quill.

Perhaps, had circumstances been otherwise, he might have been allowed to take a third path in life, for he did not lack academic ability. Whilst at school he had learned that the brothers of some of his peers were in training for other professions – as botanists, geographers, astronomers, historians, men of letters. It had crossed Rosolino's mind that he might have the makings of a reasonably good schoolmaster; or he might even have had sufficient talent to write a book, like cousin Omfrio Cacciatore. Yet here he was, sentenced to the constricted existence of a life in Holy Orders and harbouring a dreadful fear that all he would do was fail, not just himself, but all those around him.

Don Rosolino Lovetta clutched the brass pocket watch with his name engraved upon it, feeling its movement tick-tick-ticking through his hand. Each passing second was a relief, one second which he would never have to suffer through again, and one tick closer to the blessed moment when his pain and tribulations would cease to matter. The best that he could hope for was that the life set before him would be in some way meaningful – and mercifully short.

1777

FORTUNATO FONTANELLA

The timing of Fortunato Fontanella's arrival at Casa Paradiso had not been chosen accidentally. There could be no more auspicious date than the seventh day of the seventh month of the year 1777. Being a man of superstitious leanings, Fortunato set great store by such details. What was more, the date fell on a Monday, by far the most propitious day to embark upon new beginnings.

Fortunato tugged at the rains to halt his horse and jumped down from the cart, then stood with his elbows resting on the gate, taking in his new home.

'What do you think, Calendula?' He asked, addressing the horse. 'I'd say the place is looking even finer than when we saw it last year. Needs a good spruce-up, that's for sure. I'll get on with the house and you can make a start on the garden. Best get cracking, eh?'

Calendula snorted in agreement. She'd done admirably, pulling the laden cart all the way from Verona. Fortunato was not usually in the habit of burdening her with such a heavy load over such a long distance, but she had undertaken the task without complaint. He had brought only his valuables and vital personal possessions with him. He would send word to have his furniture delivered soon, but there was a lot to do before that could happen. Fortunato drew back the bolt on the gate, led Calendula into the yard and unhitched her from the cart. 'Make yourself at home, girl,' he said, patting her flank.

How Fortunato Fontanella, a retired merchant from Verona, had come to be the owner of this out-of-the-way property on the outskirts of the little village of Pieve Santa Clara was, as were most things in Fortunato's life, the result of guidance given by his mother, God rest her soul. She had always dreamed of a life in the country, far away from the grime and the chaotic bustle of the city; and Fortunato had spent the best part of four years searching for just the right place. At a conservative estimate, he had viewed over ten dozen properties, many of which would have been ideal for his needs, but Casa Paradiso was the one which Mamma had wanted. Her choice could not have been clearer. On the sunny spring day when Fortunato had first been to see the place, there had been a sudden rain shower followed by a rainbow; and not just any rainbow – a full arc, visible from end to end, shimmering in magnificent iridescent splendour across the Lombardy Plain. Mamma's decision left no room for doubt.

Certainly, the house needed some work to make it comfortable as it had been empty for over a decade and had been neglected for considerably longer, but aside from that, it fulfilled each one of his mother's criteria. Such a pity Mamma hadn't had the chance to experience the place whilst on this earth, but there was no reason why she could not enjoy it now. Fortunato couldn't feel her presence yet, but he was sure she'd catch up with him before too long. It was probably better that way as there was so much to be done and his mother's company, although never unwelcome, could be a distraction.

Fortunato unloaded his box of equipment from the cart and laid out what he needed on the doorstep. Firstly, his swan feather and bundle of dried sage, rosemary and lavender; secondly his pouch of salt which had been blessed by a blind gypsy; and lastly his protective crystals – white quartz to attract the positive and black tourmaline to transmute the negative energies. Kissing his mother's lucky amulet, which he wore on a loop of leather around his neck, he performed the entrance rite, turning first to the North, then the East, then the South and West. Some believed that it was favourable to spit three times on the doorstep before entering a new home, but Fortunato considered this to be a silly superstition, as well as a rather unsavoury practice.

With his herb bundle and crystals in hand and his pouch of blessed salt tied around his waist, he opened the front door and announced in a firm yet friendly voice, 'I am the new keeper of this house. I mean no harm.' There was no immediate response, which was a good omen, as malevolent spirits were usually quick to react. Satisfied that he could begin the cleansing process unmolested, Fortunato lit the bundle of herbs and stepped into the hallway, ensuring that it was his right foot which crossed the threshold first.

It was an undeniable fact that spirits resided in old houses. There was nothing to be afraid of in the great majority of cases. In layman's' terms, one could equate the presence of departed souls in one's house to lodging in close proximity to one's human neighbours. Anyone who had lived in a crowded city, cheek by jowl with other people, was aware of those above, or below, or next door. One might hear echoes of their footsteps and conversations; laughter, arguing, or the sound of babies crying through the walls. And it was not just sounds which one might detect, for smells could carry too; whether it be the aroma of a delicious dinner cooking on the stove; or the soapy waft of drying laundry; or some sort of nasty pong. All of this was perfectly normal, and most neighbours did their best not to cause a nuisance. Obviously there could be bad neighbours too, who might be prone to disagreeable behaviours. When dealing with such people, one would first try to reason with them. If that didn't work, one might be forced to threaten consequences. In the worst of cases, one would have no choice but to move somewhere else. These same premises applied to cohabiting with spirits.

Fortunato's spiritual sensitivity had been passed to him from his mother. It was a compelling subject, and therefore rather a shame that scholars didn't take the trouble to study the workings of the paranormal more seriously. After all, this was the age of reason and enlightenment. Science was advancing at a gallop, with recent discoveries made relating to alchemy, phrenology and mesmerism, to name but a few. Yet sadly, most practitioners of what was considered supernatural were nothing but charlatans who gave a bad name to those, like Fortunato and his mother before him, who truly understood the realm of mystical phenomena.

Fortunato made his way methodically from room to room, cleansing the atmosphere by sprinkling handfuls of blessed salt and fanning the fragrant, purifying smoke from his herb bundle with the swan feather. He paid careful attention to the areas where psychic energies were susceptible to stagnation, such as dark corners, cold fireplaces and the space beneath the staircase. He was most relieved to find that the house had been thoroughly emptied of the previous owner's possessions, as these could also trap unpleasant forces and cause them to fester. A family feud had been mentioned by the notary who had formalised the purchase, therefore the risk of bad energies lingering was very real. The sale had been greatly delayed and had nearly fallen through when the daughters of the late owner, a fellow by the name of Moreno Lovetta, had disputed a debt he had secured upon the house.

Despite anything which might have gone before, Fortunato was heartened to find that there was nothing foreboding. All the spirits he encountered seemed perfectly benign. Some noticed him, others chose to ignore him and carried on with their everyday business.

Satisfied with his preliminary cleanse, Fortunato placed his crystals in the most central part of the house, left the energies to settle and went back outside, where he took a little time to survey his domain. This was indeed a heavenly spot, a *paradiso* in every way, with a sweeping panorama of rich farmland stretching as far as the foothills of the Apennine mountains. Fortunato planned to have a paved area laid exactly where he was standing, where he could set out a table and chairs for outside dining. That had been high up on the list of Mamma's requirements. 'Find a house from where we can enjoy both the sunrise and the sunset,' she had said.

Beyond the terrace, he would have his kitchen garden. There were already a few fruit trees, although most were past their prime, so he would plant new saplings. This region was perfect for growing apricots, peaches and plums, and he had promised Calendula her very own apple tree. Further along would be his *pollaio*, where he would raise chickens and ducks – only for their eggs, of course, as Fortunato did not eat the flesh of living creatures. He would definitely procure a few nanny goats, as he was particularly partial to goats' cheese; and a milking cow too, but all in good time.

Calendula was at the far end of the plot, near the boundary fence, munching on a patch of clover.

'Have you seen Mamma?' Fortunato called out. The horse looked up, sniffed the air and shook her head. Fortunato took a deep breath, attempting to sense a sign. His mother's approach was usually heralded by a gentle scent, like rose water and jasmine, but Fortunato detected no such auspice. He was not unduly concerned. His mother would arrive when she was ready. After all, this was as big a move for her as it was for him, and just like their mortal counterparts, older souls moved more slowly.

Whilst he waited for the house to be ready for the second stage of purification, Fortunato made his way to the barn. He had not appreciated quite how large the building was on his previous visit as his attention had been focussed on the house, and now that the barn had been emptied of the former owner's things, inside it appeared even larger. One half was open all the way up to the rafters; the other half had a mezzanine floor, previously used as a hayloft. This part was accessible via a wooden ladder. At the far end of the ground floor, beneath the mezzanine, was a row of animal stalls, still in usable condition and complete with mangers – perfect quarters for Calendula, and all the space needed was a good sweep and some fresh bedding.

'Come and take a look at your new stable, Calendula!' Fortunato called out, and a few moments later, the horse's head appeared in the doorway, yet she seemed disinclined to advance any further. 'It's all right, girl,' Fortunato reassured her, but despite his encouragement, she flattened her ears and backed away. He knew better than to force her, because Calendula was an extremely sensitive creature and her refusal to set hoof in the barn was a clear indication that something wasn't right in there. Spirits commonly lodged in outbuildings, and perhaps Calendula sensed that whoever was occupying the barn had previously been unkind to animals. Fortunato closed his eyes, attempting to attune his senses to the problem, yet the barn felt as empty as it looked.

'What is it, girl?' Fortunato repeated, and Calendula, who still resolutely refused to cross the threshold, whinnied and pointed her muzzle towards the hayloft, so Fortunato climbed the ladder to investigate, and as he did, he was startled by the fluttering of a bird up in the rafters. What bird it was, he couldn't tell as he had only glimpsed it from the corner of his eye. It was of medium size and pale in colour, so a pigeon, most probably. Surely Calendula hadn't been spooked by the presence of a bird?

When Fortunato opened the hayloft hatch to let in some daylight, he found that it too had been emptied, with the exception of a small wooden trunk with rope handles of the kind one might use when travelling. Strange, he thought, that both the house and barn had been so thoroughly cleared, yet this had been left. Perhaps it had been forgotten. On top of the trunk was a pile of what Fortunato initially thought to be cinders, but on closer inspection turned out to be droppings – ashy white in colour and containing tiny bits of fur and feather and bone. A beam spanned the hayloft, directly above the trunk, so clearly it was the favoured roosting spot for a bird; maybe the bird he had glimpsed a moment previously. But he was no authority on droppings, so whether it was a pigeon which had produced them, he couldn't say; not that it mattered, anyway. Fortunato knocked aside the pile with the toe of his boot and lifted the lid of the trunk to find a priest's cassock, neatly folded and in seemingly new condition, but rather short in length and narrow in the shoulder, so clearly made for a very diminutive man. Beneath this was a sparse array of personal items – a shaving brush; a hair comb; a string of rosary beads worn smooth by prayer and a Certificate of Ordination issued by the Bishop of Bergamo to a Rosolino Lovetta.

At the bottom of the trunk, Fortunato uncovered a thick sheaf of papers, wrapped in a cloth and tied with a piece of cord, which on closer inspection revealed itself to be a stack of letters. As Fortunato leafed through them, he found them to be precisely ordered by date. One had been written every month, beginning in October 1742 and ending in June 1760. The ink had faded somewhat, but the signature at the bottom of each was legible as 'Rosolino'. Fortunato presumed that this must be the same Rosolino whose name was on the Certificate of Ordination.

The first letters were written in an unsteady, childish hand. Their contents were much the same, with the young boy, whom Fortunato deduced must be residing at a boarding school, begging to be allowed to return home and promising that he would help his father in the fields and wouldn't be a nuisance to his sisters. Clearly the child was pining for his mother, for several letters spoke only to her, expressing longing and the yearning to be held in her arms and to be tucked into his bed at night with a kiss. Fortunato, who understood only too well the bond of love between mother and son, could not help but be acutely distressed by the small boy's anguish. Wiping his eyes on the cuff of his shirt, he continued reading.

With the passing of each year, Rosolino's handwriting matured into an elegant monastic style, and as it changed, so did the tone and contents of what was conveyed in each letter. Those written between 1749 and 1751 spoke frankly of a school where harsh punishments were meted out for seemingly trifling misdemeanours. Then briefly, during 1752, the mood was angry, rebellious even. Rosolino recounted how he had run away from school, only to be found a few days later and returned. He had been lashed, placed in isolation and fed only stale bread and water for a week. He apologised for the unevenness of his calligraphy, blaming it on the fact that during the course of his punishment, his fingers had been broken. After that, there was no expression of feelings. Each letter opened with a few perfunctory observations about the weather and continued with comments on scriptural matters.

The last of Rosolino's letters was a short note, addressed only to his father. Fortunato read it aloud, *'In my efforts to make everybody proud, all I have succeeded in achieving is financial ruin for you and insurmountable unhappiness for myself. I am deeply sorry. I know that my actions can never be forgiven, but I have not the strength to continue.'* It was these three lines which made Fortunato's heart stop, for he understood that this was a final note in every way.

As Rosolino Lovetta's suffering poured from the pages into Fortunato, he found himself so weakened that he crumpled to the ground. It took some time before he was able to recover his voice, and when at last he could speak, he called out gently, 'Rosolino. I can help you. Come to me.'

A spirit was there, somewhere, but clearly too frightened to manifest, so Fortunato took the tarot cards which he carried in his pocket at all times and began to shuffle them slowly, encouraging the tormented soul to appear. He fanned out the tarots face-down, and with his left hand resting on the note, he entreated the powers of providence to guide his right hand to the card which might provide some guidance. The attraction which possessed him was immediate and strong. Without hesitation, he reached for the card which spoke to him the loudest and turned it over. It was *The Hanged Man*.

Many meanings could be read into this card. It could be a warning to disconnect from old habits; to make a sacrifice for the greater good; to find the courage to make a change – but its interpretation could also be literal, and Fortunato understood that in this case, it was. The revelation of this card, along with the note, left no room for doubt. Don Rosolino Lovetta had taken his own life.

As Fortunato considered this dreadful event, something made him look up. There, perched on the beam, directly above the trunk, was a small, pale grey owl, and it was staring directly at him. This must be the bird which he had mistaken for a pigeon, and the bird which had produced the droppings. Fortunato was possessed by the certainty that this owl was a *spiritus animalis*, a human soul manifesting in animal form. Such transferences were not uncommon, and usually occurred when a soul needed to be noticed because they had something of importance to communicate, or an earthly task to complete which only living humans could undertake.

'Rosolino?' Fortunato repeated, and the owl neither moved nor broke off its gaze. Fortunato reached for a second card. It was *The Tower*, symbolising personal crisis.

'Let me help you,' he said again. 'I will not judge.'

The bird blinked its yellow eyes, took off and fluttered back up into the rafters, out of sight, so Fortunato consulted the cards once more. Firstly, he besought the powers of the universe to give indication of Rosolino's wishes, and the card he turned over was *The Hierophant*, the interpreter of sacred mysteries and the most common symbol relating to traditional family values and academic institutions. In view of what he had just learned from Rosolino's letters, this was not a surprise.

With *The Hierophant* held firmly in his hand, Fortunato entreated, 'Show me what must be done,' and he reached out for another card. Again, the providential attraction was strong. He turned over *The Magician*, representing the power of the mind and working towards a goal by using one's wisdom to guide the path of others. That was all very well, but what was he to do with this information? Perhaps it was because he felt so exhausted by having absorbed the priest's suffering that an answer did not come to Fortunato immediately. If only Mamma had been there, she would have known. Fortunato placed everything back in the trunk exactly as he had found it, closed the lid and climbed back down the hayloft ladder.

Calendula was waiting for him outside the barn, and it was evident that she sensed his weakened state. She snuffled, rubbing her muzzle gently against his shoulder. Fortunato rested his head against her neck and sighed, 'What Mamma said when we first came here was true. It is not I who need this place, but this place which needs me. But what must I do? I can't bring Rosolino Lovetta back.' Calendula gave him a little nudge in response. 'Yes, you're right,' Fortunato conceded, 'I'm too tired to think straight. The answer will come.'

Although several hours had passed and by now Casa Paradiso should be ready for the second stage of purification, Fortunato was not in the state of mind to do it. The anointing ceremony would have to wait. He had intended to camp out in the house until his furniture arrived, but he wasn't comfortable about sleeping in there before it was ready, and he sensed that his presence would be of comfort to Rosolino in the barn, so he unloaded his bedding from the cart and carried it up into the hayloft. He unrolled his mattress, orientating it towards the south-west to promote a sense of calm, and laid the most precious of his crystals – uncut amethysts and moonstones – on his pillow.

Fortunato ate nothing that evening, as was the practice when attempting to attract a prophetic dream. Having performed a short ceremony with a blue candle to enhance his psychic attunement, he lay on his mattress in silent contemplation, clearing his mind of all thoughts except that of being visited by mystical guidance. But his tiredness from both the long journey and the encounter with Rosolino was so overwhelming that Fortunato fell asleep before his preparation was complete. He was awoken in the middle of the night by a *chip-chip-chirrup* call. The broad, bright crescent of a gibbous moon, framed perfectly within the rectangle of the hatch, shone a pallid glow into the hayloft. The owl was on the beam with its yellow eyes fixed upon him. With one hand on his forehead and the other resting above his solar plexus, Fortunato willed the contents of his dream to return, but nothing came to him. There had been no prophetic dream. Tiredness swept through him once more and he lapsed back into sleep.

As dawn broke, Fortunato was roused from his slumber by the melody of the dawn chorus, and he lay for a time looking up into the rafters. The owl was nowhere to be seen and did not appear when Fortunato called out Rosolino's name. Now, with the benefit of a reasonably good night's rest behind him, he decided that the best he could do was to be patient and to trust providence that whatever he needed to undertake on Don Rosolino Lovetta's behalf would reveal itself in good time.

That morning Fortunato busied himself with the rest of the house-cleansing and anointment, and it was as he was performing a divination ceremony to decide which bedroom should be his and which should be his mother's that he heard a voice call from outside. When he looked out to see who it might be, Fortunato almost fell out of the window, for there, standing in the yard was the form of a priest. Although he had seen many ghosts and apparitions in his time, Fortunato had never encountered one which could speak so clearly, or which manifested within such a seemingly solid structure.

'Don Rosolino!' He exclaimed.

The priest shook his head and said, 'No. I'm Don Marco, parish priest of Pieve Santa Clara. I'm here to welcome you to the village.'

Fortunato couldn't deny that he was extremely disappointed, but not wishing to seem rude, he gathered himself and gave a cordial smile. Don Marco added, 'I've also come to bless your house, if that might be of interest to you.'

'Certainly!' Fortunato replied, for despite the steadfastness of his mystical beliefs, he was also devoutly Catholic when applicable; and a blessing was a blessing, after all. Best to cover all eventualities.

Don Marco turned out to be a very amenable fellow, and once he had sprinkled a little Holy water around the house and recited a benedictory prayer, Fortunato invited him to tarry a while and toast his arrival with a tot of cherry liqueur made to his mother's recipe. They spoke for a time about village matters and suchlike, and once Fortunato deemed that he had won the priest's confidence, he asked Don Marco whether the name Rosolino Lovetta meant anything to him. Immediately Don Marco's expression saddened. He crossed himself and replied, 'Yes. Although I did not know Rosolino Lovetta personally as I have only been assigned to this mission since the departure of my predecessor, Don Bergoglio, Don Rosolino's tragic story is well-known in Pieve Santa Clara.' Don Marco went on to recount how the young curate had been discovered hanged from a beam in the hayloft on the eve of his departure for his first posting in Lecce. The Lovetta family had, understandably, been devastated, and his predecessor, Don Bergoglio, had taken it particularly hard. Don Bergoglio had resigned his parish duties with immediate effect and had lived out the rest of his days in a monastery, undertaking the most extreme fasting, mortification, self-flagellation and other such acts of penance.

Feeling that he could place his trust in Don Marco, Fortunato inquired, 'Could I ask you to perform a Rite of Absolution for Don Rosolino?' He knew this to be a considerable request, for suicide was a mortal sin, and within the edicts of Canon Law, the priest was well within his rights to say no. Don Marco nodded, clearly giving the matter consideration, and stated, 'Although there are many within the church who remain entrenched in their refusal to offer forgiveness in such matters, it is my belief that one should not look upon any sin in isolation. A starving man should not be punished for stealing a crust of bread, despite theft being prohibited in the Eighth Commandment. One should consider the man's state of starvation before condemning him for the act. Therefore, I believe that we must first investigate the circumstances which drove Don Rosolino to take his own life.'

'I have all the evidence you need,' replied Fortunato, and he invited Don Marco to accompany him to the hayloft. The second reading of Rosolino's letters was no less disturbing for Fortunato, and Don Marco pronounced himself equally distraught. 'I see absolutely no reason to deny forgiveness,' he said. 'Quite the opposite, in fact. Never during my fifteen years in the priesthood have I come across a case which requires it so desperately. My estimation is that the soul of Don Rosolino remains trapped in a state of purgatory, and it is only through forgiveness that it might be freed.'

Fortunato looked on as Don Marco clasped his hands and closed his eyes in prayer. He did the same, although he did not pray to God as he considered the priest better placed to deal with that particular conversation. Instead, he focussed his thoughts on Rosolino, extending his love and his comfort and urging him to accept the forgiveness which was being offered to him. The silence, which continued for some time, was broken by Don Marco reciting the Act of Absolution.

'... *Through the ministry of the Church, may God grant you pardon and peace. I absolve you from your sins, in the name of the Father, and of the Son and of the Holy Spirit.*'

Fortunato added his voice to the final 'Amen', although he considered this Act of Absolution as only a first step. Fortunato felt from deep within that action needed to be taken; that the appearance of the owl was a rallying cry. Still, having won Don Marco's confidence, he did not want to spoil it, as he feared he might, by mentioning a *spiritus animalis*. The Church did not endorse such beliefs.

Don Marco's expression remained troubled. He cast his eye over the stack of letters and said, 'The methods used within young Rosolino's education shock me deeply, and I believe that something must be done to ensure that no innocent child is subjected to such wicked, torturous treatment again. I will contact the Bishopric of Bergamo immediately and demand an investigation into the methods used at the *Collegio Francescano*, and I will not rest until these scandalous practices are exposed and action is taken to remedy them.'

With that, Don Marco took his leave, pledging to keep Fortunato abreast of any developments. Fortunato went back to the hayloft, hoping that the owl had returned, but there was no sign of it, so he took out his tarot cards once more. 'Guide me,

Rosolino,' he said as he began to shuffle, but stopped suddenly, for he sensed a change in the atmosphere. A light scent of rose water and jasmine flowed into his nostrils. 'Mamma! At last!' He exclaimed, and relief overwhelmed him. Before he could inquire what had taken her so long and whether she had enjoyed an untroubled journey from Verona, she asked, 'How much money do you have, Fortunato?' An odd question, considering the circumstances.

'Plenty,' he replied. 'Enough to see me through comfortably to the end of my days, with a considerable amount left over.'

'And when you leave your mortal body, who will benefit from it?'

'I don't know. It is unlikely that I will ever marry and have children at my age. And I promised you that I wouldn't leave a single *centesimo* of the family fortune to my cousins as they were so rude to you.'

'Indeed, and I would be most upset if you left them as much as the mud from the sole of your boot.'

'Mamma, why are we talking about inheritance now? I need your help in the matter of Rosolino Lovetta.'

Fortunato sensed his mother laughing, in the way that she did when he couldn't see something which was right under his nose. Her spirit voice rang out in a tone which was almost mocking, '*I am the key to a future bright, a seed sown deep to set minds alight. In youth I'm small, a mere suggestion, but grow I will to teach life's lessons.*'

Fortunato buried his face in his hands. 'Why must you madden me with your riddles, Mamma?'

'Think, my boy.'

'I don't know. You want me to plant something?'

'Tut-tut, Fortunato. Go to the back of the classroom.'

As Fortunato echoed, 'The classroom?' the thing which should have been obvious revealed itself. 'Of course!' He exclaimed, feeling his hair stand on end. 'I know what I must do!'

The rose water and jasmine scent faded almost instantly, signalling to Fortunato that his mother had left. When he looked up, the grey owl was in its usual position on the beam. It blinked its yellow eyes and gave its *chip-chip-chirrup* call.

'If it is your wish, I will open a school for the children of Pieve Santa Clara, providing free and nurturing education. No child will ever have to endure corporal punishment, and no child will have to suffer the wrench of being separated from their family. If this is your desire, Rosolino, give me a sign.'

As the words left Fortunato, something small and shiny fell from the beam and landed with a metallic thud on the lid of the wooden trunk. Fortunato scrambled to see what it was. It was a brass pocket watch, inscribed with the name 'Don Rosolino Lovetta'. The bird chirruped one last time, took to the wing and flew out of the hatch. Fortunato never saw the little grey owl perched on the hayloft beam thereafter, and this was all the confirmation he needed that the tortured soul of Rosolino Lovetta had found its peace. He buried the wooden trunk and its contents, along with the pocket watch, in the garden – then planted a rose above it to mark the spot.

True to his word, Don Marco initiated an inquiry into the methods used at the *Collegio Francescano* and received word from the Bishopric of Bergamo that steps were being taken to reform the rules concerning the instruction of its students. Don Marco was also of great help to Fortunato in his endeavours to establish a school. Within a year, a school dedicated in the name of Don Rosolino Lovetta opened its doors, providing free and nurturing education for the children of Pieve Santa Clara.

Fortunato had a little refurbishment work done on the house, decorated it to his taste and cohabited peacefully with the handful of benign spirits who had opted to remain in residence there. Outside, he had a paved area laid, shaded by a grape vine, and furnished it with a table and chairs and a comfortable bench from which he could enjoy both the sunrise and the sunset with his mother. Beyond the paved area was a well-stocked kitchen garden and an orchard of peach and plum trees, as well as an apple tree, planted especially for Calendula, who now had no qualms about being stabled in the barn. Fortunato's *pollaio*, populated by three dozen chickens and ducks, produced eggs all year round. The nanny goats and the dairy cow provided more milk than he could use. His barn was quickly filled with families of cats.

All-in-all, Fortunato enjoyed a fulfilling retirement. He befriended many of the villagers of Pieve Santa Clara, a number of whom came to have their cards read. Don Marco was a frequent guest at dinner.

At night, when Fortunato lay in his bed feeling pleasantly fatigued from his hours spent in company, or simply pottering around in his house and garden, the silence around Casa Paradiso was intermittently punctuated by animal calls – foxes and dogs barking; the mewling of cats, both belligerent and amorous; in early summer, the songs of frogs and toads; an occasional distant wolf-howl – and every now and then, the *chip-chip-chirrup* of a little grey owl.

1782

ERIDEA PONTI

Widows without income, property, or pension, such as Eridea Ponti, were faced with two choices – the first was to remarry, but she hadn't fancied that much, and in any case, no worthwhile man had shown interest. Being poor and past the peak of her childbearing years did not make Eridea the most sought-after kind of widow. The second option was to find employment, but with no family or friends willing to look after her six-year-old daughter, Marianna, Eridea's prospects were greatly restricted. The Marchesinis had said that she could bring her daughter with her if she wanted to come and help during the next harvests, so long as she accepted remuneration in flour. That was all very well, but the harvests weren't until the following year; and in any case, was Eridea supposed to pay her rent and clothe herself and Marianna with *flour*? And what was she to do to survive for the other forty weeks of the year?

Desperation had taken hold and Eridea's troubles had spilled out in the confessional. She had gone with the intention of seeking absolution for only one thing – to admit to Don Marco that she had been just one sleight of hand from stealing a piece of cheese from a stall at the market, and that it was not her conscience which had stopped her, but the suspicious glance from the trader, who had clearly understood her intentions. She'd been starving hungry, and it was that which had driven her to contemplate it; although she realised that was no excuse. But the thing was, she just hadn't been thinking straight. Neither she nor her daughter had eaten a hot meal for over a month – closer to two, in fact. A widows' charity had given her bread, for which she was extremely grateful, but the dried beans and beets which they had also provided were of little use as she had no firewood on which to cook them.

Once that first truth had tumbled out, it had unleashed a torrent of buried disgrace. Eridea hadn't had money for her rent since her husband had died, and to begin with her landlord had shown great compassion, suggesting that she could clean his house and wash his laundry as an alternative to payment, which she had done. But as the weeks passed, the landlord's conditions had changed, and what he had asked of her was ... Eridea's voice fractured. She couldn't bring herself to speak of such a shameful thing. Suffice to say, on threat of immediate eviction and pursuit via a magistrate for her rent arrears, she had submitted to her landlord's exactions. Eridea had seen no other option. Her inability to pay the arrears could have had her sent to the debtors' gaol; and then what would have become of her daughter, Marianna? And now the landlord's impositions were increasing in frequency and growing more extreme in nature. The whole dreadful situation was beyond what she could bear.

Such was Eridea's state of distress that Don Marco discontinued the confession and ushered her to the rectory, where before anything else, he gave her a substantial hot meal. That in itself had been of great comfort. Then, in gentle tones, the priest had offered a solution.

Don Marco's dear and trusted friend, Signor Fortunato Fontanella, proprietor of Casa Paradiso, was seeking a housekeeper and nurse, proposing not just payment, but full board and lodging too. Poor Signor Fortunato had recently been stricken by a palsy which had affected the right side of his body, leaving it weakened and partly paralysed. He could no longer look after himself, or the house, or his vast menagerie of animals, without assistance. That very day, Don Marco took Eridea to meet the old fellow. Having gone through his requirements and asked Eridea what she might need or expect, Signor Fortunato had invited her to view the accommodation. Due to his physical limitations, he had been obliged to decamp downstairs, leaving the upper floor of the house entirely at Eridea's disposal, except for the south-east facing bedroom, which belonged to his mother. Eridea could hardly believe the comfort and luxury being proposed, along with a weekly payment which was more than generous. In all honesty, she would have taken the job just for the assurance of food and shelter. An agreement was reached and Signor Fortunato offered her the position there and then. Eridea considered herself truly blessed.

Even though Signor Fortunato had been living at Casa Paradiso for seven years by the time Eridea and Marianna moved in, he was still regarded as a newcomer in Pieve Santa Clara. Although many held him in high esteem for having founded the village school, there were others who considered him suspiciously eccentric for his claims of being able to talk to the dead. Some judged his occult arts a lot of hocus-pocus at best, and dangerously un-Catholic at worst. Eridea, being a devout woman, wasn't entirely sure what to make of his strange incantations and spiritual sightings, but she requested that Signor Fortunato wouldn't frighten Marianna with ghost stories, or make her doubt what she had been told, that her Papá was with God in heaven. Signor Fortunato had pledged not to cause the little girl to question this fact.

Having cared for her elderly parents until the end of their lives, Eridea was experienced in nursing. She was also very competent in the kitchen and accomplished in all matters related to housekeeping, so none of Signor Fortunato's requirements were beyond her capabilities. Yet her relief at the miraculous transformation in her circumstances was shadowed by a grave uncertainty. Eridea's great concern was how Marianna would adjust to living in a new house with a stranger, because her little girl didn't deal well with people. Some called her a disturbed child. Others thought her backward, although Eridea knew that she was not. Marianna wasn't simple-minded, just a bit of a puzzle, and different to other children.

There were certain things which Eridea avoided, namely noisy or crowded situations, because Marianna found these very difficult to manage. Visits to the village were kept to a minimum and Eridea would only go to the market first thing in the morning, before it was busy. Attending church was traumatic, so Eridea rarely went to Mass because she didn't have the heart to deal with the anguish it caused her daughter, or the aftermath. When something had upset Marianna – and many things did – a muteness would overcome her, and her silence could last for days.

Eridea worried herself to the point of madness, with her greatest anxiety being what would become of Marianna if she was no longer there to protect her. It wasn't a baseless fear. Life could change in the blink of an eye, and recent events were proof of it. One moment her husband had been in rude health, the next he'd caught one of those sicknesses which came from the canal; and three days later, he was dead. Eridea tied herself up in every kind of knot whenever she thought about it, which was often.

Considering it best to forewarn Signor Fortunato, Eridea explained, 'Marianna has always been a very timid child. She's never been much of a talker, and since her Papá died, it's got worse. She's barely uttered a word these past six months.' As she spoke, the sting of tears rose in her eyes, and she was embarrassed to lose her composure in front of her new employer.

The left side of Signor Fortunato's mouth gave a sympathetic smile. 'I understand, Signora Eridea, and I feel her suffering. I lost both my parents at a young age. My father passed on when I was a babe in arms, and my mother left this earth far too soon, when I was only a few years older than Marianna. But I'm certain that given time and patience, your little daughter will settle.'

Despite Signor Fortunato's reassurances, the first few days of their residence at Casa Paradiso were an ordeal. Marianna wouldn't utter a word, even to her mother. Whenever Signor Fortunato was in the kitchen, she would hide under the table and curl into a ball with her head pressed against her knees. Eridea tried everything – gentle persuasion; firm encouragement; admonishment; bribes, threats and ultimatums – but Marianna was mute and impervious to it all. Even pretending to ignore her made no difference. Eridea feared she would lose her job when she had barely started it, and that Signor Fortunato must think her a terrible mother. He had enough problems of his own without having a challenging child in his house.

At lunchtime towards the end of the first week, Marianna had once again refused to eat and would not come out from her hiding place.

'Marianna, dear,' said Signor Fortunato softly, lifting the cloth and peering under the table, 'We haven't had the opportunity to talk about your job. Perhaps you could take a seat so that we can discuss it?'

Following a great deal of patient coaxing by Signor Fortunato, eventually Marianna did as he asked, although she wouldn't look at him, or even her mother. She sat with her arms wrapped tightly around herself and her forehead resting on the table.

'Are you fond of cats?' Signor Fortunato asked, and this made the little girl glance up at him briefly.

'You see,' he carried on in a soothing tone, 'I have several families of cats living in my barn who require a certain amount of looking after, which I find too difficult now. I was wondering, might the job of Chief Cat Keeper interest you?'

Marianna raised her head again and gave an uncertain scowl. Signor Fortunato continued, 'Your duties would include feeding them and petting them. Both of these things are essential, as without contact with kind people, cats can revert to their wild ways. As I believe that you are a very kind little girl, I'm certain that they would be delighted if you were in charge. I will pay you, of course. How does twenty *centesimi* per week sound?'

Still frowning, Marianna looked at her mother for guidance as Signor Fortunato added, 'Obviously I don't expect an immediate answer. No doubt you will want to meet the cats first, and then take a little time to think about it, but I can assure you that they're an entertaining lot once they get to know you. Pesca has just given birth to a litter of kittens, although I'm not sure how many as her nest is in the hayloft and I'm unable to climb the ladder to have a look. And therein lies another problem. You see, if kittens aren't handled by humans when they're very small, they grow up afraid of people, and that would be a great shame.'

To Eridea's surprise, when Signor Fortunato suggested Marianna should accompany him to the barn so that she could be introduced to the cats, and to choose a kitten to keep for herself, she agreed with a nod of her head.

'Marvellous! Would you be so kind as to fetch my walking cane, dear?' and Marianna did as he asked.

Eridea watched as they crossed the yard together. Marianna was keeping her distance, which was probably just as well as the palsy had left Signor Fortunato afflicted with a severe giddiness, causing him to veer and stumble as he walked. Despite having the support of his walking cane, the old man was wobbling so unsteadily on his feet that he might have fallen onto Marianna if she'd been any closer. By the time Eridea had finished clearing the table and washing the dishes, they still hadn't returned, so she made her way to the barn to see what was happening.

Signor Fortunato was standing in the entrance, leaning

against the wall and clearly fatigued by his walk. As Eridea approached, he pressed his finger to his lips and made a gesture to indicate that she should come and look, but stay out of sight. Eridea peeped around the edge of the door to see Marianna sitting on a haybale with a bundle of wriggling kittens on her lap, and to her utter astonishment, she was talking to them – and not just with the odd word. Exactly what she was saying was impossible to hear from that distance, but she was chattering to the kittens in an uncharacteristically animated way.

'Shall we leave them to it?' Asked Signor Fortunato, giving his lopsided smile and reaching out to Eridea to support him.

'I can't believe it,' said Eridea, shaking her head in wonderment, 'I've never known Marianna to speak so much.'

'Please feel free to tell me to mind my own business, but your little Marianna is a very sensitive soul. I believe that she has been keeping her words and her sadness inside her so as not to cause you further suffering.' He emphasised the word 'further' as though he sensed that Eridea's life had not been serene, and his assumption was correct. Her unhappiness had long preceded the death of her husband. With sole responsibility for her ailing parents since the age of thirteen, moments of joy had been rare. She hadn't married until after their deaths, and by then, she had been thirty-two years old. The marriage had been one of economic necessity as opposed to love. It had not taken long for Eridea's husband to begin raising his hand to her, and nor had it taken long for her to understand that the best way to avoid it was to give him no cause for complaint. 'I married you because you were quiet, so stay quiet,' he would say.

Without having any of this explained, Signor Fortunato seemed to read her mind and said, 'Past sorrows should remain consigned to the past. This is a fresh start for you and Marianna, and it is of the utmost importance to me that you should be happy living here. As I have already said to you, I do not want you to feel like my servant and nursemaid, or for Casa Paradiso to feel like a lodging-house to you. Casa Paradiso is your home as much as it is mine now, and I hope that it will remain so until the end of my days on this earth. I value your companionship every bit as much as I appreciate the meals you cook and the care you take of me. Marianna will know it when you allow yourself to feel happy, secure and at ease, and she will feel it too.'

'I hope so.'

'I know so, for I took the liberty of consulting the cards on the matter.'

Eridea made an uncertain *hmm* sound, for she was very wary of occult practices, and this did not seem to offend Signor Fortunato, but when he asked whether she would be interested to know what the cards had revealed, she could not deny that she was curious.

'The card which disclosed to me your past trials was *The Moon*. It showed to me your disillusionment, your disorientation and your fears for the future.'

There was not a great deal for Eridea to say to contradict this assertion.

'And when I consulted the Major Arcana concerning things to come, I was directed to *The Star*, and there could be no better card to indicate a propitious and happy future. *The Star* is symbolic of happiness, healing and renewal.'

Despite maintaining a certain level of scepticism, Eridea was heartened to hear this and felt compelled to ask, 'Did you also consult the cards for Marianna?'

'Indeed I did. Would you be interested to know what they revealed?'

'Well, yes. I suppose I would.'

Signor Fortunato paused to rest for a moment, caught his breath and said, 'Marianna's card was also *The Star*.'

'Do you think she will ever marry, and marry a good man? I

worry, because of the way she is. I worry what will happen when I am no longer here to protect her.'

'You will always be here to protect Marianna, if you choose to be.'

With an ironic smile, Eridea replied, 'I was rather hoping to earn a place in heaven.'

'Heaven is not just one big garden in the sky. It is everywhere, including on earth, and I am certain that a woman as compassionate and caring as yourself has already earned her place there several times over. As to whether Marianna will ever marry, I did not ask that question specifically. It is perhaps a little premature in view of her tender age. One step at a time. For now, the important thing is to encourage her to express her feelings, and to speak, and for that, I'm sure she will be ready very soon.'

Marianna was ready far more quickly than Eridea could ever have imagined. She came back to the house an hour or so later cradling a light gingery-coloured kitten in her arms.

'Aha!' Exclaimed Signor Fortunato. 'Is this the baby cat you have chosen for yourself?' and Marianna not only nodded, but also smiled. Signor Fortunato turned to Eridea and said, 'I acquainted Marianna with a little tradition I have, which is to name all the animals who reside here after flowers, fruits and vegetables. So, Marianna, does this pretty little creature have a name yet?'

Holding the ginger kitten up for him to see, Marianna announced in a clear voice, 'Albicocca.'

'How perfect, for that little cat is indeed the colour of an apricot!'

Marianna spoke again, this time directing her words towards the kitten. 'Are you hungry, Albicocca? Do you need milk? We should go back to the barn because your Mamma will be wondering where you are and we don't want to worry her.'

With that, Marianna scurried back to the barn, where she remained with the cats until dinner time, and that evening she not only sat at the table instead of underneath it, but also ate every bite of her supper.

Having officially accepted the position of Chief Cat Keeper and proved herself very competent, Signor Fortunato proposed to Marianna a second job, that of Mistress of the *Pollaio*, with duties to include feeding the chickens and ducks and daily egg-collection. Every morning without prompt, Marianna would take the previous day's scraps to the henhouse and return with eggs. Signor Fortunato, who could no longer manage the walk over uneven ground to the *pollaio*, would ask after its occupants, and Marianna would willingly answer all of his questions.

Each one of the chickens and ducks had names. The big white matriarchal hen was Cavolfiore, and the name was well-suited as she did have the appearance of a cauliflower. Yet unlike Marianna, Eridea found it impossible to tell the difference between the others. The red hens – Rosa, Dahlia, Lobelia and Petunia – all looked the same to her. Which of the others was Tulipano, or Violetta, or Fresia, or Lavanda, was impossible for Eridea to tell. The ducks were equally indistinguishable. Marianna learned not only their names, but knew who had laid each egg, which was most helpful as Signor Fortunato was very particular in this matter. He claimed that each bird produced eggs with a distinct flavour and was therefore very exacting about their diet. Carrots and red fruits, he maintained, improved the eggs' taste, and when the meadow flowers came into bloom he sent Marianna out to gather dandelions, marigolds and buttercups to further enhance the colour of the yolks. By the same token, certain foods were to be avoided. Amongst the scraps, he insisted that there should be no onion peelings or garlic as this carried through to the eggs, causing an unpalatable pungent tang.

It was not just the chickens who enjoyed an exacting and nutritious diet. Signor Fortunato had planted the pasture with specific grasses to increase the creaminess of the cow's milk. For the same reason, the goats were fed corn and barley. His horse, Calendula, enjoyed daily feasts of oats and orchard grass and even had her own apple tree. Every few days the butcher's boy would come to deliver offal, tripe and liver for the cats. The animals at Casa Paradiso enjoyed better diets than many people did, and certainly far better than Eridea and Marianna had before moving into the house.

To begin with, Eridea thought it odd that Signor Fortunato did not partake in meat, because he could have afforded to every day, but amongst his many strange beliefs was that even animals had souls, and therefore it would be highly discourteous to consume them. Nevertheless, he said that if Eridea wished to dine on meat, and to feed it to Marianna, he would not object, as long as the creature destined for the table had met a quick and merciful end. Out of respect for her employer, Eridea prepared meat dishes only once or twice per week and these were eaten separately from Signor Fortunato's meals.

Very quickly there grew between Signor Fortunato and Eridea a mutual fondness. Signor Fortunato certainly had his ways, such as his habit of consulting his tarots whenever a decision, even one of trifling importance, needed to be made. He also believed that the spirit of his mother resided at Casa Paradiso, and he would talk to her out loud. The south-east facing bedroom was filled with the late Signora Fontanella's belongings, with her clothes hanging in the wardrobe and her jewellery box and toiletries laid out on the dressing table. The bed was kept made and Signor Fortunato required Eridea to air it and change the sheets regularly. Eridea thought it little wonder that he'd never had a wife but in many ways a pity, because he was such a lovely man. Despite his peculiarities, nothing but generosity, good humour and kindness flowed from Signor Fortunato Fontanella.

He kept his promise and paid Marianna twenty *centesimi* per week for looking after the cats, and the same sum for her hen-house duties. One day, as he was settling up for her week's work, Signor Fortunato announced, 'I need you to make a decision, Marianna,' and holding up a silver *soldo* – a coin of significant value – he said, 'You may choose between this money and what is in the basket which is under my chair.'

Eridea busied herself with chopping vegetables for the *zuppa*, trying not to give the game away in her expression, as Signor Fortunato had already made her party to his little plot.

Marianna considered the question and asked, 'What's in the basket?'

'Perhaps you should have a look, my dear.'

The basket was covered with a piece of canvas, and something was moving underneath it. With some trepidation, Marianna lifted the fabric and out jumped a small brown puppy.

'Is it for me?' She gasped.

'Only if you want it. You can have either the puppy, or this silver *soldo* in my hand.'

There was no decision for Marianna to make. She scooped up the little dog, which immediately began to lick her face. 'Is it really for me?' She asked again, her eyes wide and filled with delight; and once she had been reassured that it absolutely was, she burst into tears, followed moments later by Signor Fortunato, who also gave her the silver *soldo* for having made the right decision.

The puppy was an odd-looking creature. It grew to a small to medium size, but with comically short legs. Its fur was wiry, and however often Marianna brushed it, it always managed to look untidy. In view of its squat shape and light brown colour, and in compliance with Signor Fortunato's tradition of naming animals after flowers, fruits and vegetables, Marianna chris-tened it 'Patata'. The two became inseparable. Signor Fortunato would joke that Marianna had a dog-shaped shadow.

Over the space of a year, Marianna's cocoon of silence gradually unravelled. Her periods of closed-in muteness decreased in both length and frequency, to the point where they hardly ever happened at all. There came a moment of great transformation when she made friends with a boy of her own age, whose father came to tend the garden. The little boy's name was Gaetano Pozzetti. To begin with, Marianna had given him a wide berth as past wounds from unkind children had left scars. Gaetano had suffered similar experiences, for he had a stammer and therefore he too was wary of other children and avoided talking altogether if he could help it. The first time he had tried speaking to Marianna, all that had come from his mouth was a series of splutters, which had alarmed her and she had run away. This had done nothing to increase either Marianna or Gaetano's confidence.

Signor Fortunato took Marianna aside and explained, 'Consider it like this, my dear. When you walk with me, you know that you must move at a slower pace than you would normally. Much as I would love to run races across the yard, go bounding through the fields and leaping over hedges with you, these wobbly old legs of mine won't have it. The way Gaetano trips over his words is not dissimilar to my own stumbling steps. So, just as when you walk slowly with me and you reach out to steady me when I am about to fall, you can extend the same grace to Gaetano when he speaks. Patience, my dear, is key. The more patient you are, the more at ease he will feel and then his words will flow more easily.' With his usual lopsided smile, Signor Fortunato added, 'Remember that sometimes the best conversations are the ones which take their time.'

Marianna made the first conciliatory move by introducing Gaetano to Patata. Their exchanges began silently, but little by little, words worked their way in. Gaetano still stammered, but Marianna simply gave him the time to say whatever he needed to say, even if it took a while. Often though, they didn't need to speak. They found the same things funny and a glance was enough to set them off giggling. To watch Marianna and Gaetano playing together brought indescribable joy to Eridea's heart.

The growth in Marianna's confidence was evident. However, there was still the matter of her fear of crowded places. She could not remain solely within the confines of Casa Paradiso forever. Eridea discussed the situation at length with both Signor Fortunato and Don Marco, and it was Don Marco who suggested bringing Marianna to mid-week Mass as the service was the most sparsely attended. The first time, they sat in the pew which was furthest to the back, and week-by-week they moved one row further forward. Over a period of a couple of months they managed to edge about a third of the way to the front, until Marianna expressed that this was far enough. Eridea did not insist that they should advance any further. They had already come a long way.

As Marianna's eighth birthday approached, Signor Fortunato proposed sending her to school. Although Eridea understood that being able to read and write could be useful, and there had been times when she might have found it helpful herself, she feared that school would be too much for Marianna and that all the progress she had made would be ruined.

When the idea was put to her, she looked terrified and Eridea feared a regression just for mentioning it. She might have been easier to convince if her friend, Gaetano, had been planning to go too, but his parents said they didn't see the point because a boy hampered by a stammer would never have any use for reading and writing. Despite Signor Fortunato's repeated attempts, their minds would not be changed.

Nevertheless, with a little gentle persuasion, somehow Signor Fortunato managed to convince Marianna, helped in great part by the fact that he'd swayed the schoolmistress to allow Patata to attend classes too. As a result, Marianna settled into school, and although she was by no means the most outgoing amongst the pupils, she learned well, proving to all who had thought her backward that she was not simple-minded at all.

As one year led into the next, and the next after that, for the first time in her life Eridea experienced a feeling of personal contentment. She had always carried deep inside her a knot of anxiety, yet it was only once that knot loosened that she realised just how tightly tied it had been. Watching her daughter move from childhood to adolescence became a source of joy as opposed to worry. By the time Marianna turned twelve and completed her education, she was no longer plagued with the timidity which had so hindered her before. One could say that she remained a little different – Signor Fortunato called her 'delightfully unique' – and she still preferred the company of animals to people, but now outings to Mass, or to the market were no longer an ordeal. If asked, she would even go out to run certain errands unaccompanied. Marianna's kindness formed the bedrock of her character, and the gentle sway of her temperament endeared her to those she knew and trusted. Whether marriage lay in her future no longer weighed on Eridea's mind because at last she was assured that her daughter possessed the resilience to navigate through life's twists and turns, even beyond the day when she was no longer there to protect her.

The autumn of 1792 marked ten years since Eridea and Marianna had moved into Casa Paradiso, and it was during the month of September that Signor Fortunato suffered another attack of the palsy. This time its effects were even harsher and left him unable to stand, let alone walk; and neither could he feed himself or drink without assistance. Eridea cared for him with great solicitude, but with a nagging thought at the back of her mind. When Signor Fortunato died, which was bound to happen very soon, she did not know what would become of her and sixteen-year-old Marianna. She had a little nest-egg saved now, but that wouldn't last forever. Eridea knew that finding another position as wonderful as the one she enjoyed with Signor Fortunato, and in such a lovely house, would be next to impossible.

One evening, when Marianna was out seeing to the animals, Signor Fortunato turned to Eridea and said, 'The end of my time on this earth is approaching, and when I set aside this failing human costume, I would like you to have Casa Paradiso.'

Eridea wasn't sure whether she had misheard, for since the second attack of the palsy, Signor Fortunato's speech had become so slurred that he could be difficult to understand.

'But Signor Fortunato, what about your relatives?'

'Have you met my relatives, Signora Eridea?'

'No. They've never been to visit.'

'Precisely. And our history of animosity long precedes the passing of my mother. I would not willingly leave them half a bag of sand. But you, Signora Eridea, have shown nothing but patience, care and kindness towards me and therefore you are immeasurably more deserving of Casa Paradiso. I'd like to think that when I'm gone, you will have a level of security and something to pass on to Marianna.'

Eridea found herself at a loss to respond, for she would never have imagined such an act of generosity. Signor Fortunato's tone became serious as he said, 'There is one problem though. If I bequeath Casa Paradiso to you, as we are not related, you will be burdened with onerous inheritance taxes, and the sum would be such that you would have to sell the house to cover them, which rather defies the point of leaving it to you. However, this would not apply if we were married. As my spouse, you would not be encumbered by ruinous taxes. There would be a few administrative costs concerning change of title etcetera, but you need not be troubled at the prospect as I will leave more than enough money to cover the legal expenses.'

Although Signor Fortunato could no longer form expressions with his face, Eridea read a look of deep affection in his eyes. He continued, 'This may not be the customary kind of romantic proposal, and what I can offer to you is neither a traditional nor a long marriage. Nevertheless, I want you to know that my feelings for you are most deeply loving. In spite of my many foibles, you are to me a rock of support, my compass star, and a steady and affectionate companion. Your kindness is the lantern which has guided me through the twilight of my life. Should you choose to accept my offer, please understand that as far as I am concerned, our union would be far more than an administrative formality.' He paused for a moment and the twitch of his cheek indicated that he was doing his best to smile. 'So, in view of this, would you do me the honour of becoming my wife, Signora Eridea?'

Eridea took his hands in hers and said, 'Signor Fortunato, I can't put my words together in the way that you can, and even if I could, in this moment I wouldn't be able to. You have brought more joy into my life than I ever thought existed in the world. Marianna wouldn't be the young woman she is today if it wasn't for you. I love you with all my heart and more, Signor Fortunato. Of course I will be your wife.'

As Signor Fortunato could not manage a journey on a cart as far as the church, Don Marco performed the ceremony at Casa Paradiso.

Over the weeks which followed, Signor Fortunato's decline was rapid. He grew too frail to eat and could speak no more than a few faint words. Eridea and Marianna took turns in keeping vigil by his bedside to ensure that when the inevitable moment came, he would not be alone; not that the prospect of death troubled him. He had spoken of it many times to Eridea. 'Death is not the end,' he would say, 'It is but a point on the horizon which marks the limit of our human sight. Beyond it, the soul embarks upon a voyage of new freedoms and discoveries.' Then he would laugh, 'You will not be rid of me that easily!'

Having spent the night in a chair by Signor Fortunato's bedside, Eridea was awoken by a gurgling sound. The old man, her husband, had lost what little of his colour remained. His hands felt as though they were filled with cold water. He half-opened his eyes and in a voice which was barely audible, he murmured, 'Let them in.'

'Let who in?' Eridea asked, and as the words left her, she glanced towards the window. Three cats were on the sill, pawing at the glass. When Eridea opened the door she found two dozen more on the paved terrace, along with the elderly Patata and the rest of Marianna's collection of foundling dogs. Standing in the midst of them was Calendula. Eridea stood aside and all the animals came into the room. The old horse went to her master and rested her muzzle gently on his chest. The cats and dogs arranged themselves quietly on and around Signor Fortunato's bed.

Marianna came running into the room, still in her nightgown, and on seeing the sight before her, she said, 'It's time, isn't it?'

And so it was. Moments later Fortunato Fontanella's spirit took its leave and embarked upon its journey into the heaven beyond Casa Paradiso.

1824

MARIANNA POZZETTI

There was an old saying, referring to that moment when the accumulation of many minor actions caused a major reaction: *It's the last drop which makes the cup overflow.* That last drop fell into Marianna Pozzetti's cup one ordinary October evening as she sat in silence at the kitchen table with her husband, Gaetano.

She had prepared his favourite dish – polenta with butter and rabbit ragú – and she watched Gaetano shovelling it into his mouth as hers went cold in front of her. That whispering voice in her head asked the usual question: *Why does he never talk to you, Marianna?*

'Is it good?' She asked, because that's what she always did, even though she knew perfectly well that it was. Gaetano glanced up as if he'd only just noticed that she was there, but he didn't reply, not even with a nod.

'The polenta. Is it good?' Marianna repeated.

Still no reply, and it was this small, commonplace snub which tipped the last drop into Marianna Pozzetti's cup and caused it to overflow.

Suddenly the haze of her thoughts fell into sharp focus. They'd been sweet together, once upon a time, but that Marianna and Gaetano had long since crumbled away. It was difficult to remember those two people whose childhoods had been spent playing in the garden at Casa Paradiso, who had fallen in love at the age of thirteen and hadn't had the confidence to say it to one another for five whole years. They'd married within months of admitting their feelings and three beautiful baby boys had come along in quick succession, even though some people had said they shouldn't have children because they'd come out affected in the head. That was so long ago that it felt like somebody else's life. *Gaetano doesn't love you anymore, Marianna.*

Now theirs was a shrivelled existence, reduced to the routine of chores needed to keep them alive, which varied slightly only according to the season. Marianna saw to the domestic things, the cooking, the animals – Gaetano to the heavier work and the garden. Nobody ever came by to visit, not even Gaetano's family.

With winter just weeks away, the prospect of another cold season trapped in the house with only her husband's brooding silences for company was so unbearable that it made Marianna weep to think of it. As she stared down into her half empty bowl of cold polenta, just one thought filled her mind. The time had come to bring an end to this suffering. *Poison is going to be the best way, Marianna.*

Through much of that night she lay staring open-eyed into the darkness with Gaetano snoring beside her. Thirty-one years they had lain together in this marital bed. Night after night they still lay close, but never touching. They would probably die here too.

This final thought brought Marianna back to her plan. She could be selfish and just end her own life, but Gaetano couldn't manage alone any more than she could. Their lives were too interdependent for either of them to survive without the other. If she poisoned only herself, what would become of Gaetano? His life was hard enough as it was without having to fend entirely for himself.

With the boys gone, they had nobody to take care of them and they didn't have money to employ someone, like dear old Signor Fortunato had. So most probably, whoever had the misfortune of outliving the other would be packed off to an institution. Sometimes Marianna had nightmares about those places, which were so vivid that she would wake in a panic-stricken sweat, certain that she was already there, imprisoned in a tiny, green-painted room with bars on the windows. The wailing, the screaming, even the foul stench of the place felt so real that it would linger in her ears and her nostrils long after the dream had passed. It took all of her strength and reasoning not to duck for cover and hide under the bed.

Marianna put those images aside. She didn't need one of her nightmares tonight of all nights, and now that she had a plan, both she and Gaetano would be spared such a wretched end. The more she thought about it, the more certain she was that the sin she was planning to commit was not malicious. *It's a merciful act, Marianna.* For the first time in a very long time, she had something to look forward to.

She managed to doze off in the small hours and was awoken by a sliver of dawn light pushing its way through the gaps in the shutters. Marianna slipped out of bed mindful of not disturbing Gaetano and made her way downstairs. The cats were already at the window, impatient for their breakfast. They'd have to wait. The old dogs, Zucchino and Asparago, half-opened their eyes but showed no inclination to leave their beds at the side of the stove.

It had rained a little overnight, infusing the air with a damp autumnal chill. Perfect conditions for mushrooms, and best to get them early. Marianna wrapped herself in her shawls and made her way out. A silver sky streaked with pink promised a clear day ahead, but for now a feathery mist still lingered. The long grass, heavy with dew, soaked the hem of Marianna's skirt as she crossed the field to the East of Casa Paradiso, heading towards the woodland where the mushrooms grew.

Cremini and *morelle* were the safe, edible varieties, and Marianna found plenty of both on the edge of the woods. Under different circumstances, she would have filled her basket, used some fresh and dried the rest for future use; but as there was to be no future, she took only what she needed to make that evening's risotto. Venturing a little further into the woodland, she scoured the ground for *ovoli* toadstools, like the ones in fairytales, and they would be easy to spot because of the white speckles on their red caps. Yet despite a thorough search, she couldn't find a single one. There were all sorts of other mushrooms which she couldn't name, and many of them were probably toxic, but she was no expert. She needed something strong, which would do the job as quickly and reliably as possible. Eventually she came to a patch of inch-tall mushrooms, golden in colour, growing amongst the moss and lichen at the base of an oak tree. These were known as *cappello di Cinese*, Chinaman's hat, because of the pointed shape of the cap. She knew these to be poisonous. Mamma had warned her about them as a girl, and she had forbidden her own boys to touch them. There were four dozen, at a guess. Marianna had no idea how many she would need, so she picked them all and went back home.

Gaetano came into the kitchen as she was heating the milk and warming yesterday's bread in the stove to soften it. He sat down without greeting and ate his breakfast. *He hasn't even noticed you've been out, Marianna.* And it was obvious. Her skirt was soaked from ankle to knee.

As today she must give a semblance of absolute normality, Marianna set about her outdoor chores. First, she went to the *pollaio* to collect the eggs. Most of the hens were past laying, but she couldn't bear to put the birds she'd raised and knew by name in the pot. These days there were far fewer animals at Casa Paradiso because looking after them was too much work. Marianna had stopped taking in newcomers years ago. Only the chickens, a few rabbits and three goats were left, plus the two remaining dogs; and the cats, of course – twenty-four full and part-time residents in the barn at the last count. The animals were Marianna's greatest concern as there would be nobody to see to their needs from tomorrow onwards, but she trusted that the dogs would raise the alarm soon enough and somebody would come. There should be no shortage of villagers willing to provide a new home for them, apart from the cats perhaps, but they were more than capable of fending for themselves.

Once she had seen to the living animals, Marianna made her way to the corner of the North field where Signor Fortunato had established a garden of remembrance for the departed. There had been a time when she had kept it all nice, ensuring that it was neat and weeded and that the plants which marked each individual grave were well-tended. Now wild mint and marsh grass had taken over. Calendula's resting place lay beneath an apple tree, heavy with fruit. The horse had gone three days after Signor Fortunato.

Marianna meandered back towards the house. Casa Paradiso was showing signs of decline. The shutters were falling apart and most of the windows were in such a state that she didn't dare to open them, or the glass would fall out. The brickwork was in dire need of re-pointing. But these past years she and Gaetano had had neither the inclination nor the money to carry out any work. Marianna had signed papers stating that upon their deaths the house would pass to Gaetano's sister, and she would probably sell it, so the future owners would have to sort all the problems out. *It won't be long now, Marianna.*

Eventually she made her way back inside, where she spent the rest of the day tidying up; after which she swept and mopped the floors, dusted everything thoroughly and cleaned away the cobwebs. She didn't like the thought of their bodies being discovered in a messy house.

Still certain in the knowledge that she was doing the right thing, at around six o'clock Marianna began preparing the risotto. She placed a little pancetta into the skillet to flavour the butter, added the onion and left it to fry as she chopped the mushrooms. Cut into small pieces, the *cappello di Cinese* were indistinguishable from the *cremini* and *morelle*.

She watched as the saucepan of rice began to simmer. *Last chance to change your mind, Marianna.* Determining that her mind was unchanged, she stirred the mushrooms in. Once cooked, she garnished the risotto with a very generous amount of butter and an even more generous amount of cheese. If the *cappello di Cinese* altered the flavour, the extra cheese should disguise it.

Normally her habit was to wash up as she cooked, but not this evening. The smart thing was to leave the evidence so that when their bodies were discovered it would be easy to conclude that the mushroom risotto had been their cause of death. No further questions would be asked. Doubtless the blame would fall upon her, but people would think her careless as opposed to murderous. 'That daft old woman, Marianna Pozzetti, went and poisoned herself and her husband with bad mushrooms,' they'd say.

She placed the saucepan of risotto in the centre of the table. *No turning back now, Marianna.* Having ladled a generous portion into Gaetano's bowl, she scooped an equal amount into her own – far more than she would typically take, but tonight there were to be no half-measures. She looked on as he began to eat and asked, 'Is it good?'

Gaetano gave no reaction. Not even a nod.

'The risotto, is it good?' She repeated.

Still no reaction.

It was delicious, in fact. All that extra butter and cheese made it wonderfully creamy.

The only sound to break the silence in the kitchen was the scraping of their spoons against their bowls. Barely halfway through, Marianna already felt uncomfortably stuffed. *Finish it all, to be sure, Marianna.* So she forced it down, wondering how long it would take to feel its effects.

With a good third still left, Marianna's stomach somersaulted and a spasm of nausea followed. Sweat prickled over her brow. Across the table, Gaetano was still eating. There was nothing in his manner to indicate that anything was wrong, although he was barely taking the time to taste the risotto, let alone appreciate it.

When her head began to spin, Marianna put down her spoon and laid her palms flat on the table to steady herself. Her gaze travelled over the flower-print tablecloth. How intricate the pattern was, and how pretty. The yellow flowers had turquoise centres. The turquoise centres had little orange flecks. Funny, she must have had this tablecloth for twenty years and she'd never noticed the details. The more she studied the flowers and how they connected together, the more they gave the impression that they were moving. And good gracious! Her hands looked ever so strange – far too big, like an old man's hands, and the more she fixed her eyes on them, the more they seemed to grow. Marianna blinked to refocus her vision. Now the kitchen was brighter than normal, as though the room was filled not with lamplight, but some other kind of light. Everything was pulsing and tinged in a corally pink. The big arched fireplace was oddly stretched out of shape.

If this was death's approach, which it must be, Marianna hadn't expected the process to begin like this. She'd anticipated that the mushrooms would cause pain and vomiting, but now that the initial queasiness had passed, all that was left was a slightly fluttery feeling in her stomach and a lightness in her head. These sensations were anything but unpleasant.

Perhaps you should pray, Marianna. But she didn't really know what she should be praying for – not forgiveness, certainly, as despite her merciful intentions, what she had done could never be forgiven. Some sort of salvation, perhaps? Ultimately, her fate was in the hands of God, wherever He was these days. As far as Marianna Pozzetti was concerned, God had turned His back on her ten years ago, in 1814, when He'd allowed her boys to be taken.

The first whisperings of imminent war had started the year before, with reports that the French authorities were sending teams of men out all over the region to requisition metal to melt down and turn into weapons and ammunition. There'd been a big old hullabaloo when it was rumoured that they'd be coming for the church bells. In the end, the church bells had been spared in exchange for ordinary folk giving up what few metal wares they had. Surely, Marianna had thought, they wouldn't come for her cooking pots, or the garden tools? She had been entirely wrong. Those French had grabbed anything they could get their greedy hands on. What a prize when they'd set eyes on the copper cauldron in the laundry room, and what a mess they'd left when they'd torn it out. They even took the pretty, curly railings off the staircase.

Nobody had been able to explain in a way which made sense to Marianna why the Frenchman, Napoleon, was fighting the Austrians, and what it all had to do with Lombardy was beyond her. How much land did one man need, for heaven's sake? Some maintained that compared with the Austrian Emperor, Napoleon was the lesser of two evils – not that he'd brought any good to their lives. All his reforms had led to nothing but upheaval, with everything further disordered by droughts and bad harvests and blight, and the famines which followed. They were lucky to have Casa Paradiso and its land, so they'd kept a roof over their heads and they hadn't starved, although some years had been mighty lean. But what future was there in Lombardy for her sons, even though she'd taught them all to read and write? Jobs which paid enough to survive on were as rare as hens' teeth.

Shortly after, Napoleon's representatives had come into the village to recruit young men for the army. They'd said joining the military would forge youth into warriors. Soldiers were assured good food and plenty of it, and money too – regular money, whether they were fighting or just sitting around in the camp. Their wages were called the *per diem*, paid for every single day that the uniform was worn.

It was Marianna's eldest boy who'd first got caught up in the war fever, with grand talk of heroism. The youngest had not taken long to follow suit. Eventually her middle son had been drawn in too. She'd begged them all not to volunteer, but they hadn't listened. Gaetano should have put his foot down and forbidden it, instead of saying that they were grown men and he couldn't force them to stay at home. They'd been seventeen, eighteen and twenty when they'd gone, and the same ages when they'd been killed.

During the short time between their departure and their death, the middle boy was the only one who'd written, or whose letter Marianna had received. He'd described the uniforms they'd been given – dark blue jackets with white crosses on the front and hats that looked like upturned saucepans, called shakos. *'We're marching very well ...'* he'd said, *'... I miss your cooking, Mamma.'*

On April 22nd, 1814, Marianna had been trying to catch the cows at the far end of the East field when she'd heard the dogs barking. She'd turned around to see three soldiers on horseback riding into the yard, and her heart had leapt. Her boys had come home, and far more quickly than she could ever have hoped! She'd hitched up her skirt and gone running across the field towards them, calling out their names. How big and smart and strong they looked in those blue jackets with white crosses on the front, and what fine steeds Napoleon had given them! But as she drew closer, Marianna realised that the soldiers weren't her boys. By the time she reached the boundary of the yard, they'd dismounted from their horses and taken off their hats.

Gaetano was on his knees in front of them, howling, with his face buried in his hands. The soldiers had come to tell them that all three boys had been killed in battle in some foreign mountainous place that Marianna couldn't even pronounce.

Along with the news, the soldiers had brought the boys' outstanding pay, worked out *per diem*, including the day they'd died, and silver medals inscribed with the words *LEGIONE LOMBARDA* on the front and *ALLA GLORIA* on the back. 'Posthumous medals', they'd called them; whatever that meant. They were awarded to the fallen for their bravery, they said. 'The Fallen' – such a weak way to describe three dead young men – like they'd stumbled and skinned their knees. As for bravery, who could tell, and what did it matter, anyway? Dead meant dead – brave or not. It wasn't long after that reports came that Napoleon was in exile. Marianna's boys had been sacrificed for nothing under that little corporal's command. Their bodies had never been brought home, so they couldn't even give them funerals. Chances were, they'd probably been tossed into some communal pit along with a thousand other disposable young men. The animals from Casa Paradiso had been laid to rest with more decency and honour.

After that, everything went dark in Marianna's world.

Gaetano had made a wooden mount for each medal, and he'd put them on the mantel of the fireplace. It was this recollection which brought Marianna back to the present. Where were the medals now? They weren't on the mantelpiece anymore. Also, where was Gaetano? His chair was empty and so was his supper bowl, but Marianna had no recollection of him leaving the table, let alone of leaving the kitchen. Maybe he'd felt unwell and gone to lie down. She should go and find him, make sure he was all right – all right under the circumstances, at any rate.

When Marianna stood up, she sat straight back down again and pressed her back against the chair to steady herself.

Everything was swirling in strange circles, and now the floral pattern had slithered off the tablecloth and was crawling across the floor.

'Gaetano!' She called out. There was no answer, but if he'd gone to bed, he wouldn't be able to hear her from the kitchen. It wasn't kind to leave him by himself though. She should go to him and they could lie down side by side and let death take them together. But everything was moving in such a bewildering way, even the chair she was sitting on was rocking. Marianna didn't trust herself to climb the stairs, especially now that there weren't any proper railings.

Suddenly the possibility came into her mind that she might already be dead. Perhaps, she thought, this was how it felt to be in spirit form. Maybe Signor Fortunato's beliefs had been right. Marianna pinched first her arms, then her legs, but she felt perfectly solid, as did the table in front of her and the floor beneath her feet. And if she was a spirit now, then surely she would be able to see other spirits, or at least sense them?

'Mamma?' She called out hopefully. 'Signor Fortunato?' Nobody answered her.

She really should try to find Gaetano. Slowly this time, Marianna rose to her feet, steadying herself against the table. Now the movement of the kitchen had settled, although that tablecloth pattern was still on the floor. Very carefully, she made her way out of the kitchen and into the hallway, pressed against the wall to keep her balance. The front door was wide open and Gaetano was sitting on the step with his back to her. The relief of seeing him made her heart soar.

'Are you all right?' She asked. He looked over his shoulder, seemingly surprised to see her and smiled, 'Yes. How about you? Are you all right?' which was a question he hadn't asked her for years, and he hadn't stammered, which was even more strange.

'I think so,' she replied, although just like the kitchen, the hallway was moving. Marianna felt as though she was walking downhill as she inched her way towards the front door, all the time supporting herself against the wall.

Gaetano had a blanket wrapped around him. He moved across and patted the space beside him and when Marianna sat down, he tucked the blanket around her too. The intimacy of sitting pressed together was strange now, but not unwelcome. Marianna rested her head against his shoulder and raised her gaze to the sky. The stars were dancing, flickering and merging into each other. If she squinted, the starlight exploded, like fireworks being shot from arrows. The moon wouldn't keep still.

Now the certainty swept through her that they were both already dead. Her body felt oddly detached from her senses, as though it was not quite her own. So this was it. When you died, you didn't go to heaven, or hell, like the priest said, and like almost everybody believed. Your spirit stayed exactly where you'd always been. Everything was slightly altered – a bit wobbly – but hopefully you'd get used to that eventually. Where God fitted into all of this, she didn't know. There were a lot of questions to ask – such as why wasn't everybody else who'd died at Casa Paradiso there too? And there must be a fair number of them. The house was nearly two hundred years old, so it should be crowded with other spirits. These questions were so hard to pick apart that they made Marianna's brain ache. Then she thought of Signor Fortunato's mother. She hadn't died at Casa Paradiso, but Signor Fortunato had been absolutely certain that her spirit lived there. This last thought ignited a spark of joy in Marianna's heart. If Signor Fortunato's mother's spirit had moved in after her death, then her boys could come back too! They weren't damned to exist forever in that unpronounceable foreign place. She called out their names at the top of her voice, but it was Gaetano who answered, 'I feel them too.' Again, he had spoken with no trace of his stammer.

'Have you seen them?'

'I've felt them. You know, like when somebody's in another room. You can't see them, but you know they're there.'

'Are we dead?'

'No,' he laughed, 'Definitely not. Although if this was heaven or hell, it would suit me fine.'

Before Marianna could say anything else, Gaetano chuckled, 'I reckon you put some funny mushrooms in the risotto.'

'What?'

'Funny mushrooms. We used to go foraging for them when we were lads, my cousin and me. They grow mostly under the oak trees and they look a lot like the *cappello di Cinese*, but they're darker underneath. You have to be careful not to get them mixed up, because the *Cappello di Cinese* can make you really sick. But the funny mushrooms are marvellous. When you eat them, it's like being drunk, but much better.'

'We're not going to die?'

'From funny mushrooms? Haha, no!'

Mariana wasn't sure whether to admit that her actions had been deliberate, but before she could decide, Gaetano asked, 'How many did you put into the risotto?' and as there was no point in lying, she answered truthfully, 'About four dozen.'

'Good Lord!' He exclaimed, 'No wonder I'm feeling so cooked,' then he added, 'Were you trying to poison me again?'

'What do you mean, *again*?'

'Don't you remember the *zuppa* with the rat poison?'

'No.'

'The Christmas before last, you poisoned my supper. I only realised because you'd left the tin of rat poison on the sideboard with the spoon still in it.' Gaetano paused for a moment, turned to Marianna with a questioning expression and asked, 'Tonight, were you eating the same risotto as me?'

'Yes.'

'So you were trying to do away with us both?'

If they couldn't be honest with each other now, there might not be another chance, just in case the funny mushrooms did kill them, so Marianna admitted, 'Yes.'

Gaetano pondered her confession for a moment before replying in a curiously chipper tone, 'I suppose that makes it not so bad then. And last time, with the rat poison, was that for both of us too?'

'I don't remember.'

'Well, let's agree that you were, so no hard feelings, eh?'

'Don't you hate me?'

'Hate you for what? For trying to finish us both off? Not really. It's not like there's much to live for these days, and knowing you, I suppose you were just trying to be kind, in your own peculiar way.'

'But you hate me for everything else, don't you?'

'Of course not. Why would you say that, Marianna?'

'You never talk to me. You act like I'm not here.'

Gaetano looked straight into Marianna's eyes with a bemused expression.

'*I* don't talk to *you*? Marianna, this is the first time you've spoken out loud since the boys died. You haven't uttered a word in ten years!'

Marianna faltered. Surely Gaetano was talking nonsense. Of course she spoke; he just never listened. Perhaps he was trying to make her think she was mad, and that was a cruel trick to play, and it wasn't like him to be mean. She was about to get upset when he asked, 'Do you remember the Casa Santa Maddalena?'

'What's that?'

'It's the place they took you to treat you.'

'Treat me for what?'

Gaetano stroked her face with his fingertips and said, 'You couldn't speak. Catatonic shock, they called it. They said it happened because you couldn't cope with the loss of the boys, that your head was so filled up with grief that there wasn't room for anything else.'

Suddenly Marianna remembered – the infamous Casa Santa Maddalena, where they locked away the lunatics. For a moment she found herself back in that tiny cell with bars on the windows. She could smell the stench and hear the wailing and the screams beyond the green-painted walls. The instinct to hide overcame her and she shrank into the refuge of the blanket. Could it be possible that the hellish room which so often made its way into her nightmares wasn't a dream, but a real place? She wilfully blinked the thought away and the room was gone.

'You had me sent to a madhouse?'

'Not me. You were taken there after you were found wandering.'

Gently, Gaetano went on to explain how one night, not long after they'd received news of the boys' deaths, Marianna had disappeared. All the villagers had been out trying to find her. There had even been men dredging the canal. She had been found a week later, miles from Pieve Santa Clara and in a bad way, and it was the people who had found her who had taken her to the Casa Santa Maddalena.

'You wouldn't speak,' Gaetano continued, 'so you couldn't tell them who you were, or where you'd come from. The priest wrote to different parishes to ask if anyone had seen you. By a stroke of fortune, one of his letters reached another priest who sometimes visited the Casa Santa Maddalena, and he sent word back.'

'How long was I there?'

'Best part of six months, but as soon as I knew where you were, I came to get you. When I saw you, I hardly recognised you. You were thin as a rake handle and dead in your eyes. They said it was too soon to bring you home, but I couldn't leave you there. It was a terrible place.'

As Marianna tried to make sense of Gaetano's words and

piece together fragments of memory, she realised that there was a gap in her life which she had not noticed before. It began with the soldiers coming with the news and the medals; then there was a scattering of images of that horrible place, which she supposed had been dreams. Apart from that – nothing. All she could repeat was, 'I don't remember.'

'Don't try to. It's best forgotten.'

'And I haven't spoken since then?'

'Not one word, not even to the animals, as far as I know. But it's good to hear your voice now, Marianna. I'd resigned myself to the idea that you'd never speak again. Told myself to be content with the fact that you were safe here at home with me, that you could manage all the day-to-day things. I watch you do your chores and cook our meals in your dream-state, but most of the time you don't seem to have any idea that I'm here. I could be right beside you, jumping up and down and waving my arms in the air and you wouldn't notice. Yet other times, you react as though someone has said something to you when there's nobody about. I thought perhaps you might be seeing spirits, like Signor Fortunato. I've got used to it, in a strange way.'

'Do people think I'm mad? Is that why nobody comes here anymore?'

Gaetano considered her question before replying, 'Everybody knows you suffer,' so he might as well have said 'yes'.

He sighed deeply, 'But it's not just you. It's the both of us. I struggle too, Marianna. I've never shaken the grief either. I don't think it's possible after what happened, and seeing what it did to you made it worse. I've tried my best to make things better, but I just haven't been able to find a way to fix you.'

Squeezing her hand in his, Gaetano said, 'There have been moments when I wished I hadn't noticed the rat poison. I nearly ate that *zuppa* the Christmas before last, even knowing that you'd poisoned it. Death would have been a release.'

'What stopped you?'

'I had you to consider more than myself. We made promises to each other. In sickness and in health, through times flush and fallow. We said that we'd always shelter each other. What would have become of you if I'd taken the easy way out? They'd have carted you straight back to the Casa Santa Maddalena, and I couldn't bear the thought of you being there.'

Gaetano wrapped his arms around her and pressed his cheek to hers. 'But let's not think about all that, eh? Let's think about all the happy things. We used to be sweet together, remember that?'

'Of course I do.'

'I'm glad. It's nice to think back to those times. We used to laugh at the same silly things, didn't we? There was rarely a cross word between us, and never an unkind one. How lucky we were, we used to say, that Signor Fortunato had given your mother this place. We worked hard, there's no denying that, but we wouldn't have had as good a life without it. There's a lot to be said for having a roof over your head which nobody can ever take away from you, and land enough to keep fed. We did our best as parents, even when things were tough. We raised three fine, intelligent sons, despite all those people saying that we'd raise simpletons. God answered every one of my prayers when none of them was cursed with a stammer.'

'You're not stammering now. I've never heard you talk so clearly, or so much.'

'That's the mushrooms. They're the only thing that ever got rid of it, for a little while, anyway. It'll be back when they wear off.'

Gaetano lapsed into silence for a moment, and when he spoke again, his voice betrayed the deepest of regrets.

'Now that I can speak clear, and that you can hear me, there are things that I have to say. I know I should have stopped our boys when they said they wanted to join up. That haunts me every moment of every day. It's the first thought in my head when I wake and the last one when I go to bed at night. And it's not an excuse, but if I think about it, at their age, in their circumstances, I would probably have done the same. What prospects were there here for three energetic young men? The promise of adventure, with food in their bellies and pay in their pockets was too attractive to turn down.'

'Do you remember what you did with their medals? They're not on the mantelpiece anymore.'

'It wasn't me who took them down, it was you, but I've no idea what you did with them. One day they were there, the next they were gone. I've searched high and low, but I've never found them. Probably best not to have them as a reminder though. Better to think about our boys' lives than their deaths. They were good sons and good brothers, all three of them. We've not had the chance to speak of them these past ten years, and there are memories we should look back upon before they're lost. Once we're gone, there won't be anybody left to remember their lives.'

And so Marianna and Gaetano's conversation continued through the night. For those few hours, they were no longer bereaved parents, but rather mother and father to three healthy young sons whose presence, somewhere between ethereal and earthly, felt woven into the fabric of the house; entwined with every plant in the garden; even imprinted in the echoes and the murmurs of the air around them.

As the stars faded and ripples of pearly dawn light streaked the sky, Marianna asked, 'How long have we been here?'

'Many hours. The sun's not far from rising. How are you feeling now?'

'Like the windows have been opened and the light's come into my head. And the steps aren't swaying anymore. I'm still talking out loud, aren't I?'

'Sweet and clear, my love. By the grace of God we've got a few healthy years left in us, so let's try to find some contentment in them. We've got each other. We've got this house. There's nothing can be done to change yesterday, but tomorrow's not a promise, Marianna.'

They sat a while longer without speaking, with their fingers entwined and their cheeks pressed together, watching the new day unveil. As an apricot sun blushed the horizon, the sky turned from deep plum, to lavender, to blue. There was nothing quite like a Casa Paradiso sunrise, and this morning its colours were enhanced beyond beauty. As the light rose, diamonds of dew sparkled across the emerald fields. The silhouette of the mountains in the distance was painted in silvery hue.

Gaetano stood up, reached out his hands and pulled Marianna to her feet. When he opened his mouth to speak, a little of his stammer had returned. 'C-come on old girl,' he said. 'Fetch your basket. We're going to pick some more mushrooms.'

1850

BRUNO FERRARI

Bruno Ferrari had done the most stupid thing ever, and that stupid thing had turned into the worst problem of his life. He'd got Mirella pregnant, and Gianna, his wife, was going to kill him – if her father didn't get to him first.

Ten years previously, in the spring of 1840, Bruno had fallen head over heels for Gianna Lovetta because she had a cracking figure and a stable temperament, as well as countless other good qualities. Bruno had asked lovely Gianna to marry him within weeks of their first kiss. Despite her father having expressed reservations at the prospect of his daughter marrying a tradesman, once he'd ascertained that Bruno was a hard-working young man with his own guild-certified roofing business, whose feelings for his daughter were genuine, the union had been blessed. As a wedding gift, Gianna's father, who wasn't short of a few lire, had pledged to set them up at Casa Paradiso.

Formerly the house had been occupied by an elderly couple, so it was terribly outdated. Gianna's father paid for all the materials and some extra hired help when it was needed, but it was Bruno who undertook the lion's share of the renovation work. He put not only his back, but his heart and soul into bringing the old house into the 19th century. He gave it a fresh look by rendering over the outside walls, which some people said was a shame because the brickwork was a masterpiece of craftsmanship; but it was in desperate need of re-pointing, and that would have taken too long. Rendering over the lot was not only quicker, but it would help to keep the cold and the damp out in the winter; and it gave Casa Paradiso a more up-to-date aspect.

Inside, he demolished the kitchen fireplace – a monstrous great thing, caked in a couple of centuries of soot, which looked like something left over from the Dark Ages. He could probably have recuperated a bit of money by selling the carved stone mantel, but getting it out in one piece was impossible, so he broke it up with a sledgehammer and spread the rubble outside the barn doors, where a puddle tended to form. The other fireplaces weren't as massive, or grotesque, but they went the same way. Bruno bricked up all the hearths and fitted modern cast-iron stoves, which were a cleaner and considerably more efficient heating system, as well as being much safer. By the time Bruno Ferrari carried his bride over the threshold, two years to the day since he'd proposed, Casa Paradiso was like a brand-new house.

To begin with, everything had been just peachy. Gianna turned out to be a wonderful wife. She kept the house like a jewel box and she was a great cook. What was more, they couldn't keep their hands off each other. There wasn't a happier or better looked-after married man than Bruno Ferrari.

His small roofing business was transformed by a further investment from his father-in-law. With this money Bruno purchased all manner of state-of-the-art equipment as well as a small fleet of carts on which to transport his tools and supplies from one site to the next. Bruno had all the carts liveried in the same shade of red, with his name painted in gold on the side. Apart from all the roofing work he already had, Gianna's father sent a steady stream of lucrative contracts his way. Before long, Bruno's business had twenty contracted employees, seven apprentices and a small battalion of supplementary hired hands to call upon whenever they were required. In the area around Pieve Santa Clara and beyond, you couldn't pass a building site without seeing one of Bruno's smart red carts with the name *FERRARI* emblazoned on the side.

Gianna played her part in the business too. Having benefitted from a thorough convent education, she could read and write far better than most – certainly better than Bruno, who was by no means illiterate – so she took charge of all the business administration and the accounts. Bruno found her to be ruthless in monetary matters. He would note down the details of a prospective job, listing quantities of materials and labour costs, and give it to Gianna to write out as a formal quote. By the time she had finished with it, the total was at the very least, doubled. Sometimes the price was so inflated that Bruno felt embarrassed presenting it to the client; but to his amazement, more often than not, he still got the job.

The Ferrari family grew at a similar rate to the business, with four babies born in the first six years of the marriage, and all healthy. Gianna had said no more for now, and Bruno had agreed that they had enough to be getting on with for the moment – not that they didn't want more children in the future. They could afford to raise an army of them. The money was rolling in.

Yet for Bruno, all of this flourishing success felt like trying to cling to the back of a runaway stallion. He didn't mind grafting, and nobody could ever accuse him of slacking, but after a hard day's toil it would have been nice to come home and put his feet up for a little bit and talk to Gianna about something which didn't involve tiles and clout nails and rafters. It bothered him that he didn't see enough of his children and rarely had the chance to play with them. Although he did his best to be home in time to kiss his children goodnight, he couldn't spend five minutes tucking them in before Gianna would appear in the bedroom doorway, poised to pounce on him with the accounts. Bruno would eat his dinner surrounded by ledgers on the kitchen table to the sound of Gianna's endless interrogation about the day's payments and expenses and about how many hours each of their employees had worked. Then there was all the planning, with Gianna scheduling the upcoming jobs and organising what materials needed to be ordered from the wholesalers, or how much supplementary manpower had to be arranged, or which other trades had to be liaised with. The lists of things to see to were interminable. When Bruno requested being allowed to enjoy his food without talking shop, Gianna said that wasn't feasible, because within ten minutes of finishing his dinner, he'd be nodding off to sleep. He was too tired to argue, particularly because these days Gianna's temperament wasn't quite as stable as it had been previously. In fact, if he didn't do as he was told, she could be a little snappy.

It wasn't that Bruno was ungrateful for all Gianna did. On the contrary, he knew how fortunate he was to have such a capable wife. Money couldn't buy a better bookkeeper. But increasingly, life was being reduced to all labour and no leisure, and Sundays were not exempt. There were always administrative work matters to see to and a thousand things Gianna needed him to do around the house and garden. Bruno never had a day of rest, and this became increasingly wearing. Even God, who had quite a lot on his plate, had managed to take Sunday off!

As time went on, Bruno found himself delaying his return home just so he could have a little bit of peace and quiet. Occasionally he'd even pop into a tavern for a swift half after work, although never an establishment too close to Pieve Santa Clara, or word might get back to Gianna. He didn't over-indulge. He never had more than a small glass of beer, and often diluted with lemonade, but he could make it last a whole hour.

During those solitary moments spent nursing his watered-down beer, Bruno found himself longing for the simpler times, when it would be just him and a couple of workmates up on a roof, doing a good job with no constricting deadlines – the sorts of jobs where all you needed was a couple of ladders and a tool belt around your waist – not like these days, when every contract required three dozen men, fifty different ladders, complex arrangements of pulleys and hoists and acres and acres of scaffolding. Many of the clients drove him to distraction with their endless quibbling and questions and changes of mind. Chasing up payments frustrated him to the very edge of his patience.

But it wasn't just that. Bruno missed the on-site companionship which made the day pass quickly – the nonsense chatter; the meaningful conversations; the troubles shared and solutions proposed; the laughter, the jokes and shaggy-dog stories. These days, weeks could go by where he seldom laid a tile. He was too busy running between sites organising, inspecting, liaising with customers and sorting out other people's problems.

Aside from this feeling of all work and no play, there was something else bothering Bruno. Gianna kept a far tighter grip on the finances than he'd have liked. She insisted on him handing over every lira he earned so that she could divide it between housekeeping, reinvestment in the business and savings. If ever he fancied buying something for himself, even if it was just some little gadget, or a pair of stylish britches, he was obliged to justify it and would face a barrage of questions before Gianna would hand him back his own money; and often she'd refuse, saying that whatever Bruno had his sights set on was unnecessary. Never mind that Bruno worked every hour God sent; that every day he was up by sunrise and often wasn't home until after sunset. He would argue that although they were country folk, it didn't mean that they shouldn't have nice things, or that they should dress like peasants. Then Gianna would play her trump card, saying that their comfortable situation was due to her father's generosity. There was no ignoring the fact that whenever she said that, Bruno felt belittled.

His first major act of rebellion against Gianna's stifling control was the purchase of a beautiful eight-seater *calesse* carriage. One day, after a client had paid him for quite a sizable job, instead of taking the money home to his wife, as he was supposed to do, he'd gone to see the carriage dealer in Cremona and bought it on sight. Admittedly, it had been a bit of an impulse-buy, but Bruno had a passion for all things on wheels, and the *calesse* had been impossible to resist. It was some vehicle, with shimmering lacquered paintwork, a retractable hood, sprung suspension and forty-two inch wheels. According to the dealer, on a good road it could reach a speed of twelve miles per hour. There wasn't another in Pieve Santa Clara. Not even the Marchesinis disposed of such a fine, modern carriage. With the *calesse* came two handsome chestnut Maremmano horses, each standing over seventeen hands high.

However, Bruno's enjoyment of his purchase was completely ruined by Gianna, who just wouldn't stop going on about the 'outrageous' amount of money he'd spent without prior discussion, or authorisation. It wasn't as though he couldn't afford it. Just with the money he had in the strongbox, which he had built into one of the former fireplaces at Casa Paradiso, Bruno could have bought four *calesse* carriages, horses included, and his children wouldn't have gone hungry for a year.

Once Gianna had finished berating him about the money, she demanded to know what they were supposed to do with such a huge, cumbersome vehicle. Bruno had replied that they could take the children out in it on Sundays. Gianna had looked at him as though he was an idiot, and it really annoyed him when she did that.

Unusually for a woman, Gianna could drive a horse and carriage, but not something as enormous as an eight-seater *calesse*, which was reputedly heavy to steer and even harder to stop. Just hitching the horses to it required two men, and she had a bad feeling about the Maremmanos. In her opinion, and Gianna knew her horses, they were trouble. Bruno had to admit that they were a bit skittish, but argued that all they needed was more training. He didn't tell Gianna that the first time he took them out, one had spooked at the sight of a heron and almost landed him, the other horse and the *calesse*, in the Delmona Canal. Neither did he admit that what Gianna had said about the *calesse* being hard to steer and stop also turned out to be true. On his return home, Bruno had almost demolished one of the gateposts and it was a miracle that the two uncontrollable beasts hadn't charged straight through the barn doors.

Nevertheless, on principle, he'd refused to sell the *calesse*, or change the horses, because that would have been an admission of weakness. Gradually Gianna's anger had dissipated. But then someone had offered Bruno a fine, black mare – a Sella Francese Arabian cross – as part-payment for a job. She was a beauty, and her racing heritage made her fast. Technically he hadn't spent any actual money on her, but Gianna had still been furious because as well as the two recently arrived Maremmanos, Bruno already owned two horses. One was Bruno's former workhorse, an elderly mare, past her best and often lame, who spent most of her time in the field behind the house, but Bruno was too attached to her to send her to the knackers' yard. The second, an eight-year-old gelding, had been purchased not long after they'd married, and it was the horse Bruno used day-to-day to travel to and from work. It was a reliable, good-natured animal, but just an ordinary horse, and about as exciting to ride as a fireside chair. The racehorse was a bit of fun, great for taking out for a gallop. Gianna had commented, 'Great for breaking your neck, more likely.' Then, casting her eyes over the five horses now in residence at Casa Paradiso, she'd asked how many of them Bruno could ride at the same time, which had been a trick question, and he hadn't liked that at all. He let her have the last word when she said that she might as well have married a gambler, because if Bruno continued with his frivolous spending, they'd be ruined. Just as well the deed to the house was in her father's name, or the bailiffs might come for it.

All of this hen-pecking, Bruno could deal with, but the marriage had encountered another problem, which had started after the birth of their fourth child. Gianna had lost interest in the bedroom, which was an enormous disappointment to Bruno. Thinking back, he'd probably blown it out of proportion, and he should have given more consideration to the fact she'd just had another baby, and already had three children to look after, the youngest of which wasn't walking yet. But Gianna's sexual disinterest left him feeling neglected and inadequately loved. He worked hard. He helped out with the children whenever he could. He did everything the man of the house was supposed to do; yet at home, tending to his husbandly needs was always pushed to the back of the queue. These days Gianna was always too tired, and even when she wasn't too tired, she was rarely in the mood, or had something more pressing to do. You could almost say that she was hostile to his advances. Bruno might get a bit of bedroom attention twice a week, if he was lucky; and quite honestly, often he got the feeling that Gianna was only doing it to keep the peace.

Still, instead of making a fuss, he'd come up with what he considered to be a very practical solution to the problem. He thought he was being helpful when he suggested a schedule. After all, Gianna liked things to be well-planned and organised. He proposed Saturday nights for the main event and on Mondays, Wednesdays and Fridays they should make time for a quick bedtime roll-around. Without giving it a moment's consideration, Gianna had deemed Bruno's proposal as ridiculous. She said something about romance, or the lack of it, which went over his head. She then claimed that the schedule would turn sex into the last household chore of the day. Nevertheless, Bruno had expected there to be some level of compromise required and he was prepared for it, so he conceded that two week-day nights instead of three would be acceptable to him. He'd be satisfied with just Tuesdays and Thursdays, and just a bit of manual attention would do. Gianna was not at all sympathetic and cut him off by claiming that sex was yet another thing he expected her to do for him which he could very well be doing himself. That jibe was like a stab in the heart and a knee in the groin at the same time. Consequently, twice a week dwindled to once or twice a month, and it wasn't long before it diminished to almost never. Bruno felt desperately rejected.

He hadn't planned to stray, and he certainly hadn't gone looking, but Bruno Ferrari was a man in his prime – handsome and virile and fit as a butcher's dog. He knew the ladies still had an eye for him, especially when he was riding his racehorse. He also drew a fair bit of attention when he was up on a roof in good weather, stripped to the waist with his skin browned by the sun and his muscles gleaming with sweat. For the first seven years of his marriage, he'd behaved, even when opportunities had presented themselves, and he was very proud of that. But when he encountered Mirella, his resolve left him entirely.

The meeting with Mirella had come about when he'd been to price up a job in the village of San Daniele, which was situated ten miles from Pieve Santa Clara. Bruno was easily bewitched by a pretty face and a prosperous bosom, and Mirella was blessed with both. What was more, she was a nice girl, twenty years old and not the kind who put it about. He'd been her first, she'd said, and he believed her.

With hindsight, Bruno had to admit he'd lost his head for Mirella, although that didn't change his feelings for Gianna, because Bruno didn't doubt for one moment that he loved his wife. If anything, the affair strengthened his marriage because it made the atmosphere less tense at home. Mirella was easy to talk to and didn't chew his ear off about work matters, or nag him about whether he'd done this or that menial chore. What was more, she never turned him down when he was feeling frisky. Mirella's company, both in and out of bed, always left him in high spirits. Even Gianna had commented on his improved temper. She'd remarked that he was cheerful, although thinking back, she might have said '*suspiciously* cheerful'. Anyway, for a time the situation had been very beneficial and Bruno had imagined that once the job at San Daniele was finished, the affair would come to an end too.

That wasn't the way things worked out, because by then Bruno had grown very attached to Mirella and he just couldn't bring himself to stop seeing her. She was a great girl – fragrant and buttery and voluptuous and extremely accommodating; although she might have been less willing if he'd mentioned that he was married. When she'd asked, right at the moment they'd first met, he'd lied, counting on the fact that nobody would know his true marital status ten miles from Pieve Santa Clara. An older and more worldly-wise woman than Mirella might have smelled a rat sooner. A more experienced woman, one who knew the cycles of her body better, might also have been more aware of when it was safe to have relations and not. Six months into their affair, Mirella had announced that she was pregnant and when she spoke of marriage, Bruno had been faced with no choice but to admit that he was already married.

At first, Mirella had cried more than anyone Bruno had ever seen cry, and he'd felt awful. Her parents were going to disown her, she said. Her reputation would be dirt and no man would ever want her again. She was going to be one of those fallen women who brought her child up in poverty, and her shame would be a curse upon her child. Then she'd called Bruno a series of names using language that he didn't think a sweet girl like Mirella should know. As a final blow, she threatened to tell his wife.

All of this, Bruno had just confessed to his brother, who had listened without interrupting. When at last he spoke, the first thing he said was that he had a good mind to punch Bruno's teeth out, which was quite something because Bruno's brother wasn't a violent sort.

'Your problem,' his brother said, 'Is that since you found yourself with a bit of money, you think you're really something. When you're not swanning about on your ridiculous *calesse*, you're riding around on your big, black racehorse like you're more royal than the king. You're always flashing your silver around, peacocking in your fancy Sunday clothes even on a Tuesday ...'

The stream of accusations continued. The words wounded Bruno, mainly because there was a lot of truth in them. He was about to admit that perhaps the success had gone to his head, but his brother hadn't finished with him.

'What you've done to Gianna is unforgivable. You know how lucky you are to have a woman like her? There are men who'd give their right arm to have a wife half as intelligent, or capable, or beautiful. You haven't given a thought to your children. And that other girl, Mirella. Poor thing. You've ruined her life. You're a stupid, selfish bastard.'

When Bruno's brother finally came to the end of his lecture, he asked, 'So what are you going to do?'

By this time, Bruno, who'd been hoping for brotherly support as opposed to a dressing down, was close to tears. All he could reply was, 'I'm going to have to start by telling Gianna.'

Unbeknown to Bruno, Gianna was being put in the picture at that precise moment. Mirella had gone to Casa Paradiso to tell all. Thus when Bruno returned home, he was not permitted to enter the house. A frighteningly calm Gianna stood blocking the doorway with her fists on her hips and with a frostily silent Mirella standing behind her. If looks could kill, he'd have dropped dead on the doorstep. Twice.

Gianna spoke in a tone which should not be argued with and said, 'I don't want to see you or hear from you for a week. I need time to think. Come back next Saturday at noon. I will have sent the children to my sister's so that we may speak freely, but my father will be here.' She had then slammed the door shut.

As he made his way across the yard, Bruno had turned back to the house and seen the children's faces at the upstairs window, staring down at him. He forced a smile and waved. They waved back, but none of them were smiling.

Never had Bruno felt anguish as he did that week, waiting for Gianna's verdict. He was like a condemned man, anticipating the blow of the executioner's *mazzatello* to land on his neck. He suffered from hot sweats, cold sweats and palpitations. He couldn't eat a thing. Once, he'd come close to fainting. Thinking it prudent not to show his face in Pieve Santa Clara, he rented a room in another village and laid low, terrified that his father-in-law would track him down, because if he did, he'd probably blow his balls off with his shotgun.

During that dreadful week, Bruno couldn't go to work. He didn't trust his shaking legs to climb a ladder, let alone get up on a roof; although it did cross his mind that falling to his death would make his problem go away, and he did consider it briefly. If he was gone, Gianna and the children would be fine because her father would see that they didn't want for anything. But what about Mirella and the baby? He couldn't leave them high and dry.

When Bruno presented himself at Casa Paradiso on Saturday at noon, as instructed, there was no sign of his father-in-law, and it dawned on him that Gianna had used the threat of her father's presence to knock him off balance and put him into a state of fear. It had worked like a charm. Gianna was not a woman you'd choose as an adversary, especially if you knew you didn't have a leg to stand on.

Bruno's relief at not having to face Gianna's father was replaced by the bafflement of finding Mirella there instead, and looking unexpectedly at home. The reason for this he was to learn within minutes of being given permission to sit at his own kitchen table. On Gianna's invitation, Mirella had moved in.

'Unlike you,' Gianna said, jabbing an accusatory finger at his face, 'I take my marriage vows seriously, therefore the way I see it, your responsibilities are also mine. Mirella lives here now, with me and the children, and when her baby is born, Casa Paradiso will continue to be their home. Our children will be raised together, and we will both be mothers to all of them.'

Bruno's shock was impossible to hide. He remained open-mouthed as Gianna laid out the options available to him. The first was to leave, to go far away and never return. If that was his choice, he could take with him what he had brought into the marriage – the old mare, his basic roofing tools and his personal possessions. However, in recognition of his years of work to support the family, he would be furnished with a small sum of money to help him start a new life. If this was his choice, it would be final. There would be no coming back. Ever.

The second option, for which Gianna expressed a preference because it would bring only moderate disruption to everybody's lives, was that he could continue living at Casa Paradiso, but under modified terms. Gianna and Mirella would each have their own bedrooms, as would he, although his room would not be in the main part of the house. Bruno was to organise his quarters in the area beyond the laundry room. He could still eat his meals with the family, but no other domestic service would be provided. He should expect neither his room to be cleaned, nor his laundry to be done for him.

Gianna then presented him with a written list of require-ments, financial and otherwise, which made Bruno go pale. Firstly, he would have to sell all of his horses, apart from the gelding which he used day-to-day and the old lame mare, who could live out the rest of her days in the field. The *calesse* would have to go, and would be replaced with a small, practical carriage with a manageable pony to pull it, which Gianna could also drive.

So far, Bruno considered that he was getting off quite lightly, but when he saw the greatly increased sum of housekeeping he was expected to provide to keep his expanded family, he swallowed so hard that his gulp echoed around the kitchen.

Gianna continued, 'I will carry on seeing to the business accounts, administration and suchlike. But from this moment forwards, I will be paid for my services, and at a fair rate, as would any professional bookkeeper.'

Bruno was taken aback and spluttered, 'Y-you want to be paid to do the accounts as well as being paid housekeeping?'

Gianna responded with a raised eyebrow which made it clear that she was not inviting questions and moved onto the matter of Mirella's allowance. It was important, she stated, for Mirella to feel part of the structure of the family, therefore she would be furnished with a monthly stipend so that she wouldn't have to ask for a hand-out whenever she needed clothing, or shoes, or any personal item. As for Bruno, he would be paid a salary. He would receive a not ungenerous sum every month, as long as all other outgoings were covered first, and Gianna pledged never to question how he chose to spend it.

Where the children were concerned, a fund would be established for their education. Gianna intended to send them all to school – the girls as well as the boys – and this would apply to any future children born either to Gianna, or Mirella. Bruno was confused at the mention of future children, so Gianna explained that within the framework of this new arrangement, sex was not out of the question. However, Bruno should view this not as a conjugal right, but as a privilege, which he could earn not just from Gianna, but from Mirella too. Bedroom visits would be by the ladies' invitation only and at times convenient to them. It was made plainly clear that this privilege could be withdrawn at any moment and for any reason and that he had no right to appeal the decision.

'Let's see if you're a big enough man to be a husband to two wives,' Gianna said.

Bruno agreed to absolutely all the conditions and said he'd do his best. He was then made to sign Gianna's list of stipulations and told that his three-month probationary period would begin with immediate effect.

This unorthodox domestic arrangement quickly became the talk of Pieve Santa Clara. Reactions were mixed. As far as the village women were concerned, for some it was debauched and sinful and doomed to be plagued with jealousies; whilst others lauded Gianna as a heroine. There were a good deal of envious remarks amongst the menfolk, although a fair number of them commented that having two wives might seem good from far, but might be far from good.

When the parish priest, having heard numerous troubling rumours, called by at Casa Paradiso, questioning the morality of the arrangement and pointing out to Gianna that God's design for marriage was one man and one woman, he quoted a passage from the Gospel of Matthew – *A man shall hold fast to his wife, for the two are of one flesh.*

Gianna, whose convent education had left her well-versed in all matters scriptural, pointed out to the priest that the Bible contained several stories of men with two wives. Jacob, for example, was married to both Leah and Rachel. Elkanah was husband to Hannah as well as Peninnah. If the priest so desired, she would be happy to look up the references and read the appropriate verses to him. The priest felt somewhat outplayed at his own game and muttered something about that not being necessary.

Gianna went on to explain that her husband's adulterous

actions had reminded her of the importance of showing compassion and exercising forgiveness. Would she have been a better Christian if she had turned Mirella away when she had come to her in need of help? Mirella's parents had all but disowned her, but by Gianna's reasoning, Mirella was the innocent party, free of all sin except that of having succumbed to the lies and honeyed words of an older man.

Feeling rather put in his place, the priest was obliged to agree. He gave his blessing to the unusual arrangement and assured Gianna that she and Mirella and all of their children would be still welcome at Mass. He added that if any parishioner said anything disrespectful, or made them feel in any way uncomfortable, she should report it to him and he would deal with it. Gianna said that she could sort such problems out herself, to which the priest responded meekly, 'I don't doubt that for a moment, Signora Ferrari. I hope to see you at Mass on Sunday.'

Gianna replied with a firm nod of her head, 'You'll be certain to see us *all* at Mass *every* Sunday.' She then reminded the priest that despite her married status, for all but legislative purposes, she had elected to maintain her maiden name of 'Lovetta'.

Bruno fulfilled every one of his wife's conditions and passed his three-month probationary period without putting a foot wrong. To give Gianna credit where it was due, she treated him fairly, with no recriminations. He certainly never felt unwelcome, or ostracised, in his own home.

Things were further improved when Gianna employed two site managers, because by then, even if Bruno had been allowed to keep his racehorse, getting round to all the different sites had become a physical impossibility. This saved Bruno miles of travel, and as the new managers reported directly to Gianna, he was also spared hours of administrative headaches.

He was still up and off to work by sunrise six days per week, but now he could be on his way home well before sunset to spend time with his children. Nothing delighted Bruno more than chasing them around the garden or playing hide-and-seek. Gianna called him a great big kid, but she meant it nicely. When the weather wasn't good enough to be outside, the children would pile into the comfortable den Bruno had made for himself in the area beyond the laundry room and they would play with the toys he bought for them out of his monthly salary, or he would tell them stories. As for mealtimes, it was a pleasure to enjoy his food in the company of his family, and now Gianna kept the books off the table at dinner time.

With all the mothering duties and household chores shared, and in many cases taken over entirely by Mirella, Gianna's stable temperament returned – for the most part. She continued to see to all the business administration and was paid for her work. Finding herself with an increased amount of time at her disposal, she also undertook much of the liaising with the clients, which was a great relief for Bruno. Funnily enough, whenever Gianna went to present a quote, or collect a payment, nobody quibbled. She would drive out to visit clients on the two-seater *carrozza* buggy she had purchased from the carriage dealer in Cremona. The *carrozza* came with a small Cobb pony – a steady and biddable animal – which Gianna could hitch and unhitch from the buggy without assistance.

The expanded Ferrari family settled into a well-disciplined domestic routine. Eventually, even Gianna's father and Mirella's parents came to accept the unconventional arrangement.

Exactly what went on behind closed doors was the business of only those concerned, but over the following years, Gianna bore Bruno two more children, and Mirella, three. With a total of ten children and only four bedrooms in the main house, Casa Paradiso became somewhat overcrowded. In Gianna's words, they were packed in like anchovies in a barrel. Bruno couldn't disagree, and it wasn't just the house which they had outgrown. With his burgeoning business and all the equipment needed to keep it running, he had long since exceeded the capacity of the barn.

Thanks to Bruno's continuing hard work and Gianna's scrupulous saving, they could afford a bigger property. In 1861 The Ferraris secured the purchase of a *cascina* on the southern boundary of the village, disposing of an eight-bedroom house and four enormous barns. Casa Paradiso was put on the market.

1872

FEDERICO MARCHESINI

Federico was endowed with the Marchesini name, but not the wealth. The centuries-old custom of bequeathing the estate to the eldest son meant that the grand villa, its adjoining farmsteads and approximately three thousand acres of land had passed in its entirety to Federico's uncle, Ulisse. Federico's father, having drawn the lot of being born in third place – fifth if his sisters had counted in matters of inheritance – had been left nothing beyond a relatively modest trust fund. His premature death, when Federico was just three years old, had caused his widow considerable financial inconvenience. She had managed to scrape along, providing Federico with a modestly middle-class upbringing, but her widow's pension had not been sufficient to cover his education. It was thanks to the generosity of his uncle that Federico had attended a prestigious school. Zio Ulisse had seen great promise in his nephew; certainly more than he saw in his own son. For his part, Federico had been an exemplary student, blessed with both a sound work ethic and a natural intelligence which regularly saw him at the top of the class in most subjects. He had never been outside the top three, apart from the final term of his third year, when he'd been laid up with whooping cough. Taking into account his impeccable academic record, and conscious of who was paying the fees, the school waived his examinations and marked him as a pass, allowing him to spend an extended summer of convalescence in the mountains. Now, aged twenty-four, Federico Marchesini was embarking upon his career as an architectural engineer.

Despite having been born and brought up in his mother's native city of Bologna, Federico had always maintained close ties with Zio Ulisse. It was a pity that with one thing and the other, and most recently Federico's all-consuming university studies, he hadn't been back to Pieve Santa Clara for so long. Although they had been in regular contact by correspondence, they had seen one another only very occasionally over the past few years. The one-hundred-and-sixty-kilometre journey from Bologna to Pieve Santa Clara required two complicated days of travel, more often than not beset by delays which necessitated a supplementary overnight stop, even now that the new railway network could take Federico as far as Modena. A further section of track was planned to reach Cremona, but when that would be complete was anybody's guess.

Finding himself with a week's hiatus over Easter, Federico had come to the family pile for an eagerly anticipated visit. Federico and his uncle had gone out together after breakfast and now found themselves crossing the fields to the north of the estate. Spring was the loveliest season, with daytime temperatures averaging twenty degrees Celsius and seldom dropping below twelve at night. There had been just the right amount of rain to fill the canals and keep Zio Ulisse happy. The orchards were fat with blossom and the first spears of sprouting crops cast a green haze over the land.

'What is it you've planted this year, Zio?' Federico asked.

'Wheat and maize, for the most part. And *riso arborio* in the rice fields bordering the canal. But all of this surrounding us is tobacco, which is an increasingly profitable crop owing to its medicinal uses and purported health benefits.'

Zio Ulisse paused his steps, taking a moment to survey his domain. 'My dear Federico, we stand on the cusp of a new era of farming!' He declared. 'The future of agriculture is rooted not in superstition and prayer, or whichever saint's day it happens to be, nor even on the quirks of the moon's cycles, but in scientific knowledge and innovation. We now harness the power of chemical elements to nourish the soil. Nitrogenous compounds and other such agrochemical marvels are increasing yields by a third, sometimes more. These days we are the masters of the earth, no longer its servants.' As Zio Ulisse resumed walking, he added, 'As it stands there's not much point in diversifying my crops and planting anything which is easily perishable as I can't get it out of the region before it spoils. However, once the railway line is up and running, the situation will change entirely. The impact on the dairy side of the business will be transformative. Marchesini milk will become a breakfast staple in furthest-flung corners of the land!'

Zio Ulisse looked very pleased on mentioning the railway as this was the reason for their outing that morning. He was keen to show Federico the work which had been done in preparation for the laying of the Cremona-Mantova line, a stretch of which was to run through the uppermost boundary of the Marchesini estate. Ideally, Zio Ulisse would have preferred there to be a station in Pieve Santa Clara, but that would have involved a bend in the line which the planners had refused to consider for both practical and financial reasons. The station was to be in the neighbouring village of Mazzolo instead, which was only two kilometres away, and Federico's uncle was resigned to being satisfied with that.

'When one looks at the Lombardy Plain, one would think it as flat as a billiard table,' Zio Ulisse said, turning full circle to scan the surrounding farmland. 'But in actual fact, there is a gradient averaging between 0.2 and 0.35 percent, as well as areas of greater elevation and depression. It was fascinating to watch the surveyors at work. The equipment they have these days is quite extraordinary in its accuracy. I daresay I drove them to distraction with my endless questions!'

Federico smiled, for he would have done the same. His uncle shared his proclivity for all things structural and mathematical. Had he not had the responsibility of the Marchesini estate, no doubt Zio Ulisse would have chosen a career similar to his. When Federico had told him of his ambition to study architectural engineering, his uncle could not have been more delighted.

They had now reached the spot where a straight, ten-meter-wide swathe had been carved through the fields. The earth had been banked to raise the line above floodwater level and to provide a flat foundation for the tracks. The elevated corridor stretched east to west beyond the horizon in both directions. When Federico asked when the tracks were due to be laid, Zio Ulisse snorted, 'That is a question which I cannot answer with any certainty. According to the original proposal, this line should have been inaugurated three years ago. Trains should be steaming along here already. Considering the herculean feats of engineering which have been carried out in the Alpine regions, with tunnels bored, viaducts built and mountainsides blown to high heaven, laying sixty miles of track across the Lombardy Plain should have been a quick and simple task in comparison. But with all the different regional planning regulations and disorganised bureaucratic procedures, not to mention the embezzlement and corruption, one can only trust that it will come together eventually.'

Zio Ulisse went on to explain how once complete, this stretch of line would reduce the journey between Cremona and Mantova to under two hours. Currently the route could take a full day by road, longer in the wet season. 'Much of the Via Postumia is in dire condition,' Zio Ulisse continued, 'Some of the potholes are deep enough to drown a horse in. The journey would necessitate less time on the canal, but they've let that fall into a shocking state. It's so silted up and filled with rubbish that it's unnavigable in places. When I was a boy, there was a continuous traffic of *chiatte*. The amount of trade we've lost owing to neglect and lack of funding is nothing short of criminal, and this region is not alone in suffering economic stagnation owing to poor infrastructure. Once complete, the railway network will make an enormous difference.'

'They say that by the dawn of the twentieth century there will be lines all over the country.'

'The *Country!*' Spat Zio Ulisse, pronouncing the word with disdain. 'We're all supposed to be unified now; one big happy family of *Italians*. No more Duchy of Milan, or Parma, or Modena. No more Kingdom of Sardinia, or Sicily. I can't see it working myself. Don't try to tell me that the Neapolitans, the Venetians and the Genoese will all get along, or that those haughty Romans won't cause trouble. The Papal States have refused to be sucked into it, of course. They're far too keen to hold onto their wealth and nobody's been foolhardy enough to argue with God's representatives. In my opinion the question of unification should have been put to a referendum, at the very least. You can't take all these autonomous states, republics and kingdoms – many of which have been at each other's throats since the dawn of time – and homogenize them into one jigsaw-puzzle nation. As far as I am concerned, I will always be a *Lombardo*, never an *Italiano*.'

Federico already knew that the matter of Italian Unification was a sore point with his uncle, as it was with much of the older generation for whom the preceding wars and revolutions were still fresh memories. He himself was not against the integration of the state and agreed with King Vittorio Emanuele II's message, *'Meglio uniti che divisi'* – 'Better united than divided'. There were bound to be challenges and a few differences to iron out, but overall, like most people of his age, Federico considered that eventually the benefits of *Il Risorgimento* could outweigh its disadvantages. At least it should put an end to the continual spats between the disparate regions; and the common currency, all valued at the same level, was bound to simplify trade once the rampant inflation had calmed down.

Zio Ulisse patted his nephew affectionately on the shoulder and said, 'Anyway, I didn't bring you all the way here just to grumble about politics or the state of public works. There's something I'd like your opinion on. Do you have the legs for a walk before lunch?'

They descended the embankment and retraced their steps, discussing Federico's future career plans, but it was not long until their conversation turned to Federico's cousin, Zio Ulisse's wayward son, Carlo. As they reached the road, Zio Ulisse asked, 'Have you heard from Carlo of late?'

'Not since last year. He sent mother a note from Amalfi to say he would be visiting Bologna in the spring, but we never saw him. He mentioned that he was travelling the southern regions in connection to his studies.'

'Believe that and you'll believe anything. He was probably more occupied squandering my money in Naples' whorehouses. Carlo's a year older than you. He should have completed his degree by now, but he's not even halfway through his examinations, and his grades have been nothing to crow about. He barely scraped a pass last year and I venture to say that was owed more to the six cases of Franciacorta I sent to the rector of the university than to Carlo's academic efforts.'

'Is it History of Art that he's studying?'

Zio Ulisse scoffed, 'Indeed. A degree in looking at paintings. About as much use as a paper hat in the rain! It certainly won't be of much benefit to him when his time comes to take over the reins here. Carlo doesn't lack intelligence, but he lacks the good sense to use it. Still, I hope that in time he will outgrow his rashness. I blame myself for not stamping down on his degenerate habits sooner. I despair sometimes, Federico. I really do despair. Ours is a fractured, infelicitous father-and-son relationship. Just as well his mother isn't alive to suffer it.'

Zio Ulisse lapsed into a troubled silence. Federico didn't think it sensitive to ask his uncle exactly what he meant by 'degenerate habits', but he had an inkling. He'd heard it rumoured from more than one reliable source that Carlo, aside from his roistering and womanising, had acquired an appetite for opium.

There had been a time when Federico and Carlo had been not just cousins, but the best of companions too. Every summer Federico would travel from Bologna to spend two months on the family estate. What wondrous childhood holidays those had been! The boys had been free to ramble at will with just two rules to follow: don't get into trouble and be back by sunset. They'd leap from their beds at first light and spend their days running free across the fields. There were endless adventures to be had; places to explore; camps to be made; trees to climb; trout and catfish to catch in the streams. The Marchesini cousins would wait until the very last moment, when the sun was an inch from the horizon, and go sprinting back home before curfew to wolf down a man-sized portion of dinner.

All of that had changed when aged twelve, Carlo had been sent away to school in Milan. He had returned very different – full of himself, ill-mannered, spiteful, and taking every opportunity to belittle Federico, calling him the Marchesini family's poor church mouse. Carlo had attended that school for a year before being expelled, and subsequently managed to get himself excluded from several other schools for reasons that Zio Ulisse had never cared to elucidate. Federico had tolerated his cousin for three further summers, each progressively worse. Gone were the playful boyish amusements. All Carlo wanted to do was torture animals and bother the village girls. The cousins had come to blows when Carlo had kicked a hedgehog so hard that the poor creature had broken in two. Even worse had been the time when he'd locked himself and one of the farm labourers' daughters into a stable and forced her into a sexual act.

Following that, amongst other unpleasant incidents, Federico had declined his summer invitations to Pieve Santa Clara and elected to spend his holidays by the sea with his mother instead. Zio Ulisse had been disappointed, but not offended. He'd understood Federico's reasons without having them explained.

Federico knew that his uncle carried with him a great weight of uncertainty about the future of the estate. Zio Ulisse had often spoken about how the Marchesini wealth and privilege came burdened with onerous responsibilities. Over half of the families of Pieve Santa Clara depended upon him for their livelihoods, either directly or indirectly. Zio Ulisse, like his father and grandfather before him had endeavoured to nurture good relationships with their workforce. They paid fair wages and kept their lodgings in good repair. In his younger days, Zio Ulisse hadn't been above getting his hands dirty – less so now that age and rheumatism were slowing him down – but he still did all he could to be on cordial terms with all those in his employment. This was evidenced as their paths crossed with several farmhands and dairymen, all of whom he stopped to talk to, and clearly the rapport between them was one of mutual respect. Exactly how this would change with Carlo in charge was unclear, but there was no doubt that things wouldn't be the same.

On reaching the boundary of the estate, Federico and his uncle crossed the brick bridge which spanned the canal and proceeded a further quarter mile until they reached a property on the east side of the road comprising a substantial rustic house with a separate barn. Judging by the boarded-up windows and overgrown garden, the place had been unoccupied for some time. Zio Ulisse opened the gate to let them into the yard.

'What is this place?' Federico asked.

'They call it Casa Paradiso – a suitable name in its prime, no doubt, but rather more in a state of purgatory now. I acquired it less than two years ago. I should have called upon you to take a look at it before I made my commitment as clearly I didn't pay sufficient attention to its structure. I was rather bewitched by the views.'

Indeed, the house did dispose of a commanding vista, with a broad panorama of fields and pastures scattered with small clusters of woodland. In the distance, the only construction visible was the top third of Pieve Santa Clara's belfry and beyond it the hazy outline of the Apennine mountains silhouetted against the sky.

Federico followed his uncle around the house to the east-facing gable where the most noticeable feature was a gaping triangular crack, running from either side of the chimneystack almost to ground level.

'That doesn't look good,' Federico said, and this was something of an understatement. Zio Ulisse sighed, 'When I first viewed the house there was just a minor hairline fissure which I presumed went no deeper than the rendering, so I ascribed no importance to it. This rather alarming crack has opened up over the winter. Do you reckon it could be due to settlement or subsidence?'

Federico took a few moments to inspect the damage and asked, 'When was the house built?'

'According to the original deed, construction was completed in 1640.'

'In that case settlement is unlikely to be the cause. That would have occurred a long time ago, probably within a few years of the house being built. There could be some subsidence owing to geological factors or changes in the water table, but judging by the form of the crack, I don't think it's that. Can I take a look inside?'

Upon entering the room which had formerly been the kitchen, Zio Ulisse threw his hands in the air and cried out in horror, 'Holy Mother of God! Now half the ceiling's come down!' Federico stepped carefully over the pile of plaster and rubble covering the floor and looked up at the exposed rafters, the butts of which weren't fixed into the wall, meaning that at the gable end the floor above them was supported by little more than thin air and happenstance. It didn't take a trained architectural engineer to conclude that this was not a safe place to be standing. However, being able to see the bared structure made the cause of the outside crack obvious, so Federico inquired, 'What happened to the fireplace?'

'There are no fireplaces in the house, just holes for stovepipes which feed directly into the chimneys.'

'A house of this age wouldn't have been built without a fireplace in every room, and those fireplaces would have been an integral part of the structure. Whoever took them out obviously had no idea what they were doing. Do you know when they were removed?'

Zio Ulisse shook his head and said, 'I couldn't say exactly, but the previous owners carried out extensive renovations about twenty-five years ago.'

'How long has the house been empty?'

'A year or so. It was on the market for the better part of a decade because the owners were asking an exaggerated amount of money for it. They came to their senses eventually. A few sets of tenants have been and gone during that ten-year period. I suppose they were lucky that the place didn't fall down on top of them.'

'Keeping the house occupied and heated probably saved them. This sudden dilapidation is due to the chimneys having gone cold over the winter, so the mortar has frozen and thawed into dust which can no longer hold the bricks together.'

Federico ushered his uncle out of the room and told him to wait outside whilst he took a look at the rest of the house. He made his way up to the first floor cautiously, but taking a moment to stop and admire the cantilevered staircase, which was an unexpectedly sophisticated feature in a rustic property. Over the almost two and a half centuries since its installation, it didn't appear to have moved an inch. Whoever had built it was no amateur.

In the bedrooms, Federico's conclusions were confirmed by a further series of cracks not just on the eastern gable but on the western side too. The fact that the building hadn't folded in on itself was testament to its sound construction. But whichever incompetent fool had torn out the fireplaces, which Federico supposed had been not just functional but also beautiful, deserved to be publicly tarred and feathered in the piazza.

Zio Ulisse was standing in the yard wearing a demoralised expression. 'Is it salvageable in your professional opinion?' He asked, clearly prepared for the worst.

'Yes,' Federico reassured him, 'but props need to be put in as a matter of urgency to stabilise the structure. If nothing's done, give it one more winter and all you'll have is a pile of rubble.'

'And in the long term? Would building new fireplaces be sufficient?'

'I would recommend fitting iron beams to support the upper floors. New fireplaces will certainly add to the structural integrity, although they won't need to be as hefty as the original ones as long as they're properly tied in. Some underpinning work on the gable ends might be sensible too. I can draw up a schema for you if that would help.'

Looking somewhat relieved, Zio Ulisse nodded, 'That would be most useful, thank you. And perhaps you could liaise with my mason?'

Federico turned to face Casa Paradiso. Although it was a

rustic house, its proportions were gracefully elegant, giving the impression that whoever had conceived it was more accustomed to designing formal buildings. The dimension and spacing of the windows was not arbitrary, but clearly configured mathematically, using the rules of the golden mean.

Federico took a few steps back, closed one eye and approximated the ratios by measuring against the length of his thumb. This was definitely a house of architectural design as opposed to one thrown up ad hoc. It was certainly worthy of being saved from falling into ruins, and if restored, it had the potential to be a very fine house indeed. As he stood back, imagining what could be done to it and how it would look with new shutters and windows, and possibly stripped back to the original brick, a question he hadn't thought to ask came into his mind. Zio Ulisse wasn't short of properties. Aside from the main villa and farm-workers' cottages, there must be two dozen houses scattered over the Marchesini estate, so what had driven his uncle to purchase this one? Zio Ulisse looked a little embarrassed when the question was put to him.

'I bought it for you, Federico, as a congratulatory gift for your graduation. It is not my name on the deed, but yours.'

Federico was so surprised that he just looked from his uncle to the house, open-mouthed before stuttering, 'You bought me a house, Zio?'

'Yes. But I intended to present it to you in a rather less dreadful state, and obviously I will pay for all the remedial work which needs doing. My reason for gifting you this house is that I want you to have a place to call your own here in the lands of your ancestors. We Marchesinis have lived in these parts since the 1400s. I know that your life will be elsewhere, but I thought it would be a wonderful thing for you to have a home here too, and one separate from the estate.' The corner of Zio Ulisse's mouth curled into a little wry smile and he added, 'And your self-serving old uncle wants you to have more than just the reason of family duty to visit.'

Before returning to Bologna, Federico convened with Zio Ulisse's mason, who agreed with his conclusions concerning the reason for the structural problems and with all the solutions proposed. The mason suspected that the removal of the fireplaces had been undertaken by a man called Bruno Ferrari, who had lived at Casa Paradiso for some years and had been a roofer by trade. 'That unfortunate fellow, Ferrari, dropped dead not long after he moved out of here,' the mason said, 'They reckon his heart gave out.'

He then went on to recount the peculiar tale of the roofer having had two wives (at the same time), who had borne him ten children between them. The two wives were still living under the same roof in a big *cascina* at the southern end of the village.

Curious though this was, Federico was not interested in seedy village chatter, so in a tone which made it clear that he was changing the subject, he requested that the mason should chip off a patch of the external rendering as he was keen to see the brickwork beneath it. Under one of the windows, where a portion of the mortar had crumbled away, there appeared to be evidence of a herringbone panel, and this turned out to be the case. There was also some exquisite corbeling in a dragons' teeth arrangement beneath the limestone sill. It was a masterpiece of artistry and craftsmanship. However, much to Federico's dismay, the mortar mix which Bruno Ferrari had used was so excessively strong that it couldn't be removed without taking the faces off the bricks. Casa Paradiso's fine brickwork was destined to remain hidden forever.

Shaking his head, the Mason commented, 'Goes to show that you should leave the masonry to the masons and the roofing to the roofers.'

Within the week, a forest of wooden props and scaffolding

was put in place, and just in time, as by then another section of the kitchen ceiling had fallen down. Shortly after, iron beams were installed and new fireplaces constructed. The foundations of the gables were underpinned and ties were put in as an extra precaution to avoid the risk of the disturbed walls bellying out. By the time Federico returned to Pieve Santa Clara, some six months later, the remedial work was complete. Notwithstanding neglect, natural calamities, or wilful acts of sabotage, Casa Paradiso was fit to stand for centuries to come.

Although Federico was deeply grateful for his uncle's generosity, Casa Paradiso was a very impractical gift. Not only did it require a substantial investment to render it habitable, but it was also rather geographically inconvenient for Federico to visit regularly. Once the railway line from Modena was extended to reach Cremona, the door-to-door journey from Bologna to Pieve Santa Clara was cut by two thirds and could reliably be covered in a day. But by then Federico was so occupied with further studies necessary for the advancement of his career that he simply didn't have the time for anything other than very brief and occasional trips. When the opportunity to work in America was presented to him, Casa Paradiso became nothing more than a distant and bothersome encumbrance.

Federico was glad that Zio Ulisse lived to see the trains passing along the northern boundary of the Marchesini estate, but after his death in 1881, there was no reason at all for Federico to return to Pieve Santa Clara. By then he had married and settled permanently in upstate New York with his American wife.

Zio Ulisse bequeathed to his favourite nephew a considerable amount of money in his will, causing a somewhat abrasive reaction from his son, who having failed to obtain his degree had returned to Pieve Santa Clara to take over the estate. In order to relieve himself of the responsibility of the house and not ignite a family feud, Federico signed Casa Paradiso over to cousin Carlo.

COSTANZA CASTELLO

Costanza Castello was forty-four years old and therefore considered middle-aged – rather an optimistic projection, she thought; and if this was truly the mid-point of her life, how she would find the strength and patience to tolerate another forty-four years of struggle was beyond her.

Until relatively recently, apart from a little trouble with her teeth and the odd seasonal ailment, there had been absolutely nothing wrong with Costanza; but all that had changed when her mistress, the second Signora Marchesini, had decreed that servants could no longer wear clogs in her house. The clatter of wooden-soled *zoccoli* was offensive to those refined ears.

That was all very well, but Costanza, who'd been in service up at the Marchesini house since girlhood, had worn nothing but clogs all her life, as was the case for most country women. There was no sturdier or more durable footwear; or anything which was better value for money. The *zoccolaio*, who came to the village on market days, not only made and sold clogs, but also shaped them to order, ensuring a comfortable fit every time. Costanza had always owned two pairs of *zoccoli* – one for the summer, with light soles made of poplar and criss-cross linen straps to keep them on her feet; and one for the winter with thicker oak soles and a closed leather upper, which she lined with wool. Neither was now permissible up at the big house.

Signora Marchesini's ruling had been received with a lot of behind-the-scenes griping from the servants. If *zoccoli* couldn't be worn in the house, assuming they were not expected to go barefoot, or slither along the marble floors in their stockings, who was going to provide them with shoes? Not the Marchesinis, it turned out. The servants were ordered to avail themselves of soft-soled shoes, which were to be purchased at their own expense. Non-compliance with the new directive would lose them their jobs.

When the cobbler had informed Costanza that having leather-soled shoes made to measure would cost her almost a month's wages, she had laughed in his face, so he had proposed buying a second-hand pair instead for less than half that price. Those too were prohibitively expensive, and the limited selection he presented to Costanza didn't look as though they had many miles left in them. The cobbler had suggested a third option – mass-produced shoes made of rubber – although he warned that they wouldn't last like leather shoes, and they were not as cool in summer, or as warm in winter. The price was equivalent to a week's wages. Grudgingly, Costanza had tried several pairs. She could fit her feet in lengthways, but widthways, they were all far too narrow and her toes overlapped the soles on both sides. The cobbler had assured her that with wear, they would stretch. He had then remarked that she had strangely-shaped feet. Costanza had slapped her money on the counter and left the shop with her new, ill-fitting rubber shoes, feeling both robbed and insulted. Strangely-shaped feet, indeed!

Learning to walk in such flimsy footwear had taken some practice. Indoors, on smooth, flat floors was one thing, and Costanza could just about tolerate the cold leeching through the rubber soles; but being Signora Marchesini's head maidservant meant that she was often sent outside to run one or other errand. With those soft, thin soles, she might as well have been unshod, for she could feel every pebble, blade of grass and ant carcass she trod on.

This discomfort, Costanza might have learned to tolerate, but the cobbler had not warned her that those infernal shoes would make her feet sweat so terribly. Signora Marchesini had complained of a nasty smell, which she had described as being 'like ammonia, turned milk and vinegar'. Yet no matter how often Costanza washed, scrubbed and soaked those awful shoes, she couldn't rid them of the stench. Worse, the more she wore them, the more that stink soaked into her feet.

Had circumstances been different, Costanza might have told Signora Marchesini where to stick her job and her rubber shoes, but the fact was that she couldn't afford to find herself unemployed. Her husband's work situation was precarious, and that was the fault of the Marchesinis too. Costanza's husband had worked their land since he was a boy; until one day, with no prior warning, the master, Carlo Marchesini, had gathered together the farm employees and stated that he was ceasing all operations relating to the commercial dairy and that cereal crops would no longer be grown on his land. The announcement was met with a mixture of bewilderment and disbelief by the men. Some even thought he must be joking. Why close down a thriving dairy and a fertile arable farm, which were obviously turning a handsome profit? Both had been there for centuries, and since the arrival of the trains, anyone could see that business had boomed.

The reason for this radical change was that Carlo Marchesini had decided to turn his attention to silk production. The silkworms which he intended to raise ate mulberry leaves, so almost the entirety of his land was to be planted with mulberry bushes. Only a small acreage would be set aside to grow what foodstuffs his household needed. He had then explained the process of silk manufacturing at great length, but few were listening as they were more concerned about whether they could still count on employment. On this matter, Carlo Marchesini had been altogether more vague. Yes, there would be jobs available, but mainly for women. Once planted, the mulberry bushes would need regular pruning to encourage the growth of tender shoots. That was light, easy work which required neither the expertise nor the strength of a man. As for the silk production itself – tending and feeding the silkworms, and the reeling, spinning and weaving of the silk would all be carried out by a female workforce.

As it turned out, Carlo Marchesini retained a tiny fraction of his farmhands, selecting only the younger and more robust men. Costanza's husband, despite his almost three decades of commitment to Carlo Marchesini, and to his father, Ulisse, before him, had not been amongst them. That had been hard enough to swallow – but along with the job, he'd also lost the farm workers' lodgings where they'd lived since they'd married and had raised their children. The fact that Costanza was still employed by the Marchesinis made no difference to the situation. Their home was being sequestered for use by the silk-workers and that was that.

Costanza's attempts at negotiation had been unsuccessful. However, she had caught Carlo Marchesini in an unusually reasonable mood, and the master had proposed alternative accommodation, not on the estate, but quite close by, in a house which he owned but was currently unoccupied; and that was the reason the Castellos now found themselves living in this miserable hovel, Casa Paradiso. Never had a house been so inappropriately named.

Worn out by a long day of ministering to Signora Marchesini's endless dictates, Costanza limped across the yard towards the empty house. It was almost seven in the evening. Her husband was away working on the roads, which was gruelling and dangerous labour, but these days he had to take any casual jobs he could find. Still, at least with only herself to see to she didn't have to go to the trouble of cooking dinner, or washing out his linens, or any of the other things involved in looking after her husband, so she could deal with the urgent matter of her feet. Before she crossed the threshold, Costanza took off her rubber shoes and left them on the doorstep – not that airing them would make any difference. She could still smell them after she'd closed the door behind her.

The kitchen was dark, even in the daylight, because since the glass had fallen out of the rotten frame, Costanza had been obliged to board up the window. She'd been waiting for the Marchesinis to send someone to replace it for months, but just like everything else which needed attention, and the list was growing longer by the day, nothing had been done about it. Costanza couldn't even hold back the rent, as she was well within her rights to do, because the Marchesinis deducted the money directly from her wages.

As there was no running water in the kitchen, Costanza hobbled through to the laundry room, which was a laundry room in name only. There was a trough and a water-pump, but the cauldron had long since been removed, rendering the space redundant for its intended purpose. It was the foulest part of the house – dank and fusty and rank with mildew. The black mould made Costanza cough every time she went in there. She'd wedged an upturned bottle into the drain to stop the rats coming up, but they still got in. There was no shortage of holes in the walls and gaps under doors. All the missing windowpanes didn't help the vermin situation either.

Costanza filled a saucepan with water and took it back to the kitchen to heat on the stove, but as she hadn't been at home to feed wood into the firebox, the plate was barely tepid. The water was going to take forever to warm.

'Lord Jesus, give me strength,' sighed Costanza, carefully easing off her stockings and being mindful of not touching the parts which had been in contact with her feet. Despite having changed the dressings at lunchtime, patches of pink-tinged pus had already bled through. Very cautiously, she began peeling off the strips of fabric, which were stuck fast where the blood and pus had congealed. Ideally, she should soak off the dressings, but she'd been up since before sunrise and she was in need of her bed, so she pulled them off, doing her best to ignore the pain. Her feet, a red, wretched mess of cracked skin and open sores, looked as though they'd been boiled. These days, having strangely-shaped feet was the least of her concerns.

Costanza's problem had begun not long after she'd started wearing the rubber shoes, with just a little itchy patch between two toes of her right foot. It was worse if she scratched it, so she'd learned to ignore it. But within the space of a few months the issue had spread to the other toes too, and then to the ball of her foot, and before she knew it, the whole sole had been afflicted. And then the condition had taken over her left foot too.

Having tried every home remedy she could think of, without success, Costanza was faced with no other choice than to pay to consult a doctor, who diagnosed her affliction as *tigna*, otherwise known as ringworm of the foot. He explained that the condition was fungal in nature and that it thrived in a warm, moist, enclosed environment, such as rubber shoes. Costanza should stop wearing them immediately and revert to *zoccoli*. That, Costanza had replied, was not going to be possible.

To alleviate the condition, the doctor had prescribed potassium permanganate baths, which had definitely helped, but the solution turned Costanza's feet a purplish brown, which leeched through her dressings and stained her stockings. Signora Marchesini had remarked that the wearing of 'dirty' stockings was unacceptable, and when Costanza had explained the reason for the staining, the awful woman had ordered that she should remain at home until such a time that her affliction had passed. This was no act of charity, for Costanza knew all too well that her pay would be docked for each day of work she missed, and as her wages only just covered the rent, she couldn't afford that. She stopped the potassium permanganate baths and the *tigna* came back with a vengeance. Someone had suggested she should try carbolic acid because that didn't stain, but she must have used too much because it had left her feet so raw that they wouldn't have burned more if she'd put them in the fire. It hadn't cured the condition. In fact, it had made it worse. The carbolic acid had eaten away the flesh on her feet and turned the patches of cracked skin into open sores which, no matter what she did, would not heal.

Now Costanza relied on the old-fashioned remedy of saline solution, which didn't really remedy much, but provided temporary relief. As soon as the water on the stove had warmed a little, Costanza mixed in a quarter pound of salt.

Sucking the air in through her teeth, Costanza braced herself and slowly eased her toes into the basin of water. She might as well be plunging her feet into a nest of hornets. Her fouled stockings and bandages were lying in a crumpled heap on the kitchen floor. Although she kept the thought entirely to herself, sometimes she would imagine stuffing her contaminated dressings in the Marchesinis' shoes. It was a wicked thing to think, and she should probably have brought it up at confession, but she didn't want the priest to think badly of her. Still, there were times when that dreadful pair really deserved it.

Costanza had been the first Signora Marchesini's maidservant up until her death. They had got along well and over the years you could say that they had become good companions. The first Signora Marchesini, the youngest daughter of some minor Sardinian aristocrat, had no illusions about why the Marchesini family had selected her as an appropriate bride, for she disposed of the right sort of noble pedigree and had brought a reasonable dowry into the marriage. But once she'd managed to produce two sons, as far as her husband was concerned, she had expended her usefulness. Hers was a melancholic existence, rendered all the more desolate after the boys had been sent away to school. She had always longed for a daughter, she said, but two successful and seven miscarried pregnancies had spoiled her figure. With her youthful bloom faded, her husband no longer visited her bedchamber. Costanza could see that no matter how opulent your surroundings, no matter how many servants you had to cater to your every need, you could still be as miserable as sin. Sharing her troubles with her head maidservant became a common practice for the first Signora Marchesini, and without exception, the troubles were caused by her husband. Carlo Marchesini was, and still remained, a nasty piece of work – arrogant and rude and overbearing, and an uncontrolled philanderer who couldn't keep his hornpipe in his britches. In his house, the younger maidservants went about their work in pairs, as following various incidents, no domestic girl could risk finding herself alone with the master. At night, those who slept in the servants' quarters in the attic of the house bolted their doors and wedged a chair-back under the handle.

With his first wife barely lukewarm in her grave, Carlo Marchesini had absented himself, supposedly to see to a business matter. To everybody's astonishment, he had returned not two weeks later with a replacement wife, and it was a rather distasteful coupling by anyone's standards. Carlo Marchesini was fifty and some years old – big and fat and gouty and greasy as lard. The new Signora Marchesini, his junior by over thirty years, looked like a delicate porcelain doll at his side. All the servants, including Costanza, had felt sorry for the girl, but what a venomous little viper she'd turned out to be!

The honeymoon hadn't lasted long, and now, four years into the marriage, the Marchesinis lived at opposite ends of the house and if ever their paths crossed, they would either exchange a slew of insults, or they would ignore each other. Occasionally, objects would be thrown.

Having grown bored with his new wife very quickly, Carlo Marchesini focussed his attentions on the silk business. His promise of jobs for women had been kept, but not as everyone had presumed. No positions had been made available to local women. Young girls had been brought in from the region's orphanages instead. The scheme had been dressed up as some sort of philanthropic venture, but the truth was that as long as he provided them with basic food and lodgings and a little bit of schooling, Carlo Marchesini didn't have to go to the trouble of paying his child workers for the long hours they put in each day.

The distant eight o'clock strike of the church clock brought Costanza back to the present. Ideally, she should soak her feet for longer, but she had to be up again before sunrise, and her bed was calling her too loudly to ignore. She patted her feet dry with a clean towel, then put it in a bucket with her used bandages and stockings to be boiled when she had time, whenever that might be. She couldn't afford to take a day of rest anymore. She hadn't had a whole day away from the Marchesini house since before Christmas, not even a Sunday.

Making a conscious effort to keep her thoughts as far away from her feet as possible, Costanza went to bed, but she hadn't yet closed her eyes when she was startled by an urgent rapping on the front door and the calling of her name. She recognised the voice outside as belonging to one of the kitchen maids from Villa Marchesini.

'Costanza! Come quick! The mistress needs you immediately!'

'What's happened?' Costanza called back, scrambling from her bed and fearing that it must be something very serious. For all her demands and silly orders, Signora Marchesini had never had her summoned from home before.

The kitchen maid replied, 'Odetta Colombino's dead!'

'No!' Gasped Costanza. 'How?'

'She died in childbirth.'

'That's impossible. Odetta Colombino is a child.'

'It's definitely her and it was definitely the birth that killed her. They found her in one of the mulberry fields with the cord still attached, but the baby's alive. Please come quickly, Costanza. The mistress is in a terrible state about it and she's asked for you specifically!'

Costanza reached the door just in time to see the maid disappearing out of the garden at a running pace. She stood for a moment, trying to make sense of what she'd just been told. It was terrible if a girl had died in such circumstances, but she didn't believe that it could be Odetta Colombino. Odetta couldn't be older than twelve and she was small for her age. And why was Signora Marchesini so upset that she required her immediate presence? That woman didn't give two figs about anyone but herself. Three of the silk-workers, one of the gamekeepers and a dairymaid had died the previous winter of bronchial pneumonia and all the Signora had done was to complain about the inconvenience of the staff being absent to attend so many funerals.

Costanza dressed quickly. She should put fresh dressings on her feet, but that would take time, so she grabbed a pair of clean stockings and put two pairs of her husband's socks over the top. Never mind the rules, she was going to wear her *zoccoli*. With the sun already setting, she hobbled her way up the North Road, still not believing that Odetta Colombino could possibly have given birth.

At the big house, a pitifully small corpse was laid out on the table in the scullery and covered with a white sheet. All around, the domestic servants and silk-workers stood in silence. The housekeeper lowered the sheet and beneath it was indeed Odetta Colombino, still wearing the blood-soaked clothes in which she had been found. Her young face had turned a livid grey. A wilted sprig of mulberry was clasped in her little blue hands.

Costanza had seen plenty of dead bodies in her time. Most had been old, or at least old enough to have had a run at life. The younger ones were harder to look at, but seeing Odetta, this child who had died in childbirth, gouged at her heart so deeply that she felt a physical pain from it.

She turned to the housekeeper and asked, 'The baby's alive?'

'By some miracle, yes. It's a little girl and she seems perfectly all right. She's been taken to a wet nurse.'

'How was this kept hidden?'

All the women gathered in the kitchen wore the same bewildered expression. Nobody had an answer.

'Who did this to Odetta?' Costanza demanded, although clearly that question had already been asked. The women glanced at one another with lowered eyes as the housekeeper replied, 'It was the master. He admitted it.'

Turning to one of the silk-workers, who herself was not much older than the lifeless child on the table, Costanza asked, 'Did any of you know of this?'

The girl, whose feelings of guilt were evident, replied with a regretful nod. 'There was talk of it,' she said. 'Odetta never told us, but there's been suspicions. And not just with Odetta, with other girls too.'

'Has he touched you?'

'No. Not me. The master likes 'em small and pretty.'

Costanza felt the blood freeze in her veins. She was shocked, but not surprised. Looking down at the floor, the girl admitted, 'He takes 'em to the old hunting lodge in the woods and has his way with 'em. They're all ashamed, but they can't say no, or they'll be sent away and won't have no job. And he says that if they tell, we'll all lose our jobs.'

With that, the girl buried her face in her hands and began

sobbing, 'We're all of us sorry. We haven't known what's best to do. And we didn't think anyone would believe us if we told.'

Addressing all of the gathered women, Costanza asked, 'Do any of you not believe this?' and it was clear that not one single person doubted the truth of the silk-worker's statements.

Costanza turned to the housekeeper. 'Where's the master now?'

'In the chapel, praying.'

'Praying for what? For his own salvation, I'd venture. Beseeching God to keep the authorities away.'

The outrage which overcame Costanza Castello could only be described using the most profane language. There were laws against this sort of thing, and for good reason. Without another word, she stormed out of the scullery, heading for the chapel, but was stopped by Signora Marchesini, who was waiting for her on the staircase with a look of furious impatience on her face.

'What took you so long, Costanza? Upstairs, now!' With that she turned and hurried back up the stairs in a swish of silk skirts. Costanza hesitated, but if she didn't follow the mistress's order, there was bound to be a terrible scene. Carlo Marchesini could stew a little longer. In the meantime, there was no shortage of things which needed to be said to his wife.

Signora Marchesini was waiting in the study, standing before that awful portrait of her husband – the most recent one, where the painter had taken twenty years and fifty pounds off him, but he'd captured his arrogance perfectly. It took all of Costanza's restraint not to spit at it at the best of times. Signora Marchesini began to speak immediately.

'You've heard what's happened, and that addlebrained imbecile husband of mine has admitted to it. Obviously, he will recant his misguided confession. I need you to make it clear to the staff that what they think he might have said whilst overwhelmed by shock and grief is incorrect. You are to ensure that nobody spreads the rumour that he had anything to do with what happened to that little trollop. No word of this filthy scandal must leave this house. The shame would ruin us. We'd lose both our reputation and the business.'

'Is that all you care about? What about Odetta?'

Signora Marchesini scoffed, 'The girl's dead. Nothing can be done about that, and before you ask, I don't give a damn about a whore's bastard issue either. Frankly, it would have rendered matters simpler if it had been left to perish in the field.'

'It's a baby, Signora Marchesini. A little girl.'

'I don't care if it's a dog, Costanza. I need you to arrange to have it sent away.'

'Sent where?'

'How should I know? Have it sent to a farm or something, where it can be of some use when it's older.'

Costanza stood immobile, at a loss to express the depth of her disgust. Signora Marchesini, unaccustomed to having her demands unmet, fixed her eyes on her and said, '*Well?*'

'Well, what?'

'Well, go on! Go downstairs and speak to the staff! Tell them that in the heat of the moment, my husband was overcome with grief and confusion and confessed to something which he did not do.'

'No,' replied Costanza in an icily calm voice. 'I will not mop up your mess, Signora.'

The woman pursed her lips. She was angry, undoubtedly, but did not seem altogether surprised by Costanza's resistance. She sneered, 'How much money are you after? I am prepared to increase your wages and waive the rent on the house. But obviously I will need confirmation that you have carried out your part of the agreement first.'

'I haven't agreed to anything, Signora, and nor will I. And if you think that I would take your paltry bribes, then you are as stupid as you are cold-hearted.'

Signora Marchesini stepped forwards and brought her face close to Costanza's. Her voice was like a snake's hiss. 'If you do not do as you are bidden, it goes without saying that you will be seeking both a new employer and a new landlord, and good luck with it because your references will be anything but glowing. You'll struggle to find a position cleaning latrines. But that aside, the law is clear on matters such as this. Carnal knowledge of a girl under the age of fifteen is not punishable under certain circumstances. For instance, if the girl instigated the act in the first place, or it can be proven that she was not pure before the act took place. Have no doubt that my money is plenty good enough to ensure that witnesses can be found to corroborate one or both of these facts. And be reminded of this – should you have any foolish notions of reporting the matter to the authorities, consider that my husband is on very friendly terms with many men of significant standing, including several judges and magistrates, all of whom would not hesitate to vouch for his integrity.'

In that moment Costanza cared nothing for the threats of unemployment and homelessness. Her thoughts were for Odetta Colombino, and she knew that there would be not one person of decent moral character who would have a bad thing to say about the girl, or her reputation. She had been a quiet, innocent child, and young for her years. The notion that she might have seduced the master, or that she had willingly agreed for any man to touch her was not only malicious, but also ludicrous.

Costanza said nothing, for her actions would speak louder than any words. Satisfied that she had won the argument, Signora Marchesini dismissed her, and satisfied to let her think as much, Costanza turned and marched out of the study, stomping her *zoccoli* as loudly as she could, despite the pain it caused her feet.

She found Carlo Marchesini in the chapel, prostrate on the altar steps. He looked over his shoulder when he heard the sound of Costanza's clogs.

'Thank heavens, Costanza!' He said in a broken voice. 'I knew that I could count on you.'

'Count on me for what, exactly?'

Carlo Marchesini appeared puzzled. 'My wife has not told you the plan? I made rash admissions with no thought for the consequences for my wife, or for the business on which so many people count for their livelihoods. Have you told the servants that I was not in a sound frame of mind when I confessed? I was terribly upset seeing that girl in that state.'

'You mean a *dead* state, Signor Marchesini?'

The master took a deep, stuttering breath. 'Yes,' he sobbed, although there was not one single tear dampening his face. 'Such a dreadful thing ...' then he gathered himself remarkably quickly and added, 'I will retract my confession and make a formal statement to the effect that I had no knowledge of the girl's condition, or of who might have been responsible for it. I can assure you that I will not try to lay the blame upon anybody else.'

'How very noble of you, Signor Marchesini,' replied Costanza, and the master seemed astonished that his servant should reply with what was quite clearly contempt.

'I,' he began, evidently confounded, 'I ... I have strayed from virtue's path, Costanza, and for that my heart is heavy with remorse. But as you have witnessed for yourself, and many times, there is no love in my marriage – a hasty commitment that I fell into unwisely, blinded by beauty and youth, and with the loss of my dear first wife still raw. Be assured that there was no force involved with Odetta. The girl was deeply devoted towards me, and my spirit mirrored that same affection. You must understand that this was an act of love –'

Costanza did not allow Carlo Marchesini to finish his sentence. She slapped his face so hard that her hand still stung as she spat, 'If that is what you call "love", your idea of it is mightily twisted! You think anybody would believe that Odetta, or any of the other girls for that matter, let you put your filthy hands on them willingly; that being subjected to your wicked lust was in any way invited?'

'Odetta never said "no".'

'Of course she didn't! How would a child, who wasn't even twelve years old when you violated her, find the courage to refuse a man in your position?'

'I never meant for events to unfold as they did, and I am resolute in my desire to make amends for my lapse in judgement. I will undertake a pilgrimage to seek forgiveness before God. I will pay a generous endowment to the church, perhaps open a fund for orphaned children.'

'So in your opinion, saying you're sorry and throwing a handful of gold coins in the church collection box will make things right?'

With his hand still resting on his slapped cheek, Carlo Marchesini stammered, 'W-what else can I do?'

'You can consider the child instead of yourself, for a start.'

It was clear to Costanza that this was the first time that such a thought had entered his mind. The master remained open-mouthed as she continued, 'Ensure that a decent, loving home is found for the little girl, and that everything she needs is provided for, not just now, but in the future too.'

'Of course,' Carlo Marchesini replied, although Costanza did not trust his promise. 'And if, *when*, I do this, you will speak to the staff? They all look up to you, Costanza. They'll do as you say. And naturally, I will compensate you for your trouble.'

'How? By upping my wages by a few lire and not charging me rent?'

'If that would please you, yes.'

'*Please* me? You suppose that you can buy yourself out of the pain and suffering and death you have caused by offering me a little bit of money and the right to live in a hovel without paying for the pleasure of it?'

Carlo Marchesini swallowed hard, 'What further services may I render to ensure that the details of this sorry situation go no further than the confines of this house? Please, you must understand that if this regrettable matter was to become public knowledge, the repercussions would be grave, and not just for me, but for all the people who depend upon me, including yourself.'

Costanza looked directly into the master's eyes. She was not even slightly scared of him, and he knew it. The customary self-importance of his expression was replaced with a fearful dread, which increased as Costanza spoke.

'I know that reporting a man as rich and well-connected as yourself to the authorities would be pointless, but it is not the authorities you should be afraid of. You are despised, and not just by those of us who are obliged to work for you. You are hated in the village for more reasons than I have time left alive to list. If you think that what you have done can be swept under the carpet, and that I can stop people speaking of it, you are an even greater fool than everybody, including your wife, says you are. News of your actions will be all over the village by daybreak tomorrow, even if I keep my mouth sealed shut – which I will not. The villagers will see to it that justice is served.'

Before Carlo Marchesini could reply, they were interrupted by his wife running into the chapel screaming, 'There's a mob outside!' and moments later the house echoed to the din of hammering on its doors and the smashing of windowpanes. Within seconds, the clamour of angry voices and stomping boots filled the big house.

'Costanza! Stop them!' The Marchesinis shrieked in unison. Costanza turned and left the hideous pair cowering behind the altar.

The entrance hall of the house was filled with men armed with pitchforks and shovels and shotguns. They were led by the mayor, a strapping fellow by the name of Lovetta. News of the silk-worker's death had spread even more quickly than Costanza had anticipated. Although Odetta Colombino's death had ignited the spark, the villagers' wrath had been smouldering for a long time. Everyone was angry with Marchesini for his exploitation in all its forms; for his conceit and his arrogance; for the way he flaunted his status and his wealth to those whom he had stripped of their livelihoods, and even their homes, on nothing more than a vainglorious whim.

'Where's Marchesini?' Demanded Mayor Lovetta.

Gesturing towards the chapel, Costanza replied, 'In there, with his wife.'

'And where are the domestic servants and silk-workers?'

'In the kitchen.'

Mayor Lovetta signalled to some of his men, 'Get the women out of the house and to a safe place. Costanza, go with them!'

'No,' she replied, 'I'm going home.'

Outside the house more armed men were gathered, waiting for orders. A sweetish burning smell filled the air. Costanza made her way down the long, curving driveway, crossing paths with men in pairs and groups, and as she reached the main entrance to the Marchesini estate, she stopped by the brick gateposts to take stock of the vision, both dreadful and beautiful, laid out before her.

The fields had been set ablaze; the flames' ferocious appetite consuming every leaf and twig and branch of Marchesini's precious mulberry bushes. Great plumes of smoke billowed upwards, obscuring the sky and casting a pall over the fields. And the noise! The customary silence of the night was ruptured by a great commotion of shouts near and distant; by the stomping march of hobnail boots; by the roar and crackle of the land on fire and by the strange siren wail of the flames. Along the North Road packs of men hurried past Costanza, carrying lit torches and lamps and all manner of improvised weapons.

'You shouldn't be out here alone!' One cried, and several offered to escort her, but Costanza was having none of it. 'I'm not alone,' she said and continued walking, covering her nose and mouth with her shawl and blinking the ash from her eyes.

When at last she reached the brick bridge, she saw the womenfolk of Pieve Santa Clara gathered on the far bank. The village farrier and the blacksmith, both on their horses, were blockading the bridge and warning them to come no further. The women wanted to know if the rumours were true, and Costanza confirmed that they were, but she had no desire to remain with them to watch the spectacle unfold. She limped her way through the crowd and along the quarter mile of road to Casa Paradiso. Her feet were so numbed by pain that she could barely feel them.

Costanza took her final few steps to the door of the house. No doubt she had lost her job and her home with it, yet these problems felt like a relief.

'May the devil take you to where you belong!' She cried, picking up her rubber shoes and launching them with all her might into the smoky darkness. Her curse was directed not just at her infernal shoes, but moreover at the Marchesinis.

Carlo Marchesini was spared the lynching that most thought he merited, although it was reported that he nearly died of fright when Mayor Lovetta and his men stormed the chapel. He got off with a good scaring and a bit of a roughing-up.

His wife fled at first light the following day; returning, it was presumed, to wherever she had come from, and taking as many valuables as she could cram into her carriage. Yet it was not just heirlooms and antiquities which the second Signora Marchesini carried away, for she also took with her one final bequest from her husband – an infection of syphilis – and it was this disease which did for Carlo Marchesini some eighteen months later. His death was neither swift, nor dignified, and it was certainly not mourned. As far as Costanza Costello was concerned, and with common agreement from the good people of Pieve Santa Clara, it was an ignominious end, and richly deserved.

1926

AUGUSTO PONTI

Augusto stepped out into the freezing, foggy night and slammed the door behind him. As he wrestled into his coat, he cursed that he hadn't grabbed his hat, or his scarf; but he wasn't going to go back inside to fetch them, not with Mina in such a terrible temper. Much as he loved his wife, and there were countless wonderful things about Mina, sometimes she could be so unreasonable and obstinate. He'd left the house because she was becoming spiteful, as she was prone to do when she was losing an argument.

Turning up his collar, Augusto hunched into his coat and started walking across the piazza. A spit of icy rain was falling. There was just enough moonlight to see the time on the church clock. It was approaching midnight and there wasn't another soul out, but his friend, Pietro Castello, should still be up. Augusto needed not just a listening ear, but some practical advice too, and Pietro was the best person he knew to provide both.

A dim glimmer lit Pietro's kitchen window. From outside, Augusto could hear a pretty melody of notes being plucked on a guitar and Pietro's voice singing *Va Pensiero*. He hesitated, wondering whether it was perhaps too late to impose, and stood shivering on the doorstep with his arms wrapped around himself and stamping his feet in an attempt to keep warm. Needles of sleety rain pecked at the back of his neck. Once the song had reached its end, he knocked. At worst, Pietro would ask him to come back tomorrow at a less unholy hour.

On opening his door and seeing the thunderous look on Augusto's face, Pietro asked, 'Has Mina thrown you out?'

'I've thrown myself out. I know it's late. Am I disturbing you?'

Pietro smiled, 'Well, I've got nowhere to be and I'm in no hurry to get there. Come on in, Augusto.'

The small kitchen was thick with a haze of woodsmoke and tobacco and illuminated only by the open fire and a paraffin lamp hanging above Pietro's chair. One entire wall was lined with shelves, bowing under the weight of countless books. A large advertising board propped against the dresser read: *PIETRO CASTELLO – Brickwork. Stonework. Traditional Techniques & Modern Excellence.* Pietro could turn his hand and his mind to anything. He was the cleverest man Augusto knew. As there was nowhere to hang his coat, he slung it on top of a pile of newspapers.

Pietro cleared a stack of books from a chair and placed it opposite his own by the fire. 'What's troubling you, my friend?' He asked, pouring out two glasses of warmed wine.

Augusto began to speak the moment he sat down. 'I need to tell you something, but Mina will kill me if she finds out I've spoken to you.'

'Nothing will go further than this room,' replied Pietro as he set about rolling a cigarette.

'Mina owns a house.'

Pietro looked up from his half-rolled cigarette and raised an eyebrow, then frowned, 'Where?'

'Along the North Road. Casa Paradiso.'

'That derelict place? My father's aunt, Costanza, lived there for a while, years back. Remember dear old Costanza? She had terrible trouble with her feet ... But hang on, I thought the Marchesinis owned that house?'

Augusto faltered. He hadn't wanted to mention the Marchesinis. Whilst widely known in the village that Carlo Marchesini had fathered a child with a very young silk-worker, the child's identity as Augusto's wife, Mina, remained confidential, except to a select few, and Mina was adamant that it should remain that way.

'They might have owned it at one time,' Augusto replied vaguely, 'but Mina's been its owner since she came of age.'

Obviously puzzled, Pietro rubbed his chin and said, 'You've never mentioned it before.'

'I didn't know until yesterday. Just as we were about to eat our supper last night, we got a knock at the door from a bailiff saying he's come to recover five years' worth of property taxes owed by Mina. I told him it was a mistake because Mina doesn't own a property, but he wouldn't have it. He said that the taxes have to be paid within ten days, or there'll be a big fine on top. And if Mina won't pay up, or can't pay, he'll come back with another order to take things to the value of the debt. Well, I invited the fellow in, saying we needed to clear it up. I said, "Look at where we're living, man. Do you think that if my wife owned a house we'd be renting these two rooms?" So he shows me a piece of paper and says it's called a *Rogito,* or something like that, and it's got official stamps on it as well as Mina's name and he says that it's proof she's the legal owner of Casa Paradiso.'

Pietro, who was still wearing his puzzled frown, struck a match to light his cigarette and asked, 'What did Mina say about it?'

'Well, there's the thing, because as I'm arguing with the bailiff, I realise Mina's being awfully quiet, and you know Mina, if there's something that's not right, she's not shy about voicing it. But when I looked at her, she just looked at the floor.'

Augusto contemplated his wine before continuing, 'By this time the bailiff was getting a bit leery and asking if we've got the money, and I said no, of course we didn't have five years' worth of taxes just sitting around in a drawer. The sum he was demanding was more than Mina and I bring in between us in two months! We live week-to-week, day-to-day, sometimes. So then he started asking about what we own of value, and I said, "We've got nothing. We're modest country folk. I work the canals for my wages, and my wife breaks her back in the fields, and if she didn't grow most of what we eat, there'd be no food to put on that table you're eyeing up." But the bailiff wasn't having any of it. He said the taxes are due and that's that. I tried to appeal to his better nature and I told him that I'm financially responsible for my brother too, and Luigi's still at school and I want to keep him there until he's fourteen, at least. I didn't get much of a crack at school. I had to go out to work when I was ten. I don't want it to be the same for Luigi, even though we could do with the extra income. Our small wages are already stretched beyond their limits.'

Describing the encounter made the sweat drip from Augusto's brow, and he gulped down the remainder of his wine in a single mouthful. As Pietro refilled his glass, he asked, 'So what happened?'

'The bailiff wouldn't budge. He started waving more documents under my nose and he asked, "Can your wife read?" I replied, "Yes, and so can I," so he slammed the papers down on the table and told me to read them and said that Mina had to sign them and if she didn't, she could end up in prison!'

'Did Mina sign?'

'We didn't see any other choice. We were both scared witless when he started making threats about prison. But really, I don't have any idea what she's signed her name to. I did have a go at reading the papers, but reading is one thing, understanding what's written is another.' Augusto pulled the documents from his jacket pocket and unfolded them on his lap. His finger traced along the lines of writing as he struggled to decipher the words. Some were so long and unfathomable that he had to break them up. He looked at Pietro helplessly and said, 'I don't know what *es-pro-pri-a-zione*, or *pi-gno-ra-men-to*, or *Ordi-nanza di Res-pon-sa-bi-li-tá* means.'

'Let me see,' Pietro said, and holding the documents up to the firelight, read them in silence.

'Is it true that Mina could go to prison?' Augusto asked anxiously.

'In a worst-case scenario, yes,' Pietro replied, handing the papers back to Augusto, 'but only if firstly, she is able to, but refuses, to pay the taxes; secondly, if she disposes of insufficient goods to be sequestered in lieu; and thirdly, failing all of that, if she declines to surrender the property to the Revenue Office instead.'

Although this was only marginally less incomprehensible to Augusto, he understood the third part. 'What? They could take the house if we don't pay the taxes?'

Pietro nodded, but reassured Augusto, 'That's a complex process, and it would have to go through the courts, which would take a very long time indeed. I don't think you should worry about that. The best thing you can do is to settle the taxes owed, and if you can't manage that in one go, offer to pay in instalments.'

'Right ...' mused Augusto, feeling as though his options were either the frying pan or the fire.

'Hang on a minute,' Pietro said with a quizzical expression, 'How did Mina come to own the house in the first place?'

'It was left to her.'

'Who by? Mina was a foundling, wasn't she? I thought she'd been abandoned up at the Marchesini farm as a newborn and that nobody knew where she'd come from.'

This was indeed what everybody had been told, including Mina, until she discovered otherwise. It was only when she had come of age that the identity of her parents and the scandalous circumstances of her birth had been revealed by her foster-mother.

Augusto considered the best way to frame his answer without giving anything away which would embarrass Mina. He was going to have to stretch the truth. Wrestling between the discomfort of lying to Pietro and upsetting his wife, he shrugged, 'You know how it is when babies turn up out of wedlock. People weave all sorts of stories to hide the shame. Well, as it turned out, Mina's father was a married man, so when Mina's mother fell pregnant it was all kept hushed up. But the fellow must have felt some sense of responsibility for what he'd done because he put Casa Paradiso in Mina's name with instructions that she should have it when she turned twenty-one. The first Mina learned of it was when she came of age and got a letter from a notary informing her that she was the owner of Casa Paradiso. She didn't tell me about it. Says she threw the letter in the fire. And she admitted that since then she's had a tax bill from the land registry every year and that she threw all those in the fire too.'

As Augusto swilled the wine in his glass, his expression darkened. 'I can't deny that I'm angry with her for not saying anything, Pietro. I understand that Mina's uncomfortable with people knowing she's illegitimate, not that it's any secret, and not that it should matter. Babies are born out of wedlock all the time, and it's hardly their fault. I knew she was illegitimate long before I married her and it made no difference to me. But not telling me she's inherited a house? It hurts that she should keep such a secret. And what makes it worse is that we must have walked past Casa Paradiso a thousand times together, and more than once I even said that it was a pity to see a handsome house like that being left to fall down. She already knew she owned it by then and she didn't say a word.'

Pietro took a long drag of his cigarette, clearly deep in thought, before asking, 'So what's Mina going to do with the house?'

'Mina says she doesn't want it and that she wouldn't live there if you paid her a million lire. And she says she won't sell it because that would be like taking blood money. I tried to reason with her, I said, "That's all very well, but it doesn't change the fact that you own Casa Paradiso and that you're responsible for it, including paying the taxes." But you know my wife, she doesn't always listen to reason, and when she gets an idea in her head ...'

'If it was up to you, what would you do with the place?'

Without hesitation, Augusto replied, 'I'd make it our home. It's crazy to own a house and not live in it. I went to have a look at it earlier, and it's a mess – no more than a shell, really, but it's still in one piece. The roof looks all right. I couldn't see any cracks in the walls. But I'm no expert on these things. I was hoping that maybe you could come and cast your builder's eye over the place. I'll need an idea of what it might cost to get it habitable. I was thinking, we could get one room cleaned up and the rest we could sort out bit by bit. It's a big house for the two of us, but hopefully we'll be blessed with children eventually. And there's a part built onto the side which looks as though it used to be some sort of laundry area, and two decent-sized rooms beyond that. So, I was thinking that when my brother, Luigi, wants a place of his own, he could have that bit. Casa Paradiso could be the Ponti family home, not just now, but for generations to come.' Pausing for a moment, Augusto reeled himself in from his flight of fancy and redirected himself to practical matters. 'Well, there's a lot I'd like to do,' he sighed, 'but it all boils down to money. Or more precisely, lack of it.'

Tapping the ash from his cigarette, Pietro said, 'The government's giving financial assistance to make rural properties habitable. It's part of Mussolini's attempt to stop people leaving the countryside, or worse, leaving Italy altogether and emigrating overseas for a better life. There's funding available.'

'I don't know about that, Pietro. Debt's easy to get into, but getting out of it is another matter entirely. And with this tax bill to pay and everything ...'

'The government money isn't a loan, it's a grant.'

Augusto received this information wide-eyed. 'You mean it doesn't have to be paid back?'

'That's right. And the grants cover pretty much everything. Structural work, internal refurbishment. Even connection to state utilities. They've already put electricity pylons along the North Road, and in the spring they'll be laying pipes for mains water.'

Still not quite believing what he was hearing, Augusto gasped, 'We could have electricity? And running water? *Inside* the house?'

'Absolutely. And a modern bathroom with hot running water, and a W.C. too. No more trips to the outhouse in all weathers and no more putting your foot in your chamber pot when you get out of bed in the mornings.'

Bristling with excitement on hearing these promises which sounded almost too good to be true, Augusto asked, 'Who do we get the money from?'

'The Department of Housing and Rural Regeneration. You'll need to make an application. The paperwork's a bit of a headache, but I can help you with that. You have to prove you own a house and haven't got the money to repair it, which shouldn't be difficult. Even the Marchesinis have had a grant. My Pa and I did a fair bit of work up at the big house last year and it all came at zero cost to them.'

Augusto laughed, 'How could the Marchesinis claim to be short of money?'

'They're not nearly as rich as they look. Carlo Marchesini squandered most of the family fortune in one way or the other. After he died, his son inherited the estate, but no business or working farm to go with it and no money to keep the buildings in good repair.'

Blowing a smoke ring into the air, Pietro continued, 'Anyway, anybody can plead poverty if they've got the right connections, and Carlo Marchesini's son is in balls-deep with the Fascist Party. He's one of the secretaries of the Regional Federal Directive.' Pietro's mention of the Fascist Party carried with it a tone of wary scepticism.

Augusto had scant knowledge of the political landscape and never read the articles on the front pages of the paper if they were about the government. He just skipped to the local news and the sports section. In all honesty, he couldn't be certain which side he'd voted for in the previous elections. The initials the parties called themselves by were very similar, which made things confusing. A candidate had come to talk to the canal-workers, and he seemed like a sound fellow, and he'd made some sensible pledges, so Augusto had promised to vote for him. But once in the polling booth he couldn't remember whether the man represented the P.N.F., or the P.L.I., or the P.S.I., or the P.L.D., so he'd just crossed the first box and hoped for the best.

Nevertheless, he did know that Benito Mussolini was the Prime Minister, and it seemed to him that over the past few years he'd done a lot of good for Italy. Now there were pensions for invalids and old people, and benefits for families with children; and with all the government's big public works projects, you'd struggle to find a man without a job, unless he didn't want one. Since the Via Postumia had been widened and tarmacked you could get to Cremona in twenty-five minutes on the bus. A brand new hospital had been built not far away, in Tuttisanti, and you could use it for free.

When Augusto mentioned these things, Pietro's expression of doubt did not lift. 'Call me cynical if you will,' he said, 'but I think it's all bread and circuses.'

'What do you mean by that?'

'It's the strategy Roman emperors used to employ to control the population. Keep the masses fed and distracted and you can maintain authority and do whatever you please.'

Now feeling even more out of his depth because he knew even less about history than politics, Augusto ventured, 'Well, that poster of Mussolini which was on the noticeboard by the church said that we're all united under fascism now, and surely that's better than fighting? At least if we're all getting along, we shouldn't have to fear another war.'

Pietro reflected for a moment before replying, 'Time will tell,' and blowing a second smoke ring into the air, he added, 'If I were you, Augusto, I'd hurry up and apply for a grant whilst there's still something to be had. Mussolini's throwing money around left, right and centre at the moment to win favour, but that can't go on for ever. Once the national debt becomes un-serviceable, we'll all be back to eating beets and beans.'

Fuelled by the prospect of having money to spend on the house, Augusto began picking Pietro's brains as to the best way to tackle the renovation of Casa Paradiso. He only stopped when he noticed the lateness of the hour. Pietro had a glassy-eyed expression, as though he was suppressing a yawn, which was understandable. The clock above the fireplace said half past one.

'I'm sorry,' apologised Augusto, rising to his feet, 'I've kept you up far too long. I'd best make my way home. Thank you for all your advice.'

As Augusto was retrieving his coat, Pietro asked, 'How do you stand with paying the property taxes?'

'We can scrape together some of it, and the rest we'll have to try and borrow somehow.' He then added in a resigned tone, 'I suppose I'll have to sell my bicycle.'

Pietro went to the dresser and took out a sugar tin from which he removed a small fold of banknotes. 'Here,' he said, pressing the money into Augusto's hand, 'This will keep the bailiff quiet, and I'm in no hurry to have it back.'

'Are you sure, Pietro? I didn't come here to ask for money.'

'Take it, my friend. I couldn't bear to see you part with your bicycle. And we don't want to be visiting Mina in prison, do we?'

Augusto made his way out. Now the fog was so thick he could barely see five paces ahead of him. He stopped in the dark, deserted piazza for a few moments, and suddenly, the realisation of all that was possible in the future hit him. He and Mina had their very own place – no landlord, no rent to pay. It hardly seemed real. They'd feel like the king and queen of Pieve Santa Clara living in that fine house! And there was a fair patch of land with it too – a field in front and behind and another beside it – five or six acres from what he could see. What a garden they'd have there! They could grow everything, even more than they could eat, and make a bit of money from the surplus; hopefully enough to cover the yearly taxes, and from now on, they'd pay them bang on time. Augusto flung his arms open like wings and cried out, 'Yes!'- but not too loudly as he didn't want to wake anybody up – and danced around in a circle. Had it been earlier, he would have gone into the church to give thanks, but it would be locked up now. It was so late that even God had gone to bed.

When he let himself into the house, he found that Mina was still awake and sitting at the table with her head resting on her arms. She looked up and Augusto could see by her expression that she was sorry for the vicious things she'd spat at him earlier – some of them at least, he hoped. As he had no appetite to argue again, he said, 'Let's be done with fighting tonight, Mina.' Then, placing the money on the table, he added, 'That's from Pietro. To keep you out of prison. For the time being.'

Mina half-smiled, and this was confirmation that peace had returned. If Augusto had said something like that to her a couple of hours ago, she'd have jumped down his throat. She might even have thrown the money in the fire.

'What did you say to Pietro?' She asked.

'I told him about the house, but I spared the names and details of how you came to own it.'

Mina admitted, 'You're right, Augusto. It's madness to have that house standing there empty with us paying to rent these two rooms. We should make our home at Casa Paradiso.'

Augusto's smile stretched into a grin. Mina cast a pleading gaze towards him and said, 'But Augusto, I don't want anybody to know who gave me that house. I never want to hear the Marchesini name spoken, and I never want it revealed who my mother was, or how old she was. Perhaps we could make up as story of how we came into some money. Maybe we could say that one of us was left an inheritance by a distant relative we didn't know we had, or that our numbers came up on the *Lotto Nazionale*. People would believe it if we told them something like that, wouldn't they?'

Augusto took his wife's hand, pressed it to his lips and replied, 'If it means you'll agree to live in that fine house, we'll tell people whatever you want.'

On seeing the grin still fixed on his face, Mina asked, 'What is it, Augusto?' and he set about explaining everything that Pietro had told him. Mina listened, open-mouthed.

'Really?' She said at last, 'The government would pay for everything?'

'That's right,' Augusto nodded, all the while beaming, 'You'd better start measuring up for the curtains, my love.'

1937

LUIGI PONTI

On the twenty-seventh day of March 1937, at approximately five o'clock in the afternoon, Luigi Ponti fell in love for the second time. He bent down to kiss his first love, his wife, Teresa, then kissed his new love, their baby daughter, Graziella, now not quite two hours old.

The labour had been quick for a first one and the midwife had come just in time – not that there weren't plenty of other well-practiced women to hand. As soon as word had got out of the imminent arrival at Casa Paradiso, half a dozen experienced ladies had turned up to help. Mina had kept them all corralled in her kitchen because Teresa didn't fancy giving birth watched by an audience. Augusto had been poised and ready with his boots on and his bicycle facing the open gate, just in case a doctor needed to be called.

When she had passed the precious new life into Luigi's arms, the midwife had said, 'She's as healthy as they come.'

Luigi had held plenty of babies before, but never his own and never one so freshly born. In that first rush of awe and tender-ness, Graziella had met his gaze and let out not a cry, more of a squawk, which had sounded like '*ciao*' and made him laugh. '*Ciao*,' he'd replied, and then he'd wept, and in those two or so hours since that first introduction, he'd barely stopped weeping, such was his joy and relief that both his wife and his daughter had survived.

Beside Teresa, Graziella was asleep and taking up his half of the bed, even though she had one of her own. Luigi had made her a crib from a blanket box, taking the lid off its hinges so that she couldn't be shut in accidentally. It was a rustic bed, certainly, but bedecked with bedding fit for royalty. Teresa had been embroidering little sheets and quilts and coverlets from the moment she'd suspected she was pregnant. She had then turned her talents to the yarn crafts. Lined up on the chest of drawers were stacks of miniature knitted and crocheted clothes and two dozen pairs of bootees, all in different colours.

Luigi looked around the freshly plastered and painted room, with gleaming new ceramic tiles laid on the floor. When Mina and Augusto had said he could have this part of Casa Paradiso for himself, he felt as though he'd won the jackpot ten times over. Now what had formerly been a laundry area was his family home – just a kitchen and a bedroom, but both of good size and enough for the moment, although Luigi had ambitious plans for the future. As soon as time and finances allowed, he'd build two more rooms onto the back and add a bathroom so that they wouldn't have to share the facilities with Augusto and Mina in the main house anymore. Perhaps one day they'd need even more space, and then he'd expand upwards. Luigi liked the thought of a big family, although Teresa had made it clear that two or three little Pontis would be plenty and that if he got any crazy ideas, she'd make him sleep in the barn.

Part of Luigi just wanted to stand there gazing at his lovely girls, but he should let them rest undisturbed. As he tiptoed out, he left the door half-open so that the heat from the kitchen stove would keep the bedroom warm. It was still a bit early to go through to Mina and Augusto's for supper, even though he could already smell enticing wafts of polenta with butter and rabbit ragú. After all the afternoon's emotions, he could do with a breath of fresh air, so he made his way outside. There should still be half an hour or so of daylight left.

Patches of violets and primulas peeked out amongst the thick spring grass. Within a few weeks the garden would be bursting with every imaginable bounty – carrots, onions, beans and greens; sprawling patches of strawberries and melons, and more potatoes, zucchini and tomatoes than they could eat. There would be flowers too – yellow calendula, frondy pink cosmea, tangles of orange nasturtiums – all abuzz with bees, dancing from bloom to bloom. The scent of herbs would be so dense that you could taste it on your tongue. Mina's tireless work had turned the long-fallow soil into a veritable Garden of Eden. Fitting really, for a place called 'Paradiso'.

Positioned in between two peach trees was a wooden bench, made by Luigi from off-cuts and salvaged planks. It was his special spot, and he liked to sit there for no reason other than to admire the house. Just a few years before it had stood derelict and half-consumed by creepers. Now only the arrangement of its windows and its arched front door made it recognisable as that same once-forlorn Casa Paradiso.

He'd certainly cut his teeth on the place. His apprenticeship with Pietro and Pa Castello had set him up well, and they'd taught him not just masonry, but a thousand other sundry skills. Now, seasoned by ten years in the trade, Luigi had his own jobs and his own apprentices and there wasn't a lot he couldn't turn his hand to. With all his labour given free of charge, Mina and Augusto had managed to stretch the government grant a long way.

It had taken a month of clearing and bonfires before any renovation work could start. As they'd cut and hacked and uprooted, they'd joked about discovering a hoard of buried treasure – a stash of gold coins, or something like that. Funny, because not two days later Augusto had dug up three silver medals in the garden. They had the words *LEGIONE LOMBARDA* on the front and *ALLA GLORIA* on the back. A pawnbroker said they came from Napoleon's time – awarded posthumously to soldiers to honour their sacrifice in battle – and he'd been happy to take them off their hands for more than just the weight of the silver. The money had paid for a new water pump. Apart from the medals, they hadn't unearthed anything of value, although when he'd been putting in a drain by the doors of the barn where a puddle tended to form, Luigi had found two pieces of sculpted limestone. One was carved with a rose of the Gothic style you sometimes saw in churches, and the other with a fleur-de-lys. Neither was worth anything in terms of money, but they were beautifully etched and probably quite old, so he'd cleaned them up and Mina had them on display as curiosities on her kitchen mantelpiece now.

Luigi's gaze traced the contours of the house. Pietro Castello reckoned its proportions bore the mark of an architect's design. True, despite its relatively simple symmetrical layout, Casa Paradiso did have something which set it apart from other rustic buildings. There wasn't another house exactly like it in the village.

They'd painted the outside a creamy yellow, and the shutters in a pale green. The colours suited the house well. On the one hand, it was a shame that the pretty brickwork had been covered over, yet it was also a blessing, as it had protected the walls from the worst of the weather. Luigi had tried removing a patch of the rendering, but there was too much cement in the mix and it wouldn't come off without taking the brick faces with it. Probably best, as stripping and re-pointing the whole house would have taken him forever. He'd likely still be at it now. But when he'd discovered lintels with scrolled designs concealed under the render, he couldn't believe that anyone had covered them up. Despite having a thousand other more pressing jobs to do, he had painstakingly chipped away to expose them without damaging the carvings. He'd worn several steel brushes down to the nub in the process, and his right elbow too. It still gave him jip sometimes. Best forgotten was the time he'd almost chopped his thumb off with his chisel.

On each of the lintels he'd uncovered a carver's mark – the

initials 'C.L.'. Who 'C.L.' was, he could never know, but whoever he might have been, Luigi liked to think that he'd be pleased if he could see the house now. That was the thing with masonry – every brick you laid and every stone you set was a little piece of future history. Your labours could endure for centuries, millennia even. Luigi had etched his own initials onto a brick when he'd built a new doorstep. Someone would discover it one day and wonder: who was this 'L.P.', who had left his ghostly mark on the brick? He liked the thought of that.

Three hundred years the house had been standing sentinel, bearing the extremes of the seasons; through times of feast and famine, wars, revolutions and periods of blessed peace. Often Luigi found himself wondering about those who had called Casa Paradiso their home over the centuries, imagining the work-weary men sitting by the fireside after a hard day's toil; the industrious women tending its hearths and sweeping its floors and cooking uncountable suppers; the children who had run from room to room playing hide-and-seek. And those souls who had simply passed through – visitors, both welcome and unwelcome; dinner guests; weary travellers. Sometimes Luigi sensed something of them – a lingering ethereal presence, steeped into the bricks and mortar. If only those old walls could speak!

The house was more than just a building. It was an archive of lives, each like a chapter in a book, but nothing more than a short story, really. The span of a human existence was as quick as a blink in the endless expanse of time. Now Casa Paradiso was the Ponti family home, and hopefully it would be for generations to come; but they were just its custodians – temporary keepers of a place more permanent than any human life could ever be.

It pained Luigi that he had so little knowledge of his ancestors. He had lost his mother at the age of three and had no memory of her, just a handful of stories told to him second and third hand. His father had gone not long after his mother, leaving him and Augusto in their grandparents' charge. He wished he'd asked Nonno and Nonna more about their own parents and grandparents, but by the time he'd thought to do it, it was too late. He knew that the Pontis went back a long way in these parts and was aware of connections to families called Pozzetti, Lovetta and Ferrari – but exactly how most were related to him, he didn't know. In Pieve Santa Clara, if you looked back far enough, everyone was related to somebody else somehow, whether by blood or by marriage; and half the families in the village bore one or other of those names. He'd heard it said that his great-grandmother was called Mirella and she had been his great-grandfather's mistress, but he had recognised all their children legitimately as his own. Apparently, they had lived in a big *cascina* on the southern boundary of the village, long-abandoned now. One day he'd look through the parish records and piece together a family tree so that Graziella could see how deeply her roots sank into the Lombardy Plain.

Luigi's thoughts were interrupted by the *chip-chip-chirrup* call of a grey *gufetto* owl, perched on the electric wire which ran from the road to the house. He knew the little fellow. He lived in the hayloft and always came out ten minutes before dusk. You could set your pocket watch by him. Sure enough, the day was fading now. A light had been switched on in Mina's kitchen. The violets and primulas had folded their petals for the night.

Luigi rose to his feet and stood amongst the lengthening shadows, taking a moment to look westwards, where the sun, hovering just an inch above the horizon, streaked the clouds with coral and gold, promising a clear day tomorrow. In the morning, he would bring his brand new baby daughter outside, to be anointed by the fresh breath of the Lombard air and to be introduced to the home which would nurture, protect and become a part of her. Graziella Ponti, now not quite three hours old, would write her own chapter of history here at Casa Paradiso.

The Real 'Casa Paradiso'

The fictional house named 'Paradiso', which provides the back-drop to Graziella Ponti's story in the first three *Paradiso Novels* and now to this book, is based upon a real house built by my great-grandfather, Amilcare Scanacapra – a bricklayer by trade – in a small village in Lombardy, Italy. The village has been home to the Scanacapras for countless generations.

I have many early childhood memories of visiting my great-grandfather there. Whenever the extended family gathered, spectacular feasts would be cooked by his sisters in what today would be considered impossibly basic facilities, where the oven was wood-fired and water was pumped from the well by hand into a stone sink. Great cauldrons of broth would be simmering on the stove. On the kitchen table, broad sheets of *sfoglia* would be rolled out in preparation to make *marubini*, the lesser-known cousins of *tortellini*, and typical of the region. Their filling comprised mainly braised beef, ham, Parmesan cheese and a pinch of nutmeg, but every Mamma and Nonna had her own exact recipe. Outside, a suckling pig would be roasting on a spit and filling the air with a thickly savoury, mouth-watering aroma. It had to be cooked for many hours, until so tender that the meat could be cut with a spoon.

I remember being sent into the garden to gather herbs and pick whatever bounty of fruits or vegetables was ripe. Peaches, apricots, plums and melons grew in abundant supply. Tomatoes and marrows sprouted like weeds. I was also called upon to remove the pests, such as the caterpillars which crunched their way through the cabbages and the pesky snails which munched just about everything else. Considered a delicacy by some and a

219

supper for desperate times by others, the snails were never discarded. They were collected in an old washing machine drum and fed breadcrumbs to purge them of toxins before being cooked 'alla Lombarda' with onions, garlic, parsley and white wine. I can't say that I was ever keen.

Through my child's eyes, the house seemed like a castle – enormous and crammed with massive, carved furniture; stuffed animals and birds in glass cases; paintings and porcelain dishes and countless fascinating curiosities. The cantilevered stone staircase, my great-grandfather's masterpiece of craftsmanship, rose up three floors to an attic filled with treasure and junk. In those days, nothing was ever thrown away.

Amilcare lived in the house until his death in 1978, following which it was simply locked up exactly as he had left it, standing as a dormant relic to a bygone era. His son, my grandfather, Mario, had no designs on selling it. A lack of professional opportunities had forced him away from the region as a young man, but he would return occasionally to spend his holidays there, until declining health put an end to his visits in the early 90s. After that, the house fell into a state of hibernation, and so it remained for thirty years.

When I am asked what first inspired me to write the *Paradiso Novels*, I speak of stories told to me by my grandparents, and this is certainly true; but now, looking back with a little perspective, I think there is a deeper reason. Both my childhood and adulthood were nomadic. Wherever I lived – and there were many different places – I was a transient foreigner. Subconsciously, I felt the need to put down roots, and it was this which drove me to write books based in a fictionalised version of the place which had been home to my family for many generations.

Little did I imagine that in 2021, whilst I was living in England, with the first two *Paradiso Novels* published and the dream of writing full time edging closer to reality, I would be given the opportunity to make my great-grandfather's house my own. The proposition came about following a comment made by my mother, expressing what a shame it was that the house was deteriorating – as all old, uninhabited houses do – and complaining about the yearly taxes which had to be paid for the pleasure of owning it. My father had put it on the market briefly, but there had been no offers. The house was too run-down and out-of-the way to attract the interest of Italians. Foreign buyers were unheard of in the region. Lombardy, beautiful though it is, does not have the cachet of Tuscany. Perhaps, my mother said, only half-seriously, I could move there. After all, I was writing books about the place. I was also, rather conveniently, married to a builder who was about to retire. Sorting out the house would keep him occupied. Within two days I was packing boxes and comparing quotes from international removal firms. Five weeks later, on a foggy November night, we pulled up outside our new home.

My husband, who had only seen the place once, some twenty years previously, took one look at the dilapidated façade and jungle-like garden, much of which was growing into the house, and agreed with my mother. This project was going to fend off the potential boredom of retirement. Less rash or foolhardy souls than ourselves might not have moved straight into a house which had remained largely untouched since my great-grandfather's day, but excitement overrode common sense. We weren't too proud to glamp.

There followed a year of unrelenting renovation work to bring the old house into the twenty-first century whilst lovingly restoring its original features. Now the house is a comfortable home and shines with new life. Amilcare's massive carved furniture mixes perfectly with ours, although we haven't yet tackled the attic. Amongst its piles of treasure and junk, we've found a couple of family tombstones. No decision has yet been made as to what we will do with them. They will, at the very least, end up in a book.

The long-neglected garden is once again bursting with flowers, fruits and vegetables. I still go out to pick the caterpillars off the cabbages, but now the snails I collect by the bucketful are not destined for the pot. Instead, I take them for a long walk along the canal which runs behind the house and release them into the shrubbery. If they are determined to find their way back to munch the plants in my garden, it will take them a while. My neighbours find this most amusing.

How delighted both my great-grandfather, Amilcare, and my grandfather, Mario, would be if they could see the glorious house with its burgeoning garden now. I like to think that in some mystical way, they can.

This brings me back to the book, *Casa Paradiso*. Living in the house of my ancestors has instilled in me a deep connection to my roots. The house is a repository of memories, a place where past and present intertwine and where the stories of those who came before me continue to inspire my own journey and my own writing. A house endures through time, long outliving the human souls who are its temporary guardians. The Casa Paradiso portrayed in this book, although over two centuries older than the house which served as its muse, is born of this feeling. For all its fictional characters and artistic license, it is in many ways a love-letter to the beautiful house I now have the privilege of calling my home.

I hope you enjoyed your visit to Casa Paradiso.

Francesca Scanacapra
August 2024
Casa Paradiso

Milton Keynes UK
Ingram Content Group UK Ltd.
UKHW031826051124
450760UK00005B/127